DROP ZONE

A MINA KANE NOVEL
BOOK SIX

AMANDA CARLSON

In 2105, getting things to tumble from the sky is possible.

After ex-marshal Webb's torture at the hands of a Syndicate fixer, it's time to figure out who was involved and hold them accountable. After a deep confession from Webb, Mina realizes the risk the fixer poses, and authorization comes for her and her team to track him down. The laser fires hot when a Syndicate team searches the fixer's unit and the colonel-in-arms' DNA is identified.

Everyone involved with the case must stay well under the radar or it'll place Mina and the entire department in jeopardy. That means completing an unprecedented mission in hopes of bringing down a notorious crime ring for good. With the help of her partner, Lee Adams, and the extremely talented hacker Harmony Biggins, they hatch a plan that qualifies as the most ambitious of Mina's career.

The race is on, and with the help of the colonel-in-arms, they just might pull it off.

Other Books by Amanda Carlson

Jessica McClain Series
Urban Fantasy
BLOODED
FULL BLOODED
HOT BLOODED
COLD BLOODED
RED BLOODED
PURE BLOODED
BLUE BLOODED

Sin City Collectors
Paranormal Romance
ACES WILD
ANTE UP
ALL IN

Phoebe Meadows
Contemporary Fantasy
STRUCK
FREED
EXILED

Holly Danger
Futuristic Dystopian
DANGER'S HALO
DANGER'S VICE
DANGER'S RACE
DANGER'S CURE
DANGER'S HUNT
DANGER'S FATE

Mina Kane
Futuristic Thriller
TOTAL ENHANCEMENT
PERFECT PLANT
CUPID'S BOW
VID STAR
CODE TEAL
DROP ZONE

"HE DIDN'T ANSWER." Mina hefted up a tall, weirdly shaped vase. Round on top, spindly at the bottom. "I already told you. I called him twice this morning, and he didn't pick up. What is this? Does it hold flowers? Or ashes of the dead?"

It was eight thirty in the morning, and she and Kaylee were running late. It was Mina's fault. Getting out of bed had taken some serious effort. She'd had only around four hours of restless repositioning. There'd been no sleep involved.

Or if there had been, it'd been unrecognizable.

Now that she was up, she had a lot on her mind.

First and foremost, Vincent Kramer had brought the house down with his lips last night, contributing to the majority of her sleeplessness—to the point where Mina had been experiencing some kind of ghost-lip fixation. She would absolutely swear, to anyone who asked, that Vince's lips were currently touching hers.

It might be becoming a problem.

Second on her mind was Norman Webb. She was acutely aware that the ex-marshal, who was in a government medi-unit healing from injuries he'd sustained at the hands of a Syndicate fixer, should rank first in her brain. But the phantom-kissing thing was extremely distracting.

She was, of course, anxious to find out how Norm was doing. The main agenda, after they took her partner, Lee Adams, a celebratory new-residence gift, was to meet with Norm and figure out a way to deal with this fixer, a man by the name of Wilbert Waterbury, who'd been released from a box a month prior.

They needed to solve this quickly and efficiently with the least amount of blowback. It wasn't going to be easy. The Syndicate had a long reach and an even longer memory.

There was also the pesky faux audit to worry about. Mina hoped Duncan McAllister, the director of the CIU, had found out who'd ordered it. She wanted to check that off her list, too.

She yawned, halfheartedly covering her mouth with the back of her hand. She was going to have to take a dose of Jump if she wanted to stay fully functioning today.

"Here, give it to me." Kaylee took the vase, turning it upside down to inspect the bottom. They were standing in an aisle of Print It. "I wouldn't put anybody's ashes in this thing. Looks like it would topple over if you blew your nose near it." She set it down. It wobbled, threatening to fall before evening out, which seemed like a miracle, considering. "And if you yawn like a cobra gulping down a fat, juicy rat one more time, an air breather is going to escort you over to the platform section so you can lie down." Kaylee settled her hands on her hips. "What's with you, anyway? I've been waiting to hear what happened last night with your new smoking-hot hunk of burning love since we walked into this store. If you don't spill your ever-lovin' guts soon, I'm going to dig the stinky secrets out of your body with...this."

She snatched up something that looked like a kitchen utensil people had used years ago to cook real food. Either that, or it was a pet excrement scooper.

When Mina didn't respond right away, Kaylee swatted the air with the thing, taking a few steps forward. "I want details, and I want them now." She swished the thing downward. "The only tidbit you've offered up is he hasn't answered a couple of calls this morning." She batted it upward. "So what? The man's tired. You kept him up all night." Swish, swish to the side. "He's sleeping in like a normal person who doesn't work full time. Or even part time." She gave up on the pooper spatula and set it back on the shelf. "Does he even work at all? I mean, what does he do all day? No wonder he's still asleep."

Mina shrugged, trying to hold back another yawn. It came out in a weird half growl. There was no good way to stifle a yawn. "I don't know. He does media interviews, but there can't be that many in a single day. Ambrose is keeping track of him with a couple of guards. Other than that, I have no idea."

Ambrose Bernard was leader of the French Protectorate and subsequently Vince's boss. He wasn't very happy with Vince at the moment. Vince had gone rogue, and Ambrose was making him pay.

Kaylee puckered her lips, making kissy sounds. "You haven't asked because you're too busy sticking your face in his." She stopped, brows arching in concern. "You did stick your face in his face, didn't you?"

Mina meandered down the aisle without answering.

Her friend caught up with her in a second flat. "In case you've forgotten, we don't keep stuff like this from each other." She guided Mina around to face her. "We're best friends. I goss on everything. You know it all. From Tanya loves Tangling Tonsils to Porcupine Jones, the man who lives to creep me out. Who I absolutely never slept with." Her eyes made a slow roll toward the ceiling. "Okay, so we might've occupied the same bed together...once. Oh, never mind." She visibly shivered, rubbing her arms through her emerald-green flow shirt. "You know almost every single detail of my love life. You can't ice me out now."

Mina picked up a decent-looking lamp, successfully suppressing a grin. Much easier than a yawn. "How about this? Looks kind of Lee-like. It's brown and sturdy. These knobs on the sides make it look owlish."

"Are you kidding me?" Kaylee huffed. "We're not buying that. We're not lamp people. And why aren't you answering me? Did he break up with you? If he did, he's going to get a solid kick in the—"

"He didn't break up with me." Mina chuckled. "Stop being so dramatic. We're not even a real thing yet." Were they? Maybe they were. Mina sighed. "I just…I'm still trying to process everything. It's all jumbled up in my brain, and it makes it hard to figure out what I'm feeling. We kissed last night. It was incredible. So much so, that it feels like he's kissing me constantly. Vince's ghost lips won't leave me alone. And no, he didn't stay over. We're taking this slow." That decision had been debatable as she'd tossed and turned in her platform all alone. "I'm glad we are"—if she kept saying it, it would be true—"because I'm having trouble reconciling having feelings, or even allowing myself to have feelings, for a guy who was once my best friend. When he's in front of me, I see grown-up Vince. But when he leaves, all these memories of us as kids flood back, and I get"—she shrugged—"a little weirded out."

"Leave it to you to get weirded out kissing a guy with dreamy ghost lips when ten million people, and I'm being conservative with that number, would enter into cohabitorship with him, no questions asked."

Mina laughed. "Yeah, but most people didn't watch him grow up. We spent a lot of time together. During those years, I never felt a single romantic feeling toward him. Not a one. It was probably because we were together constantly." Mina mulled it over. "But at the same time, I can't wait to see him again and latch on to those plump, delicious, silky lips. Damn, he's a good kisser. Phenomenal. Possibly the best kisses I've ever had."

There was no possibly about it. It'd been the most romantic, highly charged interaction of Mina's life to date.

The ghost sensation tingled again.

She refrained from running her fingers over her lips like she wanted to and settled on rubbing them together. Aggressively.

Kaylee did a little jig. "See? That's what I'm talking about. More of that please." She pivoted back and forth in place, hips swaying, beckoning Mina with both hands. "Dee-tails. I need some of those sweet, sweet dee-tails. Kissing, stroking, lip-locking, nails-scraping, head-bobbing, dee-licious dee-tails. Feel free to get down and dirty. I'm in need of some sweet, sweet dee-liiight." She stopped. "Seriously, this dry spell sucks. I need to find someone with magical ghost lips. No fair."

"Okay. Okay." Mina giggled. "But you have to promise to stop dancing. This is not the time to break into song. Why do you have so much energy, anyway? You left the ceremony at the same time we did. You should be yawning right along with me."

"Like a good girl who knows what she's doing, I downed a hyperbiotic this morning and pretty much ate my breakfast in my medi-pod. It does the body good. And don't you dare lead me off-topic. What else you got? And anytime is a great time for a song." She started snapping. "Oh, there once was a man named Viiincent. He kissed like he had a biiig fat—"

Mina grabbed Kaylee's arm and dragged her forward, laughing. "No more. We have to get serious about this. My mentorship is spiraling down the grinder as we speak. Right now, Lee is wandering around his new high-rise wondering what to do and second-guessing if he'll be able to stay there or not. We're bringing over some printed treats and whatever we find in the next aisle."

She guided them around the corner.

The aisles at Print It were enormous—two meters wide and stacked higher than a giant could reach. Whatever was found on a shelf could be printed in any color, many in several variations. You could purchase a particular item, but the merchandise was really there to spark an idea.

Mina scanned the row. "Well, this is unfortunate. We can't really give him a gel-cush seat insert." She gestured to one side. "Or a child's plush toy." Gesturing to the other. "Why aren't they better organized? It should be groupings of similar items."

Kaylee glanced around. "I think we're in the yellow section."

"Yellow? Why would color matter?"

Neither of them shopped here often.

"I have no idea, but do you see anything that isn't the color of a drab sunflower? Or, more accurately, the color of mustard diluted with burnt carbon?"

"Hm. You're right. That's a lot of yellow. It's also the worst color. These actually look like rejects to me." Mina picked up a large urn that could be used for a houseplant or possibly something to keep prewash clothing in? Hard to know. "Who would buy this?"

"I'm pretty sure it's one of those decorative floor stand thingies. You put branches in it."

"Why would you put branches in it?"

Kaylee snorted. "Honestly, I've never met anyone with less of a fashion sense than you. When you move residences, you go with whatever decor is already inside. But some people—most humans—love to personalize their space. They like to add their own planetary twist on things. And for what it's worth, I think branches are pretty. Something natural in our sterile world." She took the urn from Mina. "But this one is hateful." She stuck it back on the shelf. "That yellow color not only hurts the eyes, it offends the soul."

"I have plenty of fashion sense," Mina argued as Kaylee led her out of the land of yellow. "Just because I don't care about dotting my residence with tchotchkes doesn't mean I don't enjoy decorating. I just haven't had the time or energy to spend on it yet."

"Keep telling yourself that."

Mina snorted. "Let's get Lee some plushy dry wraps. Those are fun and functional." They walked down the much larger main aisle, glancing at the digital signage, trying to make sense of it. "Where's the fiber section?"

"Over there, I think," Kaylee said, gesturing. "And while we search for the most boring gift available in this entire, massive, sensory-overloading store, keep spilling. We're not done here."

"We might be done here. I told you about the amazing kissing. That was it."

"Your storytelling is as weak as a tot slurping fruit sauce out of a retractable straw. I like the ghost-lip stuff. Give me more of that."

"My storytelling is excellent. And there just isn't much to tell. He kissed me. I liked it. We stopped. I kind of wished he'd stayed over. He said he'd meet us at Lee's this morning, made it seem like he was into it, didn't answer my calls, now we're here."

"Proof to my point. Effective storytelling involves highly descriptive adjectives and leave-you-on-the-edge-of-your-seat cliffhangers. You just gave me bullet points. That was excrement, not excitement."

Mina yawned. "Yeah, you're probably right. I'm sorry. I'm just not all here this morning."

Kaylee stopped abruptly, turning to Mina. "Look, I get it. You're hung up on him not answering this morning. You went to bed blissed out, ready to jump into this new relationship, then Kramer gives you another setback by blocking you, which you file away as yet another possible lie he fed you. It makes sense, given what's happened recently between the two of you." She began to walk again. Mina followed. "But I can promise you that's not what's happening. He didn't answer because he's either in a kiss-bliss coma, or something came up. Something important."

"How can you possibly know that? You have no proof."

He could've lied again. Mina wasn't ruling that out.

"I know because every single person in that room last night saw how you guys looked at each other. There's no impersonating that much electric current. Even when you were apart, you sought each other out, giving each other silly grins and head bobs, holding hands under the table when you thought nobody was looking."

Mina made a face. "You were watching us?"

"Not like a creeper. Jeez." Kaylee laughed. "But it was hard to miss. It was also endearing and sweet and perfect and smushy. There was so much current, all the male and female agents who might've sought Vince out to—I don't know, flex their assets and give him a flyby—didn't. They didn't because they saw he was taken. That his heart was not up for grabs. So believe me when I say the man is not avoiding you." She turned down another aisle. "And if you weren't so lovesick and paranoid, you'd see it, too."

"I'm not lovesick," Mina protested. "Or paranoid. I'm… cautious. I'm practical. I'm a realist."

"Then get real on this. Kramer is into you. He's fallen down a deep crater hole, and you're the only one in there with him. So relax. He'll call you. You'll see him again, and it will be fabulous." She waggled a finger. "And if you don't give me excellent details dipped in hot buttery fudge dipped in scintillating sprinkles the size of baby elephants next time, this relationship is over, and I'm moving on." She marched up to a shelf and grabbed a stack of dry wraps in a pretty aqua color. "We're getting these. Boring, but useful. Come on, let's go."

Mina trailed her best friend in the entire world. "You're never moving on. You're stuck with me. For. Life. Who's not being a realist now?"

"Try me and see."

"LEE, THIS PLACE is fantastic!" Mina exclaimed. It really was. The rooms were bright and airy with high ceilings. Even though the overall space was compact, it had a comfortable, lived-in feel. The standard residence furnishings were colorful, but not overwhelming.

She walked to the four good-sized solar-catch windows that spanned the living area. "The view is incredible, too. Very spec. You're high enough to see over most of the standard high-rises. I can see the harbor in the distance and some greenery from Atlas Park. Well done."

"Thanks," Lee replied, his face one big, beaming smile. "I'm really happy. I know it's not huge, but it's so much bigger than my last residence. I honestly don't know what I'm going to do with all the space."

Kaylee picked up a decorative bowl, arching an eyebrow at Mina. "This is pretty. I love all your personal decor items, Lee. Really makes the place feel homey."

Mina chuckled. "Way to rub it in."

Lee bobbed his head between the two of them, obviously missing what was happening. "It was my mom's. It was passed down from her mom. I think my great-grandmother used to put sweets in it or something. I'm not sure."

"Personal items make a place sparkle," Kaylee said, turning to mouth, "See?" at Mina.

"Kaylee is just picking on me," she told Lee as she eyed a pretty vase. This one was purple glass, perfectly symmetrical, not at all weird. Lee did have a lot of personal things, and they looked nice. "Don't egg her on. She thinks it's weird I don't have many sentimental items in my residence."

"Try zero," Kaylee said. "Not weird, just sorta bot-like. I always thought you were an air breather. Maybe not? Come over here so I can take your temperature."

"Har," Mina quipped. "And I do have sentimental stuff. I just haven't unpacked it all yet. It's in a box in my utility closet where the mover bots put it. I told you, I haven't had time. I've only been in that place for a few weeks, but I plan to at some point."

"How long have those special items been in that particular box?" Kaylee asked, hands on her hips. "I'm thinking since you moved out of your parents' residence. I've certainly never seen a single speck of anything."

"Possibly. Does it really matter? Instead of being hung up on this, we should be oohing and aahing over Lee's new residence," Mina instructed.

Kaylee was right. Her rightness wasn't any less annoying. That aluminum storage box had remained unopened since Mina had moved out of her childhood home. She probably could've found the time to take some of the items out, but she hadn't.

Now she wondered what was in there. She'd completely forgotten.

"Harmony Biggins is requesting entrance into the building," a standard female sim intoned. "What are your orders?"

"Allow access," Lee answered.

"Access confirmed."

Lee said, "I haven't personalized my sim yet, but I'm planning to."

"Of course you are," Mina said. "However, it might have to happen later." She checked her cuff. "I sent Norm a message on our way over. They're releasing him from the medi-unit within the hour. We need to be there. He can't go back to his residence. McAllister is working on setting something up for him, but Norm is pushing back in typical Norm fashion. Says he's fine and all that. Doesn't want us to fuss."

"You mean fuss enough to keep him alive so a monster mobster doesn't slice him into tiny, decorative ribbons?" Kaylee said.

"Exactly," Mina said. "I'm going to have to convince him he has to go somewhere safe until we figure out a plan."

It was going to take some creative persuading, but Mina would prevail. She was crafty like that.

"Maybe Pormal?" Lee questioned. "I don't think the Syndicate has ties there."

Mina considered the idea. "They might not have contacts inside Pormal itself, but they definitely do in the outskirts, which is too close for my comfort."

"Yeah," Lee said. "That's true."

"Harmony Biggins has entered the tube and will be here in twenty seconds," the sim said.

Lee walked over to his door, placing his thumb on the government smudger, leaning his eye into a retinal scanner, grinning enough to break his teeth. Agents were required to have increased security. Lee was doing his best impression of a geek-out.

But it wasn't actually an impression, it was the real thing.

He yanked the door open as the tube chimed.

Mina could hear Harmony's hoots from here.

Kaylee shook her head. "Trying to teach that girl to keep a low profile is going to be the hardest thing I ever do."

"Karmaseeker, this is super-duper, mega, static spec!" Harmony bounded into the room, taking everything in, missing nothing. "I can't wait for it to be my turn! Getting out of my stupid stinkhole will be a dream come true. But this"—she swept her arms around—"is heaven." She walked over to Lee and clapped him on the back. "Well done." She shoved something into his hands. "This is for you. Don't make a big deal about it." She skipped over to the windows to stand next to Mina. "Pretty sweet setup, huh?"

Mina nodded. "The sweetest."

"When do you think, ah, it'll be my turn?"

"Slow down there, star-streaker extraordinaire." Kaylee walked toward them, chuckling. "You're not even out of the natal phase yet. Good things come to those who have more patience than a child hoarding treats. You've passed a few tests, nothing more. Agent Adams had to wait over a year and a half for this, not to mention he solved a case big enough to garner him a gold commendation." She inclined her head toward Lee. "Well done, by the way. That was a super-fun party." She swung back toward her mentee. "You, on the other hand, have some proving to do."

Harmony crossed her arms, one hip on its way to full jut. Mina was coming to understand that it was her most natural position.

"You mean disarming a missile full of poisonous gas that could wipe out an entire city isn't good enough? Or how about shutting down and reworking the vid feed of a Syndicate member?" She dropped her arms, taking on a pleading pose, clasping her hands in front of her, knees bent, bottom lip protruding. "Those two alone should at least grant me a level one in a boring housing unit. Anything would be better than what I have right now. You could sneeze, and my residence would fall over."

Mina burst out laughing. Kaylee had just said the same

thing about the vase. "How can you two be the same person?" She glanced between the two of them, shaking her head.

Kaylee rolled her eyes. Harmony went back to arm crossing, hip jutting, and foot tapping.

"Harmony, you're welcome to take up a housing request with Director McAllister," Mina said. "It's up to him to decide timing, levels, and everything else. For now, let's all take a quick tour of Lee's place, then he and I need to get moving. Norm's being released soon. We need to be there." She threw her some small hope. "I bet if you help us bring down a fixer of the Syndicate, you'll get approved for a new residence in no time."

A gurgle came from Lee, and they all turned to look.

He held a small, square piece of tech in his hands, glancing down at it in awe. He slowly brought his head up, homing in on Harmony. "Is this...a Jupiter sonic accelerometer?"

"It is," Harmony answered. "I told you not to make a big deal about it."

"But...but," Lee sputtered. "There's only, like, three of them in existence."

"What's a Jupiter phonic accelerometer?" Kaylee asked as she and Mina moved toward Lee to see what it was.

"Sonic," Harmony said. "And there are actually five. I know, because I only made five. They measure microvibrations in the gravitational constant."

Mina was a little worried that Lee might fall over in his

ecstasy. She moved closer to brace for it.

"You made these?" He was as incredulous as Mina had ever seen him. He looked down at the tiny cube in his hand, his face full of wonder.

"Yeppers," Harmony replied. "I spent a lot of years by myself with my dad's toolkit." Her father, Strum Littlefield, was a renowned hacker who'd just gotten sprung from many years in a box. Mina hoped their reunion was going well. Seemed like it was. "It helped that he'd already figured out how to build one. I just finished his work. It's not that overly complicated, other than, of course, my technocoded software. There's a super-tiny sonic aural transmitter that measures dynamic acceleration through the—"

Kaylee held up her hand. "Okay. I'm going to have to stop you two right there. Although this conversation is hyper fun and supes scintillating, we have an ex-marshal to save and a Syndicate fixer to fix." She gestured at Lee. "Show us the rest of your place, then we're streaking out."

Harmony and Lee bopped their heads together as they walked, continuing to chatter about the exciting, five-of-a-kind tech.

Mina cackled. "Who knew we'd be enjoying domestic duties together like shopping for home goods, buying practical gifts, and trying to keep our children in line? Oh, how times have changed."

"Very funny," Kaylee groused. "We are not those people. We don't buy lamps, and we don't enjoy practicality. But at least your kid listens. Mine's going to spend all her time trying to dig herself out of the naughty sinkholes she keeps jumping into."

"No, she's not." Mina chuckled. "I adore her energy. Not to mention her brilliance. She's just young. But she's completely moldable. You've done an excellent job so far." They came to a stop, glancing in to see Lee's impressive sleep room. It was roomy with a good-sized platform and a sleep pod. "Wow, Lee," she said. "Have enough beds in here?"

Her partner blushed. "I...um...I requested a sleep pod, which the residence delivered, but they, um, left the platform." He scratched his head. "I have to figure out what to do with it."

Harmony hopped on top, giving it a few quick bounces. "I wish I had room for this at my place. It's totally phantasmic." She cocked her head at Kaylee. "But my place is a teensy, tiny little elemental cave. This thing would take up all my remaining space."

"Your living arrangements are not up to me," Kaylee answered primly. "As Agent Kane so nicely detailed, help bring this Syndicate asshelmet down, then we'll talk."

"That shouldn't be too hard." Harmony sprang off the platform, the rust-color sheets now mussed. "The guy's basically under residence arrest. We've got time to play."

"I don't know if we're going to be given the authority to pursue this," Mina said. "First thing we have to do is talk to Norm and shuttle him somewhere safe. Did McAllister say anything to you two about plans moving forward?"

Mina and Lee had left the scene to attend their audit, while Kaylee, Harmony, and Vince had figured out a way to make it look like Norm had broken out of Wilbert Waterbury's residence.

Kaylee shook her head. "Nope. I think everybody is just waiting to hear what Webb has to say."

Mina glanced at Lee, giving him a nod. "We have to get a hold of McAllister before we meet Norm. Do you want to do it on your new screen? Or should I call him on my cuff?"

Lee smiled enthusiastically, on top of an already enthusiastic grin. "Let's do it on a screen. The biggest one is out in the living area."

He led the way, and Harmony skipped after him. "My screen is like a junked craft blew up and one of its panels attached to my wall."

Once they were all assembled, Lee put in the call.

"Agent Adams," McAllister said. "Is this a new-residence celebration?"

"A small one," Lee replied. "I just arrived a few hours ago."

McAllister scanned the room. "Looks like a great space. Congratulations."

"Thank you, sir," Lee said.

"Norman Webb is going to be released within the hour," McAllister said.

Mina nodded. "We're planning on being there. Have you found a safe place to keep him?"

"Not yet," McAllister said gruffly. "I wanted him

installed in a safe room at Government One so we could keep a better eye on him until we see what Waterbury's next move will be, but he's turned us down."

Sounded like Norm.

"It's going to be a bit of a struggle to get him to consent to protection, because he prides himself on his well-honed evasion tactics," Mina said. "But I plan on winning that argument. Have we gotten approval to investigate Waterbury yet?" Mina didn't want to sound too hopeful, but a little hope rang through anyway.

Their boss frowned. "I've put in a request, but have not received any confirmation. I cannot sanction a full government operation until then."

"That's unfortunate," Mina said. "Wilbert is going to visit his residence this afternoon and find Norm gone. It would be optimal if we were there to capture the moment."

"I agree," he said. "But to buy us more time, I plan to have the counselors restrict Waterbury's movement until late this afternoon. A full day, if they can manage. But that might be unrealistic, as he will understand that there's been interference within the system, which we don't want."

Mina nodded. "Did you get my request about funding Phineas Raphael's vacation?" Mr. Raphael, a civilian, had allowed them to use his residence at the Meridian, Waterbury's high-rise, the day prior. Mina didn't want him embroiled with anything to do with the Syndicate.

"I did, and I'm looking into it."

"Vince is putting him up at The Bella for now. The colonel

has also let me know that we have further permission to use Mr. Raphael's residence for the remainder of this operation, if we so desire."

Mina didn't want to think about what that was costing Vince, but she was thankful for it.

"Noted. I will make that decision after we have a debrief from Norman Webb," McAllister said. "The details of his capture and torture are to be recorded on a veribox and reported immediately. That evidence will help me secure this case. If you can locate a place he'll agree to go to for safe keeping after your interview, all the better. Agent Poston and Harmony Biggins, I want you at headquarters. I have a small op for you to complete. If we get authorization to deal with Waterbury, all four of you will be working together." He addressed Mina. "What about Colonel Kramer? If he wants to continue with this investigation, he has my approval."

"I'll pass that along when I speak with him," Mina said. "I'm sure he'll appreciate being included." She resisted the urge to check her cuff for messages. She'd approved his calls to go straight through this morning and would've heard if he'd called.

McAllister nodded. "I'll be expecting a report soon. That is all."

IT WASN'T SURPRISING to find Norman Webb standing alone on the roof of Government Four, appearing disgruntled and a little put out when Mina and Lee arrived.

The drone door opened.

"Save it, Webb," Mina instructed, corking any excuses before they spilled out of him. "Get your backside in this craft so we can talk."

Norm leaned over, refraining from actually boarding, calling, "I told you I don't need any guarding! I'm fine. I know how to protect myself. You told me the kid left town. So we're good. Go complete an op that matters."

"So help me," Mina started, "if you don't get inside this drone in the next three seconds, I'm leaking a juicy story to the media about how you have an uncontrollable... feline addiction." It was the best she could come up with on short notice. "Ex-marshal of the US government is obsessed with his four-legged friends. His residence is crawling with them. The smell is atrocious. His neighbors complain about constant meowing. I can see it splashed everywhere. The goss rags love that kind of stuff. They eat it up. They'll probably give you some snappy moniker, like Catman Webb or Hissy-Fit Norm. I'm sure the younger generation you work out with at the exercise dome will think it's hysterical, particularly when it flashes across all the screens while you're all there together." Lee blinked at Mina's thin attempt to shame the ex-marshal into compliance. She shrugged, muttering to her partner, "You got anything better?"

"No," Lee answered. "But look, here he comes." In a lower tone, he asked, "Can you do something like that? Leak a fake story to the media?"

"Not exactly." Soft stories such as the one she just described aired all the time. Nobody took them that seriously. The government had a direct line to the media, but Mina wouldn't use it for something so frivolous. "Don't think for a second he fell for it either. He's just too worn out to put up a real fight."

Norm moved with a minor limp, one of his arms pressed close to his side. Other than that, he had no outward appearance of the injuries he'd sustained at the hands of Wilbert Waterbury, a presumed fixer for the Syndicate. It was mildly surprising, as his injuries had been egregious. Multiple fractures, bruised ribs, a mild concussion, and a puncture wound that had caused him to lose a lot of blood. It was amazing how far medical technology and healing had come.

Even though Mina might want to spare him the interview so he could focus on further recovery, they needed answers, and she wasn't leaving until she got them.

Once he was seated in the drone, he grumbled, "Okay, fine. I'm here."

"Is that any way to greet the people who saved your life?" Mina asked, keeping her tone light. She needed him happy and relaxed. "We know you're upset and angry at yourself that this happened. But we're past that. Vincent Kramer took lead on this." Norm's eyebrows rose. "Yeah, so you understand what that means. If the Syndicate finds out who broke you out of there, it's not just your double thrusters on the line, it's his, too." Mina was going to keep that from happening, whatever it took. "Harri Hampburg's life is on the line, too. Waterbury threatened to kill him to get you to comply, and even though he's in New Mexico and McAllister is keeping an eye on him, we need to make sure he stays safe. The Syndicate can find him. They can find anyone." Given enough time, since they had enough resources, that was the truth.

Norm bowed his head. "I know." He was weary down to the bone. "I'm sorry. You're right, I'm feeling mighty sorry for myself and extremely apologetic that I put those I care about in danger." He glanced up. "I know you know this, but I'm gonna say it out loud so we all understand. I'm grateful to you for getting me out of there. I wouldn't have lasted ten more minutes in that sorry hellhole. Every part of me was broken and bleeding. He did a number on me. I owe you my life."

"We didn't do it alone. I'm just glad we were able to help," Mina said. "Now we need answers. The entire story, on the record. Then we go after this guy and put him where he belongs—back in a box indefinitely."

Before Norm could respond, the sim intoned, "What is your destination please?"

"Looks like you could use a decent meal," Mina commented. "Do you know of a place where we can sit down and not be bothered while you tell us your story? Please don't say Biters. Someplace Waterbury wouldn't know. Then we'll decide together where you go after that."

"Yeah." Norm ran a hand over his face. "I got a place. Little diner called Mary Lou's. It's a sit-down-and-order kind of place, printed, reasonable prices. Run by bots. Located out of the way. Half residential, half merchandise mecca. Everybody leaves you alone. Been there a few times. Nice and private."

"Sounds ideal," Mina said. "Destination Mary Lou's diner."

"Destination entered. Travel time three minutes and thirty-seven seconds," the sim confirmed.

Mina didn't prod Norm during the ride. She let the ex-marshal settle and work on getting his head back in the game.

Instead, Lee filled him in about his new residence. His excitement was infectious.

"Sounds like a great place, kid." Norm chuckled. "I'm looking forward to being invited over."

Lee nodded enthusiastically. "You will be. I'm hoping to have some kind of a get-together soon." He worried his thumbs together. "I've never done that before. Entertain anyone. No room in my last place. But I'm looking forward to learning how."

"You'll be a natural at it," Norm encouraged. "All you need to do is print up some goodies and have fresh drinks available, and your job is done. Oh, and pipe in some music. People love music, especially when it's set to mood circles on the screen. Really sets the tone for the evening."

Lee smiled, soaking it all up.

"Landing at Mary Lou's diner in thirty seconds," the sim announced.

They set down and exited.

Mary Lou's resembled Biters in that they were both single-story cinder block stand-alone buildings. That's where the resemblance ended. Mary Lou's was covered in jaunty red paneling and had huge solar-catch windows and a red and white awning wrapped around one whole side. There were also a fair number of drones in the lot.

"Don't worry," Norm said, moving toward the door. "The booths are spaced out. We'll ask for one in the back."

They followed him inside.

"Hi there, and welcome to Mary Lou's. How many in your party?" A perky bot in a red and white uniform with a paper hat perched on one side of her brunette head greeted them at the door.

"Three," Norm said. "Someplace in the back. No company."

"Certainly, sir." The bot's name tag read Sarah. "Right this way."

Sarah led them to a generous booth in a back corner. No other diners were close enough to overhear. The clientele consisted mainly of families and a couple of elderly couples.

The interior was exactly like the exterior—lots of red and white. The floor was well-worn, alternating black and white tile. The booth was made out of a glossy red material.

The bot gestured for them to sit. As they did, they ran their cuffs over the approval pin set into the tabletop. It connected with a bank stamp that told the restaurant that they had borrows to spend here.

For privacy reasons, no other information was shared.

"There are a variety of ways to order," the bot explained. "The easiest is through our holo menu. Just enact the sensory button on the table, and it will display. When you're ready to order, simply tap the item you're interested in or verbalize your request. Disengage holo when you're finished. If you make a mistake and order something you don't want, simply say 'error' out loud. If you would rather use a board, they are right inside that opening." Sarah gestured to a small drawer built into the wall. "Just tap your request into the board, and it will be sent to our kitchen. Your food will be brought out as soon as it's ready.

Would any of you enjoy a refreshing drink to start?"

"I'll take a coffee with a shot of dairy-sub, no sweet," Mina said.

Norm said, "I'll have the same."

"A bubbly for me," Lee said.

"We have every flavor of bubbly available in the entire galaxy," the bot chattered happily. "Strawberry blaster, grape grapple, kiwi kidder, mango bloom, summer kiss, lime twist are a few standard examples. We can mix them, we can add ice cream, we can add—"

"Lime twist is fine." Lee blushed. Once the bot left to take care of their drinks order, he muttered, "Sorry."

Mina tapped the holo menu, and an enormous 3-D menu popped up in front of them, covering the entire table. She'd never seen one so big. Mina and Lee were on one side. Norm sat on the other.

"The eggs any way you can get 'em don't disappoint," Norm said, his face superimposed with holo menu from Mina's vantage point. "They're printed with just the right amount of trace. A personal favorite is the old-fashioned hash scramble."

"That sounds good." Lee selected the option with his finger. The words shifted and turned green.

Mina chose a lemon raspberry scone. "I already ate breakfast. Eggie made me some delicious French toast." It was possible Mina had a certain someone from France on the brain today. No, it wasn't possible, it was a fact.

Once everyone finished ordering, Mina hit the button,

and the holo menu popped out of sight. She reached in her pocket and drew out a veribox. She didn't have to explain to the ex-marshal what this protected government recorder was or why it was necessary. She activated it, nodding toward Norm.

"If we're going to have any luck nabbing Wilbert Waterbury," Mina told the ex-marshal, "we need everything. Don't hold anything back. I want it from beginning to end. From when you first met this guy, to when you were carried out of his residence yesterday afternoon." Her voice did the stressing for her. The tone that she'd chosen brokered no room for pushback. They were doing this.

Norm sat back, contemplating. "Once I start, there's no going back."

"Understood."

"You told me on the drone ride to the medi-unit yesterday that you know who Wilbert Waterbury is and who he's connected to. Take a moment to contemplate the hellscape you're opening up and the likelihood that very bad things could be brought down upon yourself and those you love by poking into this case. There's no time frame for how long it takes either." He gestured to the two-centimeter square box on the table recording his every word. "There's no pulling it back once it goes in there. It'll be like an old-fashioned freight train running at high speed on those rickety tracks. When it bashes into you, it obliterates your body with no apologies. Only way to save yourself is if you decide to step out of the way, which you can still do now."

She studied the ex-marshal. He seemed resigned, but not overly fearful. He was doing his due diligence by warning her. She appreciated that. "Is that why you kept Waterbury's Syndicate affiliation out of the first set of charges? Because there's not a whiff of it in his file." Mina acknowledged Norm's words and accepted the consequences by moving forward. "It was cited that the two of you were friends. I find that a little hard to believe, having met Wilbert. You couldn't have been close. Was that a ruse so you could get close to him? To find something to bring him in on that wasn't connected to the mob?"

Norm sat back in his seat as the bot approached to drop off their drinks.

Once she left, Norm picked up his coffee and took a sip. "You better get comfortable. This is going to take some time. I won't leave anything out, but like I said, once this is open and presented as an official report, there's no going back. If you manage to take him in, the testimony I'm about to give will be key, and you might actually succeed in taking a chunk out of the Syndicate's hide. But once that happens, they'll react like wild animals doing whatever they can to save their existence. I've seen it a couple of times during my career. They kill magistrates, go after jury members, pay off lawyers. It's as ugly as ugly gets." He met Mina stare for stare. "Are you sure you still want to do this?"

Was she?

This was what she did for a living. She'd sworn a pledge

to protect innocents and do whatever it took to bring to justice those who would hurt them. The Syndicate had operated without a care for well over a hundred and fifty years, harming people without compunction, constantly getting away with it, becoming wealthier and wealthier as the years went by.

It was more than time for them to be held accountable.

Even more important than Norm's testimony, Mina had to make sure this case proceeded in exactly the right way. They had to bring Waterbury in on charges that would stick—and before the Syndicate knew what was happening. If they didn't, they would lose. If they were extremely lucky, and Waterbury got Babble, a powerful truth-telling serum, and multiple media stories broke at the same time, it would produce the kind of chaos needed to keep the Syndicate in a spiral. It would be like igniting a hundred fires at once. This old, rich, corrupt crime organization wouldn't know which flames to put out first or, if everything went perfectly, who started the blaze. Mina believed her agency had the wherewithal to complete the case efficiently, and if anything went wrong, the CIU had the ability to protect them.

"Yes. I'm ready."

"I WAS NEVER this guy's friend. Let's make that perfectly clear. I got close to him on purpose, made him think we were friendly," Norm started. "This goes way back. Gotta be twelve, thirteen years now. He did seven in a box, and it was at least five or six before that when she first came to me." He straightened, his expression grim. "See, it wasn't just animals Waterbury liked to hurt. It was women, too. And this one happened to be my niece. She started it all. And before you ask, no, she won't sit witness on this. He scared the ever-loving sweetness right out of her, not to mention left behind some physical scars. She moved halfway around the world to get away from him and has been living peacefully ever since. She's not in witness protection, per se, but right up close. New identity chip. I wiped her lifecheck. All the standard stuff. No record of her anywhere. Anyone who goes looking would have a hard time finding her. Not impossible, but hard enough that I feel good about it. So we deal right now that her name doesn't come up. I'm not even going to mention it. You can do a deep dive on me, and it'll never pop. If you don't agree, I stay quiet. I've already put too many people I love in the crosshairs of this evil empire. She's the only genetic relative I have left. I never married, never had kids. She's worth protecting."

"Deal," Mina answered without hesitation. She wasn't willing to risk a family member of Norm's either. "She doesn't play in this. But we still need to hear the story. All of it. If she was one of his victims, there will be others. It all adds."

"It does, which is why I'm agreeing to talk. I haven't in years. Tucked it away so it didn't come back to bite me. See what that got me? Nothing. These guys"—he leaned forward, lowering his voice, though the veribox would still pick up every word—"they don't forget. They never forget. They live by revenge. They love it more than they love breathing. I can tell you for a fact that Waterbury thought of nothing but carving me up every second of his seven-year sentence. It was his fuel. His energy. His life force."

Lee sputtered, unable to keep quiet. "Then why didn't you just move away? Do the same thing as your niece? Change your name, wipe your background. You had the means to do so. Then you would've stayed safe."

Norm shook his head. "Not a chance. He would've come after me until the day he died. Better to face it and try to get the best of him. And when I tell you I was ready and had plans in place, I was, and I did. My failure was not expecting him to come at me sooner. I was off by a few weeks. Like I told your partner here," he said to Lee as he gestured at Mina, "I had someone on the inside of Oak Lane, where he's doing his group, monitored residency. And he's doing it there because I mandated it long before he was sprung. I set it up, made sure he didn't get out without it, everything. I still have sway, my word means something. Then just like that"—Norm snapped his fingers—"he slips out like a whisper." His brow furrowed. "I should've counted on that. I should've known that the Syndicate would muck everything up. There are no new hires at Oak Lane as far as I know, so they got him out some other way. Could've been bot reprogramming." He glanced at Mina with an unspoken apology. "Had I known he was going to gain more freedom, I never would've agreed to take on the job guarding your friend Harri. Not in a trillion. I would've enacted my plan, had him come get me on my turf. Things would've gone different. Much different." Norm shook his head sadly.

"I believe you," Mina said. "You're excellent at your job. Your record is pristine. You set things in motion, thought you had the areas covered. I've been there. It's no fun when the gravity gives out."

Norm appeared crestfallen. "That's how I know I'm slipping. I should've known the Syndicate would worm their way in. Another mistake I made—because the bosses didn't try to save him at the time of his trial, didn't pull any strings, didn't throw currency at his case—is I figured he was a string they wanted to snip. That he was beneath their notice or was a toothache they were willing to pull." He took a sip of coffee. "Had no idea they were paying for his residence the entire time he was inside. I went over his file every six months from the time he went in to the time he got out, and nothing flagged. They paid for the reno and everything. They want him back. He has value. And because of that, they're not going to let him go again easily." He pinned Mina with a gaze that churned with regret. "Even if we catch him, he gets out. My bet is nothing will stick."

"Not if he gets Babble before they know he's inside," Mina countered. "By then, it's too late. He'll confess every bad deed he's done and knows about in that organization. It will be a bloodbath, a hemorrhage they can't stop."

Norm's eyebrows shot up. He looked intrigued, his face easing from sadness into hope. "Babble, huh?" He leaned forward. "And how do you figure you're going to get that approved?" Babble had been restricted a few years prior to Waterbury's case, as people who were slated to get it were ending their lives rather than face giving a confession that exposed their every ugly secret.

Mina gestured to the veribox. "Times have changed and are continuing to change. Approving violent criminals for Babble, especially ones that've already done time in a box, is getting easier. What can help our case is you providing us with firsthand incriminating evidence and my director bringing that to a magistrate. Wilbert Waterbury counts as an extremely violent offender, especially after testimony that he tortured you."

"That will only work if the magistrate isn't dirty," Norm countered.

It was a sad truth. "That's right," Mina said. "It'll be up to McAllister to find one who isn't. We have to trust he can do that. But we can't do anything without airtight evidence. And that starts with you and your story. So walk us through."

"He's an animal," Norm grunted, sitting back in his seat, relaxing by a few degrees. "It doesn't get much worse than prolonged torture with intent to kill, according to my data log."

A male service bot dressed in the same uniform Sarah wore approached their table, expertly hefting a large tray filled with their food.

The tray didn't so much as jiggle.

Not an extremely great time to break the rhythm, but they had to eat. That's why they were here.

"Here you go," the service bot said cheerfully as he set everything down in its correct place. "Enjoy your meal."

Mina picked up her scone. "I had no idea entirely bot-run eating establishments existed anymore." She reached out and paused the veribox, glancing around, making sure there were still no inquiring ears nearby. "With the Air Breathers Employment Act of 2090, I thought it was illegal. Don't they have to have at least a few humans working here?"

"This place has been here for years, so I'm pretty sure it was grandfathered in," Norm answered around a mouthful of food. "This is as good as I remember." He finished his bite and continued, "I believe the upper management consists of all air breathers, and that's enough. Some people prefer not to be bothered when they go out to consume a meal. There's another place called Manicotti's up north. Same thing. All bots working the floor."

"Is it a diner like this?" Mina said, tearing off a piece of her scone. It crumbled with the right consistency. She popped it in her mouth.

Yum.

"Nope. It's Italian. They specialize in that specific trace," Norm said. "But just like any printed restaurant, they can do you a solid and make just about anything."

"You're right. This is good," Lee said, scooping up his second bite of eggs. "Best I've had in a while."

"I bet your new meal printer can create some great food." The food was better than decent. Mina enjoyed the flavor. Some printed recipes mimicked the way food used to taste much better than others. It was usually because they'd been around so long and had taken time to perfect it. This was definitely one of those places. Mina would have to keep it in mind.

"I hope so. It's not a Magnito, like yours," Lee said. "It's an Al Dente, but it's the current model. I had it print me a quick bowl of cereal this morning. It was great." Lee beamed.

Mina was extremely happy for her talented partner, who'd earned his new residence and a decent meal printer because of quick thinking and a big brain. "Let's finish this up and get back to the story." She checked her cuff. No message from Vince. "Then I'm reporting to McAllister. Once he gets a copy, things can move forward."

Once Norm was finished with his story, she hoped like crazy they'd have something solid to go on.

"Wait a second," Mina said. "I want you to clarify. You were friendly with Waterbury on and off for four or five years before you figured out the animal-mutilation piece?"

Norm had already covered his torture, in detail.

It'd been hard to listen to, but necessary. Before that, he'd quickly recounted his years-long efforts to get Waterbury in a box, starting with when his niece had contacted him for help, through having Waterbury picked up for cashing in his dead mother's security borrows.

"Like I told you," Norm said. "It all took time to unravel. I started frequenting his haunts and finally settled on a place called Tanks. In the beginning, I didn't know he worked for the Syndicate. But it wasn't hard to spot he was working for someone." Mina understood what the term working meant. Norm had caught on early that this guy did bad things for a living. "He was agitated most of the time, left abruptly, had a new cuff every other week. Tanks is a bar that sells low-quality printed ale. Dark inside, sparse patronage, lots of bots, easy to disappear. It all fit."

"How'd you get him to trust you enough to talk?" Lee asked, rapt by the story so far. "A guy like that, you'd think he'd be distrustful and keep to himself."

Norm chuckled. "My usual was pretending to overimbibe, then I'd say stuff I knew he'd like to hear. Terrible stuff about women. How much I despised 'em and how useless they were. Fastest way to get a guy like that to talk is to be more awful and hateful than he is. It was the best acting of my career. Watched him swipe my DNA after that. Took a glass I'd been drinking out of and pocketed it. Thought I was too much of a rotting sot to notice. I was ecstatic. I was still on the federal payroll at the time, just barely, and my identity in that sector was Billy Martin, who worked as a sewer cleaner. I even paid out of my own pocket to hire a hacker to layer it deeper, in case Waterbury decided to do a dive. Figured after he checked me out, he'd either stop coming to Tanks altogether, or he'd be even more buddy-buddy. Luckily, it was the latter. Not long after that, I figured out the Syndicate angle. One night, when he left quickly after getting a summons on a brand-new cuff, my partner at the time, Xavier Carter, tailed him. Then we met up. We identified a known Syndicate member passing information to him in a park outside city limits. Have it all on vid. That's when I got my niece out of the country. The animal-mutilation information came maybe a year or two later." Norm shook his head. "Waterbury is a pro. Doesn't talk much. Lets very few things slip. He likes to consume alcohol, but he doesn't drink too much. So after years of putting in time with this guy, and getting very little, I decided to help him along one evening." Norm chuckled, leaning back, crossing his arms. "Put a little Blur in his glass. Got him talking about a bunch of stuff, but had to make it seem anecdotal. With Blur, you get relaxed, let your guard down, but you remember what you say. Didn't want him talking about anything he would regret, because that regret would come right out of my hide. That's when he told me about a stray cat he'd found and what he did to it." Norm ran his palm over his face, shaking his head. "Awful stuff. I had to act like doing something like that was normal, and who cares because it's just a cat. That was the moment I knew I was bringing this guy down if it was the last thing I ever did. It showed me what this guy was capable of. He didn't just knock women around, which was bad enough, he was a stone-cold killer who enjoyed mutilating defenseless creatures. It took me a long time to work out how to do it. Decided to leave the Syndicate out. All the way out. Best chance I had of getting charges to stick. Unfortunately, the break I needed came after I was forced to retire out of the Marshals Service. Waterbury had told me previously, at least three years prior, that both his parents were dead. Then one night, I made a point to comment that he always had a new cuff, and that had to be a pretty expensive habit to maintain.

He mumbled something about his mother's government pension paying for them. Claimed he liked collecting tech. I had him with that one, as I figured it had to be true. A guy like that doesn't say no to currency of any kind. But he'd forgotten he told me some time ago that his mother was dead. I had to recruit a few current marshals to do the actual apprehension and subsequent investigation, because I wasn't on the payroll by then."

"Were you ever inside his residence before? The one where he kept you captive?" Mina asked.

Norm nodded. "Twice. The first time was so he could show me a rare weapon he'd purchased. Happened about six months after we first met. An automatic rifle from about a hundred years ago. When he first bragged about it, I claimed he was lying, since most of those were confiscated and melted down. He was pissed I didn't believe him. So he took me there to show it to me. No hint of anyone living there with him. Place was sterile. Second time was on the pretense of me setting him up with a woman I knew. This came after I was out of the government, right before he was picked up. Told him I had to connect them personally, on-screen. The role of the woman was played by a marshal by the name of Alice Sweeney. He had no way to get her DNA, and I paid for a very extensive alt. Got me in the door. While he was busy talking to her, I excused myself to use the waste room. Found a large cooling unit in his utility room. Found the animal carcasses. A week later, he was picked up. The marshals knew about the stolen pension and the mutilation, but I left the Syndicate out. I don't know if it was a good idea or bad, but it's what I decided on. Before the arrest went down, I tried hard to figure out if he'd offed his parents—his mother, his father, or both. I found no trail. She died of some sort of rare disease several years before I'd met him. Father was MIA in the system. Hadn't made a DNA swipe in over a dozen years. Nothing conclusive. Waterbury was never supposed to know it was me who was behind his arrest. The plan was to keep me out entirely, but a young rookie messed up during interrogation, and Waterbury saw a recent photo of me. He put two and two in the same column. Added up to the guy who'd been working him over for years. The man was apoplectic. It took three or four marshals to calm him down. After that, I knew my fate."

"He was picked up for defrauding the government by keeping his dead mother's pension borrows," Mina said, "but you indicated the marshals who nabbed him knew about the mutilation piece. But they didn't have proof at the time, so they had to obtain a warrant after he was in custody?"

Norm nodded. "Yeah. Once he found out I was involved, I was able to give testimony about that. The warrant to search the residence came in quick. There was a petition to give him Babble at the time, seeing that both his parents appeared to be dead, but we couldn't prove the father's death was suspicious. The judge turned down the request. Like I said, the Syndicate never popped its head in to see about this case, unless they had something to do with the truth-serum refusal. Seemed like they didn't care too much. He was tried and put away in only a few days. The evidence was a lock."

"Seven years was a long sentence for what he was accused of," Mina said. "Did you have anything to do with that?"

Norm drummed his fingers on the table, raising a single eyebrow. He wasn't going to comment about that.

It was enough for Mina.

She thought about it. "He liked to physically hurt women, along with doling out vile verbal abuse, according to your statement. I'm assuming he spoke about that once or twice over the years. Did he give you any names? Were there any women who tried to press charges and then retracted their testimony? Was he ever in a stable relationship while you two were friendly at Tanks? It doesn't sound right that he'd have that long of a dry spell."

"There were a few women he was close with over the years, for sure. I tried to get their names. Even resorted to inviting him and a date over for dinner. He declined and never said who they were. Attempted to tail him a couple times when I knew he had a date, because he liked to brag, but he always used a drone. Never went anywhere on foot with those poor women."

Trailing a craft was almost impossible, as navigating air traffic was hectic, and the drones were piloted by sims. It wouldn't work unless the drone always set down at a public landing, as a craft needed prior permission to set down. If Waterbury was picking these women up at private residences, Norm wouldn't have been able to follow or get approval. A craft wasn't allowed to hover for an indefinite amount of time either.

Norm leaned forward. "Listen, this guy knows how to keep himself clean. Yeah, he made a mistake leaving the animal carcasses where I could find them. He likes trophies. But he won't err like that again." He gestured a hand at Mina in a conceding motion. "But if what I give you here today is enough to catch him, and you make sure he gets a dose of Babble immediately, it might be the ticket you're looking for. A quick one-two punch. Bring him in, stick him with a syringe. No delay. It just might work."

"That's what we're hoping for. To make it an absolute lock, we need your testimony coupled with irrefutable evidence." She shot a glance at Lee. "I know it was risky to try to hack into the satellite that contains vid evidence of Norm's torture yesterday at Waterbury's residence, and it would be risky now, but we need that footage. It would be enough to bring him in and put this plan into motion."

Upon digging, Lee had found that half of Wilbert's residential cams, including the ones in the utility room where he had placed Norm, were linked to a private satellite owned by Travis Blade, one of the main bosses of the Syndicate. Waterbury's desire to keep a recording of his torture of Norm as a keepsake had been a huge mistake.

Mina continued, "He would have enjoyed perusing that

footage again and again after he murdered Norm." She shot a look of apology at the ex-marshal. He shrugged. "How do we get it? Do we just take a risk and hack in?"

Lee scratched his head. "I mean, it's a possibility. We can get it for sure with a hack. But then Waterbury and the mob would have absolute proof we have it. They would have a big heads-up and could begin to refute it before it hits the government airmeld. That kind of hack would be like lighting off a hydro-cracker right in front of their faces."

Mina bit her lip. "Hm. That's not optimal. But we need that feed. It's all we have to back up Norm's testimony."

"What Waterbury wants is sitting right here," Lee said, glancing between Mina and Norm. "Like Colonel Kramer suggested yesterday, if we give him another shot at Norm, I'm pretty sure he would take it. This time on our turf. Then we can vid it ourselves."

Curious, Mina asked Norm, "You said you had plans in place to take him down. Were you going to gather evidence yourself, then call for backup?"

Norm was quiet. "Not exactly."

When he didn't readily go on, Mina cocked her head. "It's helpful to us to know what your plan was." It wasn't critical to his testimony, so he didn't necessarily have to tell them.

Norm angled his head at the veribox. Mina reached out and shut it off.

They would continue this off the record.

He sighed. "My plans didn't involve either of us surviving."

Chapter 5

Mina couldn't hide her shock. "You were willing to die to end his life?"

That was hard to believe. Norm had so many contacts—marshals and other federal agents—who would've willingly come to his aid. All he had to do was get this monster on a live feed doing some damage, and agents would've stormed the residence.

Norm shrugged, fiddling with his empty coffee cup. "Ultimately, my plan wasn't to die, but I knew the chances were high enough. Waterbury wasn't going to be satisfied with anything except my death, and he was going to make it painful. He was never going to stop pursuing me until he had his end result. He was going to do the deed in a place of his liking. Where he felt secure. Certainly not out in the open. Not at my residence. So I made peace with it. Or at least I tried."

"But you had plans in place to try and keep that from

happening, right?" Lee asked.

"I hadn't received my implants yet. That was a mistake," Norm said, regret at the forefront. "I should've had them put in the day he walked out of that box."

"Implants?" Though Mina didn't want to know.

"Yes," Norm answered. "Two. The first was a static locator." He tapped his forearm. "It was going to be placed here. So you could find me, either before or after. The other was—"

Mina held up her hand to stop him. Even though the veribox was off, she didn't want him to utter it out loud.

"Those are highly illegal." It wasn't a question.

"They are," Norm said.

"What are illegal?" Lee asked.

Mina sighed. She was going to have to inform her partner what was going on, even if she didn't want to. "Norm was going to have an echo fibrillator implanted." Norm confirmed with a small nod. "I'm assuming it was voice-activated. Those things are incredibly unstable. In order to take out another person, they need to be right next to you. Like, centimeters away."

There weren't too many implants that could kill another person and leave the person with the implant alive. Technically, echo fibs could do that, but in reality they usually killed both participants.

Norm leaned forward. "When somebody's torturing you, they're usually hovering right over you, if not in your face." He stopped, his eye catching on something over

Mina's shoulder. He snapped back a moment later. "And that's exactly what happened. Had I gotten that thing installed, he wouldn't be alive right now, and you'd have all the evidence you need. Including my prerecorded vid message explaining the plan and the code to find my static location. I figured he'd film the whole thing, so I wasn't worried about you getting that with a warrant. In the end, you'd have found my battered body, kinda like you did yesterday, and we'd have gone from there."

Mina shook her head. "That's not the way it would've gone down. You wouldn't have survived either." She glanced at Lee. "You know how an echo fib works, right?"

"Yeah. It basically nulls a heartbeat. She's right," Lee said, "you wouldn't be able to survive that." He glanced pointedly at Norm. "Technically, heartbeats pump at similar patterns. Crude tech like that can't differentiate between two things that are that similar. It wouldn't discriminate between you and Waterbury. It would shock you both."

"Not if you rile somebody up," Norm argued. "This particular fib is supposed to latch on to the quicker beat. At least that's what the dealer told me."

Mina crossed her arms, sitting back in her chair. "Another way this could've gone is that Waterbury could've gagged you. Then you wouldn't have been able to get out a voice command. He would've killed you and would've gone free."

"Nah. He likes to hear his victim scream," Norm

answered confidently. "Had to go with the implants. They're coated in silicone and wouldn't be detected by a wand. He searched me good once he got me back to his residence and only started on the torture once he was satisfied I had nothing on me. I went into that residence like an old farm animal to slaughter." He visibly shivered. "Implants were the best I had, and I still believe that. Tell me you would've done it different."

"I'm telling you I would've done it different. No question," Mina said. "I'm here, interviewing you, ready to come up with an alternative plan. One that doesn't involve any of us dying."

"The Syndicate is a sticky wicket," Norm warned. "They don't forget. Ever. If I'd gone through with my plan, and survived, it would've gone public, exposing them and their fixer. I'd be forced to go into witness protection. The Syndicate would continue looking for me, but since Waterbury had been boxed for the last seven years, my hope was that I'd rank lower on their to-do list. That way, I could stay ahead of the game."

Mina didn't comment. It was clear Norm hadn't been thinking straight. If he had, he would've seen that his plan lacked any real chance of success. She glanced around the restaurant. It was time to get out of here.

She tapped her cuff, then swung it in front of the borrow slot. She grabbed the veribox off the table and stuffed it in her pocket.

"Meal's on me. Come on, let's go."

As they were leaving, Lee asked, "What is a sticky wicket?"

Norm chuckled. "I have no idea, kid. My grandfather got the saying from his dad. Means you're in a precarious situation. Have no idea how long it tracks back. I just like the sound of it."

"It is pretty funny," Lee agreed.

Once they were out on the landing pad, Mina held off on hailing a drone. They still hadn't covered where they were taking Norm. The neighborhood around here had a lot of trees and an actual sidewalk that was free of any pedestrian traffic, foot or jetty. "Do you know if there's another public landing place around here?"

"Yeah. There's one a few blocks up to the north." Norm gestured in front of them.

"Are you okay to walk?" Mina questioned.

Norm answered hotly, "Of course I am!"

Mina quirked a brow. "As we just covered in there"—she jabbed a thumb toward Mary Lou's—"you just went through major torture. It's okay if you're a little sore."

"I'm fine to walk."

"Okay, let's go, then."

Lee leaned over to whisper to Mina, "Why are we walking?"

"Because we need time with Mr. Stubborn here to get him to go where we want. I'm not up for arguing about it in the craft only to not come up with a suitable destination."

"Makes sense," Lee mused.

They were all quiet for a few moments, enjoying the scenery. A nice break from the storyline Norm had laid out inside. They were technically within city limits, but this area was less crowded. Mostly because it was interspersed with manufacturing meccas.

The trees were a bonus. If Mina remembered correctly, her mother had told her large protests had taken place when the powers that be had decided to place manufacturing meccas within city limits. The industry had won that one, but this area wasn't a full mecca, just a handful of buildings.

Mina was glad that they'd kept the greenery.

Someone buzzed across the intersection in front of them, four meters up, on a jetty.

She glanced up, watching the drones pass by in their appropriate altitude lanes based on which direction they were headed. She wondered what the world would've felt like long ago when there were very few things in the air. More congestion at ground level, but maybe it'd been quieter? The air was constantly full of traffic now. She didn't know how loud old-fashioned vehicles had been, but maybe it'd been similar? She'd watched old vids, but it was hard to gauge the noise level.

"You can save your breath. I know why you're doing this," Norm began, gathering Mina's attention back to the task at hand. "I'm not going to any safe house. I'm fine on my own. Before this, my specialty was evasion. I plan to pick up where I left off. I can keep myself safe."

"Nobody's questioning your past. You're excellent at your job. But this is different," Mina said. "As you already stated for the record, if you'd survived your incredibly stupid decision to get an implant, you would've gone into witness protection, because, and I quote, 'the Syndicate doesn't forget, ever.' I need you in a place where I know you're protected. I don't want to exhaust any energy on worrying about your safety. That would be counterproductive. Once they discover you're not in that residence, they're going to be in full pursuit. They'll be wary about your testimony. And rightly so. While you're lying low, we're"—she gestured between her and Lee—"going to come up with a plan to put Waterbury back in a box."

"If you enact any plan, it's gonna place you and everybody else in the crosshairs of the Syndicate," Norm argued. "You should just let me handle it my way. It's between him and me anyway."

"Like hell it is," Mina countered. "We're all in this now. I told you, Vincent Kramer took lead. When the Syndicate and Waterbury find out you escaped, which will likely be by the end of the day, and if their cleanup team is as meticulous as we think it is, they will pick up Vince's DNA somewhere in that residence. He's going to be a beacon for them. We can't let that happen. My way is going to involve getting Waterbury to bring down his bosses with an injection of Babble. Then we get names, dates, deaths, who he gets his orders from, everything. Once we have all that, it will trigger a cascade of warrants, and the Syndicate will be too busy trying to bail themselves out of burning-hot lava to focus on revenge. If we do this right, they won't be able to trace it back to just one person. Their organization will be like a satellite burning up on reentry, and it will take everything they have to try to recover the losses."

"That might prove true in the beginning," Norm grudgingly agreed. "But when everything stops smoldering, you're going to bet your backside they're going to figure out who ignited that switch."

"They're going to blame it on Waterbury." That was Mina's hope. That's what they were going to plan on. "For what he did to you. It will be his own greedy revenge, and his confession, that sinks the Syndicate."

Norm's eyebrows rose. "You think so, huh?"

"I do. If we do this exactly right. But it's not going to happen"—Mina stopped walking and pivoted toward the ex-marshal, hands on her hips—"until you're installed in a safe house. You owe me. That's all there is to it."

"How do you figure?" Norm said. "I know you saved my life, but that—"

"Pormal." Mina let the word stand on its own.

Norm didn't even try to refute it. "I can explain."

"Agents don't lie to each other, ever," Mina stressed. "I asked you to your face if you knew who Quaz was, and you said no. You led us to Pormal with an agenda. Not only was Waterbury out and possibly on the prowl, your objective was to keep Harri safe, not to ensnare us in a complicated op. Did you know we'd pick up the Petra Pebbles case?" Mina had been wondering that for a while.

"Of course not!" Norm managed to sound offended. "I don't have psychic abilities."

"No, but you're well connected," Mina countered. "By the time we met you at Biters, she could've already requested a case be opened. Information could've been shot to your cuff."

Norm sputtered for a few seconds. "If I'd known that, then I would've known about the Nesbits and their connection to her. I can assure you I did not know any of it."

"Then what was your angle?" Mina frowned.

It was hard not to be upset. She felt betrayed that Norm hadn't confided in her, that he hadn't told her why she'd been summoned to Pormal and about Waterbury. If he'd been honest, they likely wouldn't be standing here right now. And the Syndicate wouldn't be about to discover that Vincent Kramer had witnessed highly illegal actions by one of their fixers.

"I didn't have an angle." Norm's shoulders hunched, his defeat showing. "I just...I just figured that if I told you up front about these people and that they were asking for help to keep the outskirts back, you would have given them the standard line about not being able to do anything. I wanted you to see firsthand, hear it coming from their mouths. I didn't want to taint it with anything you gathered from me."

Mina shook her head. "That's not how we do things, Norm." She could also go on about the fact that it meant he really didn't know her. She chose not to.

"I know. I should've told you everything up front." He ran a hand over his face. "I'm slipping. I really am."

She wasn't about to let this turn into a pity party. "To make things right, between you and me"—she swung her hand between them—"you're going to do what I say on this op. From beginning to end. No questions asked. No pushback. And after we're done, we'll see where we stand."

"I can't—"

"This isn't a negotiation," Mina cut in. "If you don't agree, we part ways right here." A challenge. One she wasn't sure he would take. Lee uttered a small squeak. "You owe it to me to make things right. I want you involved in bringing down Waterbury. And the priority is to do it in a way that doesn't put any of us at risk. It's going to take a second to figure it out. During that second, I want you somewhere safe." She glanced at her cuff. "It's ten thirty. If I have my way, Waterbury doesn't get out for another seven hours. We have time. I need to go over everything with Lee." Mina would also like to consult with Vince, if he was around. "If you don't want to make this right, then you're out completely. No second chances. This is it, Norm. Make up your mind."

They held gazes for a couple of moments.

"Fine," Norm said. "We do it your way. I guess I owe you that much."

"Yes. You do."

"Using Mr. Raphael's residence as a base to figure out the plan makes the most sense. That way, we can be near Waterbury's residence," Mina told her director through the drone's aural comm. "Then, if we need to make a quick arrest, or we witness anything suspicious, we can act quickly. Did you get a chance to go over Norm's account of his time with Waterbury?"

Mina had sent her boss the veribox report Norm had given at Mary Lou's approximately twelve minutes ago.

"I have," McAllister said. "I'm not through all of it, but he details his investigation thoroughly. However, we will need more if we want the charges to stick and want to secure the use of Babble. His testimony is not enough without solid, irrefutable proof."

"It would've been much easier had Waterbury been sloppier," Mina lamented.

"I can't say I'm surprised you got Webb to go

underground. If anyone could have convinced him, it was you," McAllister said. "Well done."

"I'm not sure if it counts as underground, since he's residing, for the time being, in a residence a hundred stories up. But he insists the Syndicate won't look for him there." Mina held off on the gripe, as she did believe Norm would be safe for the time being, even if the location wasn't her first or second choice. "He told us the unit was set up by an acquaintance with no ties to the government, under the name of someone who's been deceased for more than a decade. It's the only place he agreed to go. We checked it out, and it seems solid. The high-rise has decent security, and the scanners and locks on the inside have been upgraded. Norm knows what to look for as far as breaches. I wouldn't feel comfortable leaving him there for more than a week, but a few days should hold. The residence is also equipped with several lasers and a blaster."

"It sounds more than adequate. We can't forget that Webb is an experienced law enforcement official with more than thirty years in the field. As far as the pending Waterbury case, I will authorize the use of Mr. Raphael's residence for now. Official word has not yet come down from the committee on whether they will designate this as a case, nor is there any new information on the so-called audit you participated in yesterday." Mina could hear his frustration. It was shared. "But after listening to Norman Webb's firsthand account of his torture and pursuit of Wilbert Waterbury, and the years he put into securing an arrest, I'm fairly certain we will garner the necessary approval shortly. We have an obligation to see this through. I don't need to consult a governmental doctor of psychology, as it's clear that Mr. Waterbury, if left to his own devices, will continue to kill, either as a job or because he enjoys it, likely both. It is our priority as sworn servants of this country to protect all people from harm. This demands a response. One we will answer."

Mina was overjoyed by this news.

"I heartily concur," she said. "I'm certain Lee and I can formulate a plan to bring him in."

"Report back with any updates," McAllister ordered. "I'll be in contact if things change. After Agent Poston and Harmony Biggins are done with their task, they will be over to rendezvous with you shortly. This case will likely require more help."

He didn't name Vincent Kramer, but his use of others implied Vince's inclusion.

"I will reach out to Colonel Kramer," Mina said. "I'm certain he'll want to be a part of this, if he's not otherwise engaged. Before heading to Mr. Raphael's, Lee and I need to make quick stops at our residences to pick up our compucases and other tech."

"Harmony set up streaming surveillance of the Meridian and has been monitoring," Lee added. "She also set alerts so if anyone pops up on Waterbury's floor, she gets a ping. So far, it's been mostly quiet. Just a few residents coming and going."

"We'll contact you when we have anything new to share," Mina said. "Or in the next hour, whichever comes first."

"I'll be waiting. Good luck." McAllister clicked off.

Mina sat back in her seat, satisfied that they were going to be allowed to go after Waterbury and place him back in a box, like he deserved. McAllister had a lot of authority to call a case himself. But with something as big as going after the Syndicate, getting a ruling from the committee was protocol. If he had to, McAllister could go to the courts instead of waiting for the committee's final judgment. If a magistrate approved, it would hold up. Mina was pretty sure there wouldn't be any trouble there.

She addressed Lee. "Once you get back to your residence, grab your compucase and anything else you think we might need and meet me at Mr. Raphael's. We're cleared to use the hub and tubes and will have DNA-swipe access to his residence."

Lee looked lost in thought. "I've been thinking about all the ways we can nab Waterbury and make it stick. But one thing you said today stuck with me. You mentioned a satellite burning up on reentry." He blinked at her. "We might actually be able to do that."

Mina's eyebrows lofted up to her hairline. "That was a euphemism to describe the Syndicate watching their corruption burn up in front of them at the hands of the law."

"I know. But it might actually be our best bet to bring

Waterbury to justice. If we need what's on that satellite, the easiest thing to do would be to bring it back down to Earth so we can physically access what's on the data core."

She tried not to act overly incredulous. That plan had so many potential complications she didn't even know where to start. "Hm. That would be a mighty large task," she settled on.

Lee nodded eagerly, remaining undeterred. "It would. But if we succeed, we'd have everything we need to wrap up this case and possibly gather even more evidence against the Syndicate. It would be about getting into the drop zone and retrieving the data before the mob does. That's it, really. Satellites fail from time to time and fall back to Earth, usually from a collision or strike by a micrometeorite. Because of that, all the technology and software are embedded in a meter-thick graphene, heat-treated ball called the stable heart to make sure it survives reentry. Not everyone stores data in space, but I can almost guarantee that the Syndicate does. By doing so, they would consider it to be impervious to any physical threat. Just another practical safeguard when your main objective is to engage in criminal activity. Once the satellite flames through reentry, and nothing is left but the stable heart, fiber glides pop out with these cool steel wings. They arc up like this." He brought his arms up around his head. "They slow the propulsion way down, allowing for a semisoft landing. When the glides are enacted, so is a location transmitter. If we can get to the drop zone first, we'll have Norm's torture evidence and more. Maybe we'll even find something that would implicate Travis Blade, since he owns the satellite. If we can prove Waterbury's torture of Norm beyond any doubt with the vid currently stored up there, Waterbury would definitely get Babble, and everything would work in our favor."

Mina was impressed with her partner's line of thinking. It was clear he was no longer a rookie.

"Your idea has merit." Mina considered. "But honestly, I can't imagine we would get clearance to do such a thing." It seemed drastic. Mina had never heard of another agent getting permission to do anything remotely close to knocking a satellite out of the sky. "It makes my brain ache contemplating everything that plan would entail. Let's keep pondering. We're almost to your residence. If you can come up with a way to enact your idea cleanly"— maybe cleanly was the wrong word, but she didn't have a better one—"I'll think of a way to sell it to McAllister. We'll discuss it more once we're at Mr. Raphael's."

"Got it," Lee replied enthusiastically, nodding. "I've always wanted to be a part of something like this. It would be beyond cool to recover something from space. I've watched a couple vids about people who've done it successfully. A documentary and a regular action vid. The doc was about retrieving files that were no longer beaming back to Earth because of a system failure, but contained some sort of data that was being shared between countries to cure a rare genetic disease. They received permission from the Swiss Republic to take it down. It was pretty incredible. After they rammed it with a one-man rocket they sent up, the stable heart fell back to Earth in one piece, and they were able to use the information to make a cure. The other vid was about space bandits trying to infiltrate a satellite that was filled with currency." He chuckled. "They commandeered another satellite to do the job. But the bottom line is you need something to knock the satellite out of its orbit. The rest kind of falls together. Literally."

"Yeah." Mina chuckled. "It sounds super easy. Just knock a satellite out of the sky. No problem."

Lee shrugged. "There's so much up there these days, it shouldn't be too hard. Things collide almost on a daily basis. Everything floating in space is insured by Orbital Law to cover losses in the event of what they deem a 'space catastrophe,' which is just basically a collision of some kind with a micrometeorite or something larger. The insurance is also necessary for anyone on Earth who's injured or killed by falling debris. Some of those stable hearts can weigh up to a ton."

"You're making it sound doable," Mina mused. "I'll give you that."

"Honestly, I think we have a shot."

"Landing at Gemini high-rise in thirty seconds," the sim intoned.

"That's you," Mina said. "Must be exciting to hear the name of your new residence out loud."

"It is," Lee agreed. "I don't think I'll ever get sick of

hearing it."

She grinned. "I'll see you in twenty. I'm curious where you can take this satellite plan. Then we'll have to use our wiles to sell it to McAllister." That in and of itself would be a huge endeavor.

But maybe it would work.

Mina was stuffing the last few snacks Eggie had printed for her into a bag when her cuff beeped. It was the sound she'd assigned to Vince.

"Engage," she ordered.

Vince popped up on holo, hovering above her wrist.

"I'm sorry," he blurted before she could say hello. "I missed our meet-up this morning, but it wasn't intentional."

"That's okay," Mina replied casually, Kaylee's words from this morning pinging around in her head like a clanging bell set to the tune of I told you so. She didn't want Vince to know how much it had affected her that he hadn't been available. But there was no denying it had. "Where are you?"

"In France," he replied gruffly. "Are you in a secure location?"

"I'm in my residence alone," Mina confirmed.

"The moment I stepped foot in my unit last night, they summoned me back." His tone implied his suspicions. Someone had been waiting for him to return and had alerted Ambrose, his boss and the Protectorate's leader. "I had no choice but to comply. There was no time to formulate an audio or to send it, and even if I could've, I was surrounded by company. I've been in meetings pretty much nonstop, including on the flight back. I was just now released for a small break."

She peered closer at his holo image. He looked fatigued. She wasn't the only one who needed a dose of Jump, an approved energy booster made with natural stimulants. Mina had just taken hers.

"On the bright side, they've called you back to France," she said with forced cheer. She hoped Vince wouldn't pick up on the forced part. "It's what you were hoping for."

Vince's life revolved around the Protectorate, and the separation from his work after he had gone rogue trying to bring down Veritus had been hard on him.

Having him in France, possibly permanently, was exactly what Mina had been trying to protect herself against. Yet another reason why they wouldn't work as a couple. Maybe this was for the best.

Though convincing herself of that was going to take some time.

"It's great, and it isn't," he said. "It's almost dinnertime here, so they can't hold me for much longer. I'll check in again when I can. How's it going with Norm?"

"We interviewed him, got a full, verified accounting of his dealings with Waterbury over the years, and got him to a safe location this morning." Mina left out the fact that she'd argued with Norm to get him into hiding for his own good. "Lee and I are heading over to Mr. Raphael's. McAllister has given us the go-ahead to try to figure out how to safely box up Waterbury. Lee has some grandiose plans, which may or may not include things that float around in space."

"That sounds...interesting. Sorry I can't be there."

"Me, too."

"I miss you," he said quietly.

It went unsaid that they hadn't had enough time together.

"Um..." Mina hesitated. "I miss you, too."

Weird to say out loud, but it was true. She really did.

"I'm sure once I didn't answer this morning, you assumed I'd changed my mind." He chuckled. "Which is the furthest thing from the truth. It was completely out of my control. I was looking forward to seeing you again. The sooner the better."

Needing to change the subject—because Mina, to no one's surprise anywhere on the planet, wasn't great at talking about these things—she said, "When do you think you'll return?"

"I'm not sure. Things here are...complicated." His voice sounded strained. "I'm connecting my removal from America to what happened with Norm, even though no one has admitted it. They keep quizzing me about what I was involved in yesterday, specifically, who you are. It's been going on for hours."

"They have my name. You gave it to that guard yesterday when we were trying to get into Petra's residence."

"Yeah. I know. That might've been a mistake on my part. But it's taken me by surprise, because they know I'm in contact with the American federal government and, for the most part, have approved my involvement. It's not something that they should be suspicious about. I was briefed by your director, while accompanied by Ambrose, on the first case we worked together." He was helpfully leaving out all the things that had gone wrong. There was no need to rehash them. "My assumption is, when they decided to take a deeper check into my story yesterday, your name didn't pop in the appropriate place. Ambrose is perturbed that I'm keeping things from him."

"You might have to give him specifics to set things to rights." Mina didn't want him to lose his job because he had an affiliation with her, and her identity was cloaked.

"I signed several nondisclosures, given to me by your director, and I plan to honor my word. The French government would love deeper intel on the Americans, and their agents, but they're not getting it from me. I think they're testing me to see where my allegiance lies." He blew out a frustrated breath. "A few months ago, I would've said France all the way, but now I'm not so sure."

Mina was tempted to ask Vince how secure his comm line was, but she also knew this man was a professional. He wouldn't be talking so openly if he felt there was even a minute chance he would be overheard. Certainly not about his allegiance to the country that employed him.

"I really hope this entire inquisition is not about your relationship with me," Mina said. "I would hate for you to have a prolonged rift or lose your job in the Protectorate because of that. I can talk to McAllister. I'm sure he could arrange to send out a brief confidential memo confirming who I am and that you've played a small role in a few of my cases. That should be enough. You love your job. You're good at it. Losing it because of me would be silly." And impractical. And irrational. And a million other words floating through her head.

"My leaving the Protectorate wouldn't be solely because of you. But if things continue to worsen, I may take you up on that." She was relieved to hear it wasn't all about her. But honestly, she didn't want any part of it. It was too burdensome. "There's more to the story." Vince lowered his voice. "I'm beginning to suspect that Ambrose might be a double agent."

Mina gasped.

Not because he'd told her his suspicions, or that they might be true, but because saying something like that out loud could get him killed.

"Don't worry," Vince countered, reassuring her. "I'm on an ultrasecure channel in an isolation chamber. The walls are made of ten-centimeters-thick titanium, no tech embedded, and my cuff is connected to a nano-fiber cable. I took all the precautions available to me. We use these chambers when we reach out to our spies. Legally, these chambers have to be impervious to any auditory or vid surveillance to protect our assets. We take that very seriously." Of course the French government had spies. Every major government did. "I'm not sure when we'll be able to talk like this again, and I wanted you to have all the details. Particularly if something happens to me. I trust you more than anyone else, and you understand what these implications mean, specifically. You also have the means to help if necessary."

Mina felt a pulse of alarm run through her. "Give me a realistic guesstimate of the peril you think you're in if someone finds out about your suspicions."

"Very low. There's a chance Ambrose would act preemptively if he knew my hunch, but I know how to be discreet," Vince replied. "And, let's face it, I'm too well known now. People would notice if I suddenly disappeared for an extended period of time. Ambrose dug himself a hole when he required me to be splashed around the international media day in and day out. Now that I'm a regular on the screen, people would wonder where I'd gone and make inquiries." The media blitz was a good thing. Imagine that. "As I uncover more and more about the inner workings of the Protectorate, it's pretty clear that I've been naïve about a lot of things, not to mention entirely too trusting. It's probably why I was able to work my way up in the ranks so quickly. They wanted a lapdog. They provided the lap, and I willingly climbed in. Now that I'm waking up and asking questions, they don't like it. I don't think they'll harm me, but if they could keep me under lock and laser until they had my sworn compliance, I believe they would. I'm going to keep investigating quietly and see what I uncover."

"Be careful," Mina cautioned. Not that he needed to hear it, but still. "You are at risk of tearing open something that people would kill to keep quiet."

If he was right about Ambrose, and the news broke, it would be very dangerous. If Ambrose Bernard, head of the entire French Protectorate, really was a double agent, that would mean he was trading military and government secrets to someone or an entity, likely another government who was not an ally, for currency.

It was a stunningly huge allegation.

"I understand the implications and appreciate your sentiments," he said. "Which is why I wanted to tell you." His head moved toward something she couldn't see. "The green light is flashing. Someone's trying to signal me. I have to go. I'll contact you as soon as I can. I wish I was there to help you with your case. Next time we speak, I won't be able to be as candid, so listen for the clues."

"I will. Take care of yourself." Mina bit her lip. "I'm going to have to share your suspicions with my partner and my director. I can't keep this news from them. It won't go further than that. The added exposure may help protect you. McAllister will document what you've told me, and we can use it against the French government if necessary." What was left unsaid was if something happens to you.

He nodded. "I expected you would. I trust them both. Hope to see you soon."

Vince disappeared off her wrist.

The sense of loss was acute.

"LET'S GO OVER it one more time." Mina paced by Mr. Raphael's screen, which was situated on a wall in the living area. Lee was running real-time feed of a group of satellites. She watched as they floated across the screen like isolated ships sailing into an unknown void. Earth, in all its green, blue, and swirling white brilliance, beamed up from below. It was pretty spectacular. "I want to understand what you're describing before we try to sell it to McAllister. Have you been in contact with Harmony? We're going to need her input on this as well."

Lee was unfazed by Mina's request to get Harmony on board. He simply nodded. He knew her worth. "Harmony and Agent Poston are on their way. They should be here within five to ten. As for the plan," he began again, "in order to knock Travis Blade's satellite out of the sky, we would need permission to use something already up there. Privateers might be a good option. What's being displayed on-screen right now is live feed from the Orbital World Satellite Station. It's mandatory that everything in space be registered. They fly several cams on continuous loop for the public to see." The Orbital World Satellite Station, or OWSS, was the largest space station and was occupied by over one hundred individuals from different countries at all times. It was massive. There were more satellite stations up there, run by individual nations that were smaller, but Mina didn't know how many. "The OWSS is in charge of keeping track of everything floating around up there. Travis Blade owns ten satellites, and the one Waterbury has his cams linked to is called Currency Reigns, which is completely apt." The Syndicate wasn't known for flying under anyone's radar. It was in-your-face or nothing. "It's nestled around a few dozen other satellites and numerous space- and science-monitoring equipment. It's set to float across the screen in about twenty." He waved at the screen.

Satellites weren't the only things floating around in space. Scientists regularly released various information-gathering devices, along with telescopes, space crawlers, and sound amplifiers that worked as tenders. Twenty years ago, it'd been relatively easy to obtain the necessary permissions to put something into space. Nowadays, it was much harder and more regulated. Lee was right. There was a lot of stuff up there, and calamities happened often enough. "In order for something to be disrupted out of its orbit"—he got up and moved closer to the screen, using his hands to demonstrate—"it needs an impulse thrust of two-point-two meters per second squared for approximately four minutes." He moved an arm toward one of the satellites, like he was going to give it a shove. "That allows for a significant change in trajectory. Once the orbital space is disrupted, and the vessel moves closer to Earth, gravity does the rest."

He flashed Mina a big smile and settled his hands on his hips, like this was all Mina needed to know.

It was not.

She resisted shaking her head. "Since everything is monitored and recorded"—she gestured toward the live feed where carefully crafted technology with shiny appendages floated by—"isn't it going to look premediated if we fly something purposely into a satellite?" The whole idea was to cloak this operation so the Syndicate wouldn't get suspicious.

"It's actually pretty easy to make it look like an accident. See how these smaller vessels are positioned lower or higher than the bigger satellites?" He moved closer, pointing out a few objects that looked like mini crafts with jetties attached to their back ends. "That's on purpose. When they're released into the exosphere, their distance from Earth and which orbital zone they occupy are calculated very intentionally. Occasionally, they misfire, causing them to either accelerate or decelerate." He dragged his hands along the screen, pumping up the view of a few slow-moving objects. "They use a chemical reaction for propulsion. It's located right here." He circled his hands around the jetty structures. "Computer, show satellite collision, exhibit 1B, vid feed, at one hundred percent."

A new vid popped on the wall.

Mina watched as a smaller craft-like object, which was floating right above several satellites, suddenly began to sputter. It shook for a few moments before dropping. As it went down, it took out a large wing of the satellite below it. Then both objects plummeted out of view.

"This happens a few times a year, which is why Orbital Law requires everything up there to be insured."

Mina nodded. "I understand. But getting a government warrant"—for lack of a better term—"to do something like this seems like it would be incredibly difficult."

Not to mention extremely costly.

"I don't think so. I did a little digging into that also." Lee headed to his compucase. "As far as I can tell, it's happened a few times already." He began to type. New data appeared on the screen. "There have been two occurrences where satellites have been brought down under suspicious circumstances. The government has never confirmed or denied its involvement, and the stories were not widely publicized. But the data found in their stable hearts led to arrests, and the owners of these satellites were boxed up for pretty heavy crimes." Mina scanned the data on the screen. "One event happened in 2086, involving the Proton Asset Corporation. After its satellite was grounded, the owner and CEO was boxed for thirty-five years. He'd been embezzling and exporting chemis, which led to a trail of lost lives."

"That was almost twenty years ago." Mina began to pace. "If agents were given permission to do something like this nowadays, I would've heard about it." At least she thought she would've. "No whiff of anything like this has ever filtered down." Mina gestured to the data. "Maybe it was a military takedown. And if the US government neither confirmed nor denied its involvement, it may not have happened with governmental interference, even though law enforcement was able to get the stable heart." She paused, thinking. It was hard to know. There had to be other secret departments she was unaware of. They could've been behind it.

"I'd agree with you," Lee said, "as it feels excessive to take down a satellite, but the last time it happened was only seven years ago. It involved a privateer by the name of Malcolm Hammer." More data spilled across the screen, including a picture of a man with a long chin, high forehead, and jet-black hair combed away from his face. A pair of eerily diffracted green eyes stared back at her. He leered into the lens like he had payback to exact.

"I know that guy." Mina wagged her finger, trying to come up with how she could recognize his appearance but not his name.

"You know him by the name The Virtual Game Killer."

Mina continued to shake her finger. "That's right! That's the champion virtual gamer who killed all those women.

How many was it? Twenty-three or -four?" She shook her head. "I was just getting out of training when all that went down."

It'd been a really big story.

Serial killing was harder to get away with now than it had been hundreds of years ago. But this guy had been good, covered his tracks well. Now she knew why. It'd all been stored in a satellite.

"He enjoyed torture," she continued. Not unlike Waterbury. "He'd connect with a woman during a virtual game and steal her data...to later gain access to her residence? I can't remember all the details, other than it took them a long time to track him down." Mina gazed at the screen. "So you're telling me he was using a satellite to store his nefarious dealings, so they knocked it out of the sky?" It sounded like government interference to her. To prevent more women from being killed, it seemed a small price to pay.

The same theory would apply to Waterbury, so maybe what Lee was suggesting wasn't so extreme after all. Who knew how many people Waterbury would go after once he was free and clear? He would certainly cover his tracks. Being funded and protected by the Syndicate would only make that part easier.

Bringing the satellite down might be their only real chance to get charges to stick.

"Yes. They really knocked it out of the sky," Lee said. "According to the data, Malcolm Hammer was a genius. On the Mind Galaxy scale, he was off the charts. Graduated from advanced programming at age twelve. Built a gaming empire by twenty. He was not only a virtual gaming champ—one of the best of all time—he wrote and created all his own virtual experiences. Many of which were operated out of a massive satellite. It was one of the first of its kind, if I remember correctly. I was pretty young at the time, but I remember being awed. His MO was to invite specific people to demo a brand-new game, but in order to do so, they had to complete what he called a 'background check.' It was the way in which he siphoned their personal data. Then, once they logged into the game through his private network, he would begin to download their home sim accounts and everything personal they had connected to it. That's how he found the perfect victim."

The thought of this man with his evil green eyes preying on unsuspecting innocents made Mina furious. "Then he would set up holo interactions with the women until they felt comfortable with him. He would then convince them to meet him at a location of his choice. All of these interactions were masked. There were no records found of the holo meets or anything from the victim side, because he would wipe all the evidence clean. He controlled their sims, their cuffs, their boards. Everything. They never had a chance."

Mina whistled low. "I remember it now that we're talking about it. He mutilated them. Then he got sloppy. That's how they found him. He left some DNA behind."

Lee nodded. "He did, but everything about him here on Earth was squeaky clean. That's when they decided to take the satellite down. It's all here in the report. There's a lot redacted, but I got the gist. Maybe McAllister has clearance to read it all. I mean, what they did to catch him is what we want to do. It could help our case."

"It definitely could." Mina's cuff beeped. "This is Agent Kane."

"Hiya," Kaylee said. "We're about to enter the Meridian. Have Lee zap the lobby and hallway cams." She didn't have to tell Lee, he was already on it.

"All clear. Come on up."

"Okay. See you in two."

Mina stared out one of Mr. Raphael's solar-catch windows, hands on her hips. "If we get permission to do this, it's going to be a massive in-coordination-with endeavor. We're going to need a lot of help." She turned. "It will likely be multidepartmental, possibly involving the military. It's hard to keep something like that quiet—"

Lee sucked in a breath, his eyes locked on his compucase.

She rushed to his side. "What?"

He gestured at his screen. "When I looped the cams, I checked all the key areas. These three guys just emerged from a waste room on level ten near the public hub. They're holding some heavy-duty titanium cases, and they don't quite fit. Warn Agent Poston and Harmony. We don't want them crossing paths."

Mina tapped her cuff.

"What's up?" Kaylee asked. "We're almost to you."

"Change of plans. We've got possible company. Send Harmony through and reroute yourself back to the lobby. Jump floors, stay off of ten and fifty and out of the tubes for another five. Find a place out of sight once you're downstairs. Be ready to enact an extremely quiet tail. Three perpetrators, classic mob, holding large titanium cases."

"Got it." Kaylee didn't question her. "I'll be ready and waiting."

Mina walked over and pulled open Mr. Raphael's door, anticipating Harmony's imminent tube arrival. A ding sounded. It took Harmony under three seconds to slide into the residence. She already had her compucase open and was typing as she sat down.

"Let's see who's coming to visit, shall we?" she murmured. In less than four seconds, she homed in on them. "Oh, yeah, they do look crooked and spooky. Who wears sunshades inside? Those kinds of disguises went out more than fifty years ago. And look at their icky iced-back hair. Only goons wear their hair like that. The individual hair rows look like fat noodles stuck on top of their head with sticky elastomer. How can they not know they're announcing themselves as bad guys?" She tsked. "So dumb. But yay for us. Those cases they're holding are huge. Could be examination equipment, heavy-duty cleanup, or both. They're boarding a tube. Next stop, level fifty. Or, you know, we're wrong, and they're visiting their elderly grandmother and bringing her cases full of yummy soup." Waterbury's residence was on level fifty. Harmony glanced over at Lee's compucase. "They're in tube number thirteen."

Lee flicked his feed over, looking mildly abashed. Harmony, being Harmony, was steps ahead. "They seem really confident," he said. "Like they're on a mission."

"There's no fear in their body language." Mina watched the three men in the tube. They didn't speak and kept their heads down. "They're being cautious, but not overly so. They certainly don't think anyone is taking notice. My guess is that Waterbury figured Norm was dead. After all, he did stick him in the side yesterday." Among other things. Norm had been on the brink of death. "Waterbury must have called in cleanup, knowing he can't get to his residence until later this evening. He must be in a rage. Things didn't go according to plan. Poor, poor Wilbert."

There was no way to stop these guys from discovering Norm was not inside the residence. And with the amount of equipment they were carrying, they would perform an analysis once they found him missing, including a DNA search. That was the most logical approach anyway.

"I can shut the tube down," Harmony suggested. "Give it a nice little jerk. Make it seem like it's about to plunge. That should put some fear in them. It'll slow them down for a minute or two."

"No. We need more than a few minutes," Mina said. "We have no choice but to let them proceed with their mission.

We also don't want to give away that the government is paying attention or that there's any outside interference. We stay beneath the radar, though I'm happy we get to watch. Are you recording?"

Both Lee and Harmony confirmed at the same time with matching snorts. Of course they were.

"Here they come," Harmony said. "Level fifty, just like we thought. Grandma doesn't get her soup today."

The burly men made their way down to Waterbury's door slowly and confidently.

"They're not checking for any tampering," Mina murmured, eyes locked on the screen. "They don't think anybody's been in there." That was a good thing.

Harmony flicked a few keys on her compucase. She typed faster than anyone Mina had ever seen. "I'm inside the residence. I removed the still images last night and replaced them with my homemade video, so we have live feed. But only from the cams controlled by the sim, not the ones in the utility room that are hooked to the satellite. I'm working on audio now. It'll just take a second. I want to make sure it doesn't trigger anything or mess up the vid I planted showing Webb trying to break out."

Harmony had strung together a bunch of still images of Norm in his battered state and animated them with Waterbury's residence as a backdrop. Mina hadn't watched it yet, but she knew it was crude. It'd been the best they could do in the moment. It was meant to confuse Waterbury into thinking Norm didn't have any help, not stand up under Syndicate hacker scrutiny.

Once inside the residence, the men moved down Waterbury's short hallway single file and turned out of sight. Harmony switched to another cam, one that highlighted the front of the utility room, which had been left open and unlocked.

Mina leaned in closer.

One man glanced into the room, then waved another guy over. It took a second, but all three men began to physically panic, each shaking his head and looking at one another. Then all three split up to search the rest of the residence. It didn't take long, as there were only four other rooms.

Mina's stomach sank as she watched one of the men put his wrist near his lips.

His voice came over Harmony's compucase a second later. "The target is missing. I repeat, the target is missing."

A very faint response issued out of the man's cuff. "What do you mean the frackin' target is missing? It's not missing, it's dead. That's why you're there!"

"There's no one here, boss," the man confirmed.

"That can't be. Willie said he was in there. Locked him up himself. He hasn't been back."

"He ain't here."

"Well, then, watch some frackin' forsaken vid feed and figure out what the hell happened in there!" It came out as a bark, loud enough that Mina could catch every word. "Then swab it down. The works. Nothing untouched. That guy was a marshal, for frackin' sake. We can't have this leak and have the government snooping around. Too much is at stake right now."

Interesting.

What was at stake more so now than any other day? Likely nothing special, crime as usual for the Syndicate. But maybe not. This sounded particular. There was more than an echo of unease coming from that coughing bark over the man's cuff.

Once Mina sent a recording to Tech, they would figure out which Syndicate boss the voice belonged to. Mina imagined it was Travis Blade, but only because that would be convenient.

A man called from another room. "Willie didn't give us access to his sim. No way to play it back. Everything's 'crypted."

"Fine!" the voice shouted from the cuff. "Full sweep. Right now. I want everything. Find out how he escaped. I'll send someone over to talk to Willie. I have to get him out of that monitored frackin' jail cell." Almost too softly for them to catch, he ended with, "That guy is going to get us all fracked up the behind with his personal vendetta."

The man was fond of the word fracking, apparently.

And fond of shouting out admissible evidence.

Mina would take it.

"THE SWEEP WAS thorough," Mina reported to her director, who was positioned on Mr. Raphael's screen, where the satellite feed had just been. "They swabbed every surface multiple times." It'd taken the three men inside of an hour to get everything done. "Nobody talked, other than a few grunts. They didn't call their boss back. I sent the vid to Tech for a voice match."

"I have Waterbury on lockdown, no visitors," McAllister said. "Sanctioned and ordered by the official counseling office. He's not going anywhere, but can receive messages and will likely give authority to whoever is requesting to use his sim, and that person will subsequently watch the vid Ms. Biggins created. The vid is very rough. They will be suspicious and have it analyzed. They will hopefully think Norm had a friend help him, however, not the federal government."

Mina cleared her throat. "There's a very high likelihood

they captured Colonel Kramer's DNA in their sweep. They went over everything meticulously." She'd watched the entire thing with a sinking heart. "His DNA profile won't pop for an average search, but their hackers are the best of the best." As confirmed by Lee and Harmony, who were their best of the best. "The Syndicate won't make their findings public, but chances are they will eventually target him, even if it's just to monitor his whereabouts. He's an eyewitness to a heinous crime, perpetuated by one of their own. As you heard from the audio I sent of the thugs inside the unit, they want to keep this very low profile. Whichever boss was giving them direction must have something large-scale in the works. He called that out specifically."

Behind Mina, Mr. Raphael's door clicked open, and Kaylee walked in.

Mina nodded at her pal to go ahead and give her report.

"They were pros," Kaylee said, facing the screen. "After exiting the building, all three broke apart almost instantaneously, each moving quickly and efficiently in a different direction. I tailed one to the end of the block. He entered a high-rise and took the tube up to the roof. An unmarked craft was waiting. I'm assuming each man did the same. Even if we had drones circling the air space, we wouldn't have been able to maintain a tail. These guys were looking, too. I had to do some pretty ace pretending as a casual shopper. The one guy kept looking over his shoulder." She sat down on Mr. Raphael's compact lounger, glancing around. "Fill me in on what went down here so

I'm up on things."

"Those three came in, found Webb missing," Mina told her, "and did a full sweep of the residence. They didn't have access to Waterbury's sim, but they'll get it soon enough. They'll view it remotely with his permission. No need to come back. However, they'll likely send in a cleaning crew. These guys left without mopping up."

Kaylee nodded. "Kramer was careful when he went in to get Webb yesterday. He sprayed his hands and wore a hat, but we know DNA sprinkles."

Harmony added, "Yeah, and he had to act fast to get Webb out, so shedding will be expected. According to my data analysis, there's a ninety-nine-point-seven-five chance of them catching his DNA. Not only are the Syndicate hackers good, they have diamond-point tech. They have access to stuff that's not even on the market yet. They pay big currency for whatever's latest. If they only captured a quarter strand of Kramer's helix, they'd suss it out. And no public blocks are going to stop them. They'll know it's him inside of six hours, is my guess."

Lee, who had been nodding along, agreed. "I'd say four to six hours is accurate."

Mina hadn't shared Vince's call with anyone, as she was reporting to her director for only the first time since she'd arrived at Mr. Raphael's. She'd told Vince that she would be confiding in her director and her partner, but she had to believe that he would be okay with Kaylee and Harmony knowing as well.

She trusted everyone in this room with her life.

"I spoke with a certain colonel less than an hour ago," Mina reported. "Everything I'm about to relay is first-class confidential. No speaking of it outside this room. I was given permission by the colonel-in-arms himself to reveal this, but his safety is on the line." Everyone here knew what that meant and would honor it. Even though Harmony hadn't been sworn in as an agent yet, Mina was absolutely certain she would not divulge anything. She was a hacker first. They kept things cloaked as a way of life. "He was relocated to his home base in the early hours of this morning. Not by choice. They've been grilling him about his involvement with the US government, searching for details about the cases he's worked while he's been here, singling me out in particular. He's given them very little, as he's honoring his nondisclosures." She paused, deciding to veer even wider on the next part, not wanting to say everything out loud just yet. McAllister was on a secure channel from headquarters, but they were in a civilian's residence. One they didn't know much about. "He has a hunch that everything may not be as it seems inside his bubble." She met Kaylee's inquiring gaze. "I would compare it to the Fiefer case."

There was no case by that name, but fief was the word they used as code for double agent.

Kaylee gasped.

McAllister made a sound resembling a cough. "Are you certain?"

"As certain as I can be with the information I was given directly by the man himself." Lee appeared confused, and Mina shot him a look. He nodded, understanding that she would explain it later. "He was inside an isolation chamber for privacy. He won't be able to speak as freely the next time."

Mina wasn't worried about understanding his clues. After all, they'd been speaking a similar language their entire lives.

"This is...unprecedented information," McAllister settled on. They all seemed as shocked as Mina had felt when she'd first heard it.

"Are we talking about the king in the Fiefer case?" Kaylee asked, her voice expressing her incredulousness.

She was asking if Ambrose Bernard was the one who Vince thought was the double agent.

"Yes, we are," Mina confirmed. "But please remember, as I'm relaying what was told to me, it's all hearsay based on feelings and speculation. Absolutely nothing is verified at this moment."

"Just alleging such a thing could place him in considerable danger," McAllister said.

Mina tried not to think about what that would look like. Vince was competent. He would handle himself.

"I told him that. I also indicated that you would be open to crafting a memo highlighting the cases he's helped us with and verify who I am. Something brief and nonspecific. I figured we owed him that much since he's helped us in an agent capacity while he's been here. If that's not appropriate, that's fine. He gave one of the watchdogs my name when we were trying to get into the vid star's residence yesterday. I'm not sure how much detail you gave them when you debriefed them on the ship-jumping case, but they may require a little more." McAllister had met with both Ambrose Bernard and Vince after they'd taken the ship full of Veritus members into custody. "They seem to be targeting my involvement specifically, and the lack of information they're finding on me is making them suspicious of his allegiance."

McAllister was quiet for a few moments. "I did not name any of my agents during the debriefing. I gave them very little, in fact. If they try to figure out who you are, which it seems they are, it would be a very dry trail. I can see how that would flummox them and possibly cause them to question one of their own's intentions."

Mina figured her director had been brief with the debrief. "My next priority will be to contact him so I can fill him in about what's going on here. He needs to be informed that a large crime organization has his DNA so he can take the appropriate precautions." Mina figured this was the best time as any to move on with this case. "In light of the escalating situation with Waterbury and the Syndicate knowing there's been interference, I feel it's time to make some decisions. We've been working on a possible solution to our problem, but I'm going to let my partner explain it." She gestured toward Lee. His eyes went wide. "But before we do, let's change the channel of communication. Just to be safer. I'll summon you back up on my cuff," she told her director.

McAllister popped off the wall screen and up on her cuff in the next two seconds.

Lee maneuvered so McAllister could get a good view of him, taking the drone controls like a champ.

It was no use having Mina try to sell this plan to her director. She didn't have the information stored in Lee's brain to lay this out in a clear, objective way.

"Um." Lee cleared his throat. "There's a way for us to get everything we need to build an airtight case against Waterbury. We believe all the vid data taken during the torture of Norman Webb is located on Travis Blade's satellite Currency Reigns. Waterbury has his cams funneled to it, and I'm nearly one hundred percent certain that this satellite stores data. They keep the data up in space because it's far safer than being here. They can detect and shut down a hack in split seconds. They're ready for it. They have complex booby-traps to fry your equipment if you try to see what's on there. But they're not expecting a different kind of attack."

"And what kind of attack might that be, Agent Adams?" McAllister asked. His tone indicated he knew exactly what Lee was going to say next.

Lee didn't falter. "We bring it down. The whole satellite. We knock it out of the sky, and once it burns through our atmosphere, the stable heart that contains all the data is all that's left. It's built to withstand the heat of reentry. If we get to the heart before the Syndicate, we will have everything we need to make an arrest, and with vid of Norm's torture, I believe Waterbury has a good chance of getting Babble. That would lead to more of the Syndicate being incarcerated for crimes they've committed."

"What's stopping them from erasing the data remotely once they get the alert that it's descending out of the sky?" McAllister asked.

Mina's eyebrows rose.

She figured McAllister would start off deeming the idea out of their scope. But he hadn't. He didn't even sound shocked. It was more than surprising, but not unwelcome.

"It's technically impossible for them to do something like that," Lee said. "Once it starts to fall, emergency shutdown is enacted. Everything is powered off, no signal, no current. It's preventive so the data won't be lost during the satellite's descent and subsequent crash to Earth. The locking mechanism comes standard and can't be overridden. The Syndicate will do everything they can to retrieve the stable heart. They will move quickly. But we have the advantage. We'll know the trajectory minutes before they'll be alerted by an internal mechanism. Those minutes will be crucial."

"I like it. I like it a lot," Harmony murmured, bobbing her head. "Good thinking, Karmaseeker. That's using your old noggin to good effect. It's a big ask, but one that comes with crazy rewards." Her fingers flew across her board.

"According to history, this kind of thing has happened twice in the last twenty years."

"Lee said it's happened twice," Mina said.

"Twice within the government," Harmony amended, leaning forward, her eyes scanning quickly. She must absorb data at hyperspeed. "Or so they say. It's pretty murky, as the government neither confirms nor denies. But there are ten more times that satellites have been purposely knocked out of the sky. Which means it's way more than that, and to make it even more cryptic, many of them haven't been reported or documented in the media for whatever reason. Some have lawsuits attached, some don't." She scanned what was in front of her. "Looks like there was a pretty major one about four years ago. It was a data snatch-and-grab. Some asteroid smuggler wanted the inside scoop on what his competitor was doing. He was prosecuted and sent to a box for ten years. In most of the other cases listed on the site, lawsuits that were drawn were ultimately dropped. Insurance was paid out. Some of these people made a small fortune." She leaned back in her seat, flexing her fingers. "If we want to take Waterbury quietly and not set off any alarms, Agent Adams is one thousand percent correct. This is the way to do it. There's no other way to get that data. Cam vid that shows the fixer torturing a federal marshal will bring the house down. I'd say we have more than a few minutes' lead time to get ahead of the mob if we map the trajectory super carefully in advance. I know some hackers with pretty sweet programs built especially to do that. I bet we could get it up to ten to twelve minutes. If that happens, we get the stable heart. No question about it. We swoop in and pick it up. Then pry that sucker open. Plug in the data cards before the sneaky Syndicate knows what hit 'em. Agent Adams and myself must be on the scene. We risk losing it otherwise. After it lands, I'd say they wipe it clean inside of fifteen minutes." She rubbed her hands together, smiling like a fiend. "We're going to need somebody with crazy-big tools. And once we're in"—she snapped fingers on both hands, looking extremely satisfied—"bam. We have the data we need and anything else Travis Blade is trying to hide."

Kaylee's mouth gaped open a little. She clacked it shut. Mina felt the same way. "So you're telling us the solution to this case is to knock a really huge, really expensive satellite out of the sky? Can we even do such a thing?" She turned to Mina.

Mina didn't have an answer, but McAllister did. "Doing something like this is possible. The approval route will be...complex, requiring both committee approval and judicial warrants. But it's not impossible."

"I'll say it's complex," Kaylee muttered. "It's not like we can just hire a craft to ram it out of its lane. But getting into that nice, juicy stable heart sounds like what we need to bring this greater sucker in."

"Agreed," Mina said. "My partner's right. There's going to be more for us to find on that data core. Particularly when we heard the Syndicate boss tell the guy who discovered

Norm was missing that they couldn't risk government involvement right now."

The odds were favorable that at least something more would be stored up there. But even if there wasn't, retrieving the physical evidence against Waterbury so a warrant would be issued to give him Babble was what they'd been hoping for anyway. That alone would be huge. Anything else would be a bonus credit.

"When are they not doing something illegal they don't want us to know about?" Kaylee scoffed. "There's a pretty good chance Waterbury's cam data is up there, but there's a possibility we won't find anything else. The warrant to bring the satellite down has to be based on convicting Waterbury alone, not any conjecture, frackin' or not."

Mina nodded, allowing herself to get a little more excited about the plan. A plan she'd thought a scant hour ago would be almost impossible. "If we can get a judge on board ahead of time, prepped with Webb's verified testimony, and he agrees that if the vid feed is there and conclusive, Waterbury comes in and immediately gets Babble, it would be an arena ball goal for the win."

This might be the most complex case Mina had worked on to date. All the moving parts had to come together in precisely the correct way, or it could blow up in their faces, and they would lose their only chance at Waterbury and, in the process, tip off the Syndicate. The Syndicate would be angry at their interference. It wouldn't be a question of if they would retaliate, it would be when.

McAllister said, "If committee approval is granted, a judge will be asked to approve a warrant. That will require Norman Webb to provide an oral statement in front of that magistrate about ongoing, imminent threats to his life, as well as testimony about his torture at the hands of Waterbury. If we can do that, we have a good chance of following through with this plan. It will take me a few hours to bring this to the committee and see what their decision is. During that time, I want you four to come up with a precise work-through from beginning to end to carry this out. As soon as we have a warrant, we move. With this directly affecting Colonel Kramer, and the likelihood that the Syndicate will discover his involvement, we need a quick resolution. We owe it to him. I'll report back when I know more."

He popped off Mina's wrist.

She stared at the vacant space in quiet astonishment for a few seconds. That had gone much smoother than she'd anticipated.

This crazy plan just might work.

"Did that just happen? Tell me that just happened." Kaylee appeared as shocked as Mina. "I'm having trouble believing that our esteemed director just gave us approval to move forward with a plan to knock a satellite out of the friggin' sky."

"The Syndicate boss prefers the term 'frackin' sky.' And he did. I'm pretty sure." She still couldn't completely believe it.

But she did know this—they had a lot of frackin' work to do.

"No," Harmony argued. "If we use the Bonsai Gattaca probe to knock Blade's satellite out of orbit, the trajectory will be forty-two-point-seven. It's simulated right here. See the arc?" She tapped her screen. "That probe is massive. It's completely reinforced on the outside. I bet it won't even sustain any lasting damage. That is, if we get permission. It's owned by a privateer."

Lee shook his head, tugging his eyes from his compucase to hers. "You're not taking into account the added mass of the interior lens. When you do, it changes it to a forty-two-point-nine. Watch my sim. See there? After this, we run it through the Orbital Crunch Stream to make extra sure. That accounts for interior weight automatically."

"Oh, yeeeah," Harmony said. "I see now. Thank goodness you're here, Seeker. You and the deetz go hand in hand."

Kaylee shook her head, grinning as she turned to Mina. "Their heads have been bobbed together under one big wizard helmet for over an hour. I don't understand anything they're talking about. But I like it. It makes me feel better about what we're trying to do here."

"Yes. If it weren't for them, we wouldn't be here right now," Mina replied. "We would've been forced to hand off this mission to another hacker-agent team."

"Have you acquired shuttle transpo to get us to the stable heart once it lands yet?" Kaylee asked from her position on Mr. Raphael's lounger, compucase in her lap. Mina sat across from her on a chair. "I'm trying to figure out how we're going to crack this thing open. Not an easy task. Plus, we have to be cognizant that whoever we bring in could either rat us out to the Syndicate or be put in their crosshairs. The more we do ourselves, the better."

"Yes." Mina didn't relish getting anyone else involved. If they could, they would stick to government resources. Privateers would be in a precarious situation trying to fend off retribution from the mob. "As far as the transport goes, the government has high-level stealth shuttles, but they'd be readily identified by anyone bothering to take a look. And we know extremely interested parties will be looking, so I'm seeking out other companies." Using a rocket shuttle made the most sense. Their speeds broke the sound barrier and could get them where they needed to go the quickest.

Kaylee sat back. "You know, we're going to need the media to cover this instantaneously. Someone is going to see this thing blaze through the atmosphere and crash into Earth. Probably a lot of someones. The story we want needs to break. So how do we do that if this is a cloaked government mission?" She bit her nail. "In order to sell the story to the media and get them to run with it, we need somebody reliable, or a celebrity, or someone trustworthy to feed them a tidbit. Then the media does their own digging and finds that it's Travis Blade's satellite. Then, in tandem with that announcement, this reliable someone feeds them that an investigation is happening. Before anyone blinks, somehow a few major players are already in custody." She shook her head. "Or, you know, something like that." She slumped in her seat. "Unfortunately, it's not that simple. The Mafia is going to suspect government involvement from the get-go. I don't even know why we're trying to hide it. Maybe we should just project a giant image of us all standing in a circle dressed in syn-leather, hands on hips, waiting for that thing to touch down. That would be a more accurate, and likely a juicier, story."

"The Syndicate will suspect us," Mina agreed. "But if there's a chance we can keep them confused, we take it. You're right—media presence is key. The mob will react quickly to get their stable heart back, but if there's a media storm, they'll have to be more cautious about how they go about doing that. The Syndicate hates bad press. They take it as a personal affront. I don't know what kind of celebrity you're talking about." Mina sighed. "And please don't say Vince. He's already in their sights."

"I'm not talking about Vince," Kaylee pondered.

"But, I mean, it could be. We should technically leave all hyperlanes open. He might volunteer to arrange it. He has contacts, and he could do it from afar. By the way, have you been able to get a hold of him and let him know about the possible DNA grab?"

Mina glanced at her cuff. "No. I left him a message about thirty minutes ago. Nothing back so far."

"You're pulling your worried face." Kaylee frowned. "He's a big boy. He holds a powerful position in a very prestigious military. He's in charge of a lot of people. He has allies. He knows how to get out of a mess. He's going to be fine."

"I know. But this fief allegation has me worried. It's one of the biggest accusations—the leader of a major military force—I've ever heard about. The entire Protectorate could come crashing down, and in that chaos, Vince could easily become a casualty. If anyone finds out he's asking the questions and thinking about pulling the trigger on exposing them, he'll have a target on his back. You know as well as I do that people kill for less than that every single day."

Kaylee looked thoughtful for a moment. "I'm going to reiterate that I think he's going to be fine and can take care of himself. Until we know otherwise, we stay out of the panic zone."

"For what it's worth, I agree with Queenie over there," Harmony injected. "Big, sexy Kramer is going to be fine. He's crafty. I never got a chance to ask him if it was him dressed up in that old-man alt when he pulled one over on me." Vince had used Harmony to get to her father, Strum Littlefield, a renowned hacker who'd recently been sprung from a box. "But if it was him, like I think it was, there wasn't a hint of nervousness when he played me. I'm pretty sure he's a master. He's probably feeding his superiors all sorts of woe-is-me lines, like 'I can't wait to get back here,' and 'I hate America,' and everything he can to lead them off the scent. That's how he operates. Smooth as a creamy, silky piece of real chocolate dipped in syrupy caramel sauce."

Mina had no problem ignoring the sweets reference, but she had to come back to the first part. "I'm sorry, but Queenie?" Mina bounced her head between Kaylee and Harmony in her confusion.

Kaylee shrugged. "I told you the other day the two of us are experimenting with nicknames. Remember kidlet? Well, today she's supposed to be addressing me as the Queen of all Mentors. But apparently that nickname is too long for some to memorize." She gave a knowing head bob in Harmony's direction.

"I shortened to Q-MENT, and she didn't like it," Harmony chuffed, her eyes still on her screen. "Picky, picky."

"That was supposed to be a play on last night's G-MENT," Kaylee commented, addressing Mina like she and Harmony weren't participating in the same conversation. "Which I vetoed, of course. It wasn't that I didn't like it, it was more that it lacked pizzazz. Hear me? It has no pizzazz."

"You know, come to think about it, Queenie's not really

working for me either," Harmony snarked. "It grants you too much status. Stuff like that goes right to your head and inflates it forty-seven-point-five pounds per centimeter. Doing that on a regular basis will impede your ability to function—like, at all."

"Nah," Kaylee argued. "The brain capacity only goes up a few millimeters, not pounds, and I can deal with that. I can still get through a door. Queenie is acceptable for the time being. Maybe next time add in a nice 'of the universe' or 'nonpareil.'" Kaylee waggled her perfectly sculpted eyebrows. "For you laypeople, that means without equal, which is totally and completely the truth."

Mina rolled her eyes, chuckling.

Her cuff beeped, and she stood. "I'm going to take this. It's Quinn." She walked toward Mr. Raphael's sleep room as she ordered, "Engage, voice only. Hi, Quinn."

"Hey, sis," Quinn replied. "Is this a good time?"

"Good enough," Mina replied. "I have a few minutes."

"It's about dinner tonight. Are you going?"

"Um, what dinner?"

"Mom and Dad are home from their trip. Mom wants to have a family dinner tonight. She said she told you."

"She must've left a message," Mina said. "She only hits me at work if it's an emergency. That's our agreement. A message is probably waiting for me at my residence. I'll check after this."

"Like I told you the other day, I want to bring Daphne," he continued. "But only if you come. I don't want it to be awkward and weird for her. I mean, our parents are nice and relatively easy, but they're still, you know, parents."

"I'm sorry to disappoint," Mina said. "But there is a very slim chance I'll be free for dinner tonight."

"How slim are we talking?"

"I'd say one in twenty," Mina answered truthfully. "I have something big brewing, but there's a chance we may not get approval for it for a day or two." That would be unfortunate, but it could happen. "In that case, I'd be available. Or if we get approval in the next hour or two, I might be able to make it work, if things fall into place quickly." Literally. "But I won't be able to give you or Mom a for-sure until an hour prior. I'll tell Mom yes or no first chance I get." Mina hadn't seen her parents in a while. She missed them. It would be nice to catch up.

"I'll tell her you'll tag her later when I call about bringing Daphne," Quinn replied.

"Thanks." Mina recognized the disappointment in his voice. "I'm sorry, little brother. I understand your frustration. But please know that what I'm involved with will help a lot of innocent people. It's really important to me. That's why I do this."

"I know," he said. "I talked to Harri. He's down in New Mexico. He had to leave the city without saying goodbye. But he explained it all. He told me what you did for him."

Mina held her breath. "Did he tell you everything?" It was Harri's right—he was not under any gag order. But Quinn knowing all the key details about Bliss Corp and their dealings with Plush could prove dangerous for him.

"No, but I understood for the most part. He said he couldn't talk specifics. It was clear you helped him get away from serious trouble. He said he'll likely be able to come back at some point. He offered to let Daphne and me use his residence. I mean, we have to pay the borrows, but it's without a formal lease agreement with the bank. We said yes." Her brother's voice switched to upbeat. "It works great for us. We're actually moving into it in a couple of hours."

"That's so great, Quinn," Mina said. "I'm glad to hear Harri's keeping his residence and that you guys get to utilize it. He put a lot of effort into it over the years, and I know he loves it."

"Yeah, he's pretty bummed he had to leave, but he's pretty excited about the job down there. I guess it's a win-win for now. Since Daphne and I are splitting the cost of his unit, we can start saving." That ability to save borrows was a big deal.

"Harri is very generous. He's a great friend. Okay, I have to run," Mina said. "Tell Mom what we talked about, and I'll shoot her a message later this afternoon."

"Before you go, can I ask if you've been in touch with Vincent Kramer recently?" Quinn asked.

Mina's eyebrows shot upward. "No. Why would I be?"

It was hard to lie to her brother, but she felt like it was necessary at this moment.

"Oh, just thought maybe you'd been in contact. Mom

said she ran into him and gave him your info. She said he was really happy that you two would be able to be in touch after all these years. Then all that stuff happened with Veritus. I know he's been in town for a bit. He's all over the news. You guys were so close growing up, I thought maybe he reached out. I really liked that guy. You always did your best to include me when you could, and I appreciated that. It would be nice to catch up with him. But now that he's in such a fancy position, I bet it's hard for him to slide around unrecognized."

Quinn was correct about that. So, so correct.

"Now that you mention it," Mina said in her most casual of casual tones, "he did leave me a message about a week ago. I've been too busy to hit him back. But I'll reach out soon. It'll be nice to hear what he's been up to."

"Cool. If he's around, invite him to dinner. Tell him we'll keep our cool, and he can lie low and stuff."

Mina chuckled. "I'll do that. I've got to run. Nice talking to you."

"You, too. Stay safe, sis."

She stood there for a moment.

Vince would probably enjoy a dinner at her parents' house catching up with everyone. A pang rang through her. Mina knew these kinds of feelings would rise up if she allowed herself to imagine a life with him. But he was in France, where he belonged. It was probably better he'd been called back now rather than later.

Her lips tingled.

The sensation was much less intense than it'd been this morning. The ghost-lip fixation would be short-lived. It was a shame, because he was an incredibly good kisser.

Mina made her way back to the living area.

"The cleaners just arrived at Waterbury's," Harmony called, waving her over. "These guys look a little less goony and more get-the-job-done-y. They're carrying similar cases to the other guys, but one of them is clutching a hose. Kinda gives them away. They really should be more sneaky about it when they're, you know, cleaning up a gruesome torture scene."

They watched as the Syndicate's cleaning crew disembarked on level fifty and entered Waterbury's residence.

Things were moving fast.

Mina hoped they would start to move just as quickly on her end.

"Okay, time to get back to work," Kaylee instructed. "We've got a complicated mission to plan. We're bringing that flack-a-lacker down. And if anybody thinks different, you can kiss my queenly behind. Hey, try Queenly next time." She flashed Harmony a big smile. "That's even better."

"Yeah. I'll get right on that." Harmony giggled. "More like weenie."

"Not even a chuckle. Your sarcasm needs work. So much work."

"I'm keenly aware that you judge my wit. I will try to

ree-deem myself next time. I bow down to your masterful level o' ridicule, mockery, and cynicism. Please forgive my missteps. Do you prefer currency or coin as payment for my penance?"

"Neither. I require a stable heart."

"That, I can deliver."

"Norm, it's me again," Mina said into her cuff. "I need you to hit me back as soon as possible."

Lee shot her a concerned look from his spot at the table. "He should be there. Why isn't he answering?"

"I wish I knew," she replied. "If he doesn't answer in the next five, I'm going to have to head over there and check on him myself." She'd have no other choice.

"I'll go with you," Kaylee said. "I've dug down as far as I can on figuring out how to break the stable heart open. We have to go military. No way around it. They have all the specialized tools and the muscle we need. Once McAllister hits us back, I'll fill him in. Until then, I'm in limbo."

Mina nodded. "I found us space on a rocket shuttle, but the price is astronomical. We don't have much of a choice, since we need to retrieve the heart as fast as possible wherever it lands. So I'm on hold until McAllister gets approval. Not that I want to spend that time hunting up

Norm, but here we are." She gestured toward their partners. "Since everything else rests on Lee's and Harmony's shoulders, we can spare an hour." She grumbled, "As it seems we have no choice."

"No pressure over here," Harmony snorted. "But honestly, we've got this. We've calculated the projected gravitational acceleration in centimeters per second squared, initial velocity, and targeted trajectory once the object starts its free fall. Now we just have to decide on what we're going to use to bat it out of the sky and then calculate height in kilometers, time, and velocity per second to get an accurate read to get the timing exactly right. It's a no-brainer, really. But first, I need a snack."

"Good idea. You guys break for lunch. Kaylee and I will go check on Norm," Mina said. "Waterbury's residence should stay quiet for the rest of the day, but hit my cuff if somebody shows up. I want to know who's coming and going."

"Will do," Lee answered, barely tearing his eyes away from his compucase.

"Once we round up Webb," Kaylee suggested as she made her way toward the door, "we should bring him closer so we can keep a better eye on him. If McAllister wrangles a meeting with the magistrate, Webb needs to be there lickety-split. We can't hunt him down again. There's no more time."

"I hear you. Bringing him with us makes the most sense." More grumbling crept in. "We barely have time to retrieve him right now. Unfortunately, he's not amiable to what we want. He's fiercely independent. He's probably out running errands or something and doesn't want me to know about it."

Mina tried to shake her frustration with the ex-marshal. He had just gone through a very tough time at the hands of Waterbury. She was cognizant of that. But she was trying to keep him safe, and he was adamantly resisting. And Kaylee was right. They'd need him to report immediately to the judge when it was time. Keeping him close would ensure that would happen.

"I've summoned a craft. It'll be at public transpo in three," Kaylee said.

Mina addressed Lee. "When we get back, we need to know what you've decided on to knock the satellite out of orbit. Nobody wants their expensive space equipment broken, so the government is going to have to pay a lot of currency to get this done. McAllister has to have that information."

Lee leaned back in his seat, eyes darting away from his screen as he crossed his arms. "Harmony and I have been talking about it. We think there might be a better way. It involves hacking into the main thruster of the satellite and reversing it at full speed to deplete all the fuel. Doing so would automatically deorbit it. Then we hiccup it into a complete system failure, and it drops like a one-ton boulder. It wouldn't involve anyone else or cost us anything."

"They might catch the hack," Harmony added, nodding

along. "But I found a way to be even sneakier. We hack in as we simultaneously flip it into reverse. Its thrusters are attached to a separate signal feed, so it makes our hack almost phantomlike, and when it's over, it looks like a blip. How's that for sly? Once the satellite begins to reverse, they're going to scramble to patch it up, but we will be right there making sure they don't. Years and years of fuel reserves will be eaten up in three minutes at max speed. And the newer satellites accelerate quickly so they can bust out of one orbit to get into another, because things are crowded up there. Once the fuel is gone, we crash the system, and they'll just think it dropped out of the sky due to an error. It gives us less time to recoup on the ground—more like eight or nine minutes—as they'll get an alert sooner, like when it starts accelerating. But Karmaseeker and I have been reviewing all the options, and this one seems like the best by a lunar eclipse. The others were kinda farfetched. We don't think some scientist is just going to give up their trillion-dollar spacescope so we can ram it into the mob's pack mule."

That was one way to put it.

"Yeah." Lee nodded. "And anyone who allows us to use their stuff up there could face retribution, too. We don't feel good about that."

"It sounds like a brilliant plan to me if you can pull it off. Ultimately, you guys are in charge," Mina said. "Fine-tune it, and we'll regroup once we have Norm. McAllister, and likely the higher-ups, will like a cost-nothing solution. It's a strong selling point."

"Got it. I hope you locate Webb quickly," Lee said.

"You and me both," she said, nodding to Kaylee. "Let's go."

They made it to the hub and into their waiting craft in less than five.

"What is your destination please?" the sim asked.

"Dharma Hills high-rise," Mina said. "Private hub, level fifty, verification through concierge Tyna Bristol."

"Completing verification. One moment," the sim answered.

"Human verification, huh?" Kaylee said. "That doesn't happen very often."

"You're telling me," Mina replied as the craft rose into the air. "It's a whole thing. The hub is completely private, and entry is monitored. I'm beginning to think most of the units in that high-rise are for people evading one thing or another."

"That could be both a good thing and a bad thing." Kaylee pondered. "Good thing because security is beefed, bad thing because bad guys know stuff like that."

Bad thing especially now that Norm wasn't answering.

"Verification has been denied," the sim said.

"Connect me directly to the concierge," Mina ordered. "Continue our flight to the Dharma. Hover in a safe zone if necessary."

A regular craft could hover in place for only three minutes max, but a government drone had more leeway.

Not much, but a few minutes more. Any longer than that, and an idle drone was an accident waiting to happen.

After a brief pause, the call picked up. "This is Ms. Bristol," a prim voice announced.

"Hello, this is Agent Kane," Mina told the woman. "I was at the Dharma earlier today accompanying a guest who is occupying unit 107. That resident is currently unresponsive. I require access to the hub and to that unit, along with my partner, Agent Poston."

"Unless you're a resident here, access is denied," Ms. Bristol told them with no give in her tone. "But I will send one of my staff up to check on that unit. One moment please." She snapped off without waiting for a rebuttal, the call replaced by soft background music.

This was highly unusual.

"What's going on here?" Kaylee asked, a single eyebrow arched perfectly over one eye. "You were already in there, therefore approved by the resident. That should be enough to get you through the hub door at the very least."

"Looks like I made a mistake." Mina shook her head. "I allowed Norm to set it all up. I didn't question him. Lee and I just followed him in. We verified the security protocols in the unit, knew that you had to have human permission to land in the hub. We trusted Norm with the rest."

"He knew you'd be denied if you tried to get back in on your own."

"It's looking that way."

"I don't get it. You guys are like family. Trust moving

forward is going to be a real issue. He has to know that he's lasering holes in your relationship, not to mention your confidence in him."

"He does. There's no question about it," Mina lamented. "This is leading me to believe that Norm was holding back this morning and knows more than he was telling me. Otherwise, none of this makes any sense."

The music snapped off.

"There is no one inside that unit at this time," Ms. Bristol reported with as much prim as she had before, if not more.

"Did someone from 107 leave via the hub in the last few hours?" Mina asked. "And if so, what was his destination?"

Tyna could easily check with the transpo hub. If Norm ordered a ride out, it would be logged in the database.

"I'm not at liberty to divulge that information. We protect all of our residents' privacy to the utmost degree here at the Dharma."

"I understand, and it's admirable." Mina could get government permission to land and check on Norm, but it would take time. She didn't want to waste that time if she didn't have to. "As I've stated already, I'm a federal agent who is trying to track down an ex-marshal who is staying in your high-rise for his protection. I'm beginning to think you already know this. When I hang up from this call, I will report the situation to my director, who will immediately issue a warrant for me to investigate where said ex-marshal went. You will be forced to comply at that point. You can circumvent that and keep even more federal agents from coming onto the premises by immediately giving me that information, or allowing me access to that unit, instead of making us wait for the inevitable."

After a lengthy pause, Ms. Bristol answered crisply, "Send me your credentials. Airmeld them to the connection your craft has set up. I will review them and get back to you shortly."

Music began to play while they waited on hold for a second time.

Mina ordered the sim, "Send Agent Kane and Agent Poston badge details, level one, through the secured connection to concierge Tyna Bristol."

"Sending level one badge details," the sim confirmed.

"She's not even pretending to mess around," Kaylee said. "If that entire high-rise is a safe house, then she's going to be extremely careful about who she lets in. And I can guarantee she won't want more than two federal agents snooping around. It would make her residents jumpy. It kind of makes me happy she's checking us out."

"It definitely makes Norm safer, if he'd actually decided to stay put. We can't exactly fault her for doing her job." Even if Mina was antsy to get in.

"Let's hope badge credentials are enough for her," Kaylee murmured. "We've got work to do."

"We do. Part of that is trying to figure out what's going on with Norm. Why the runaround? Why the secrets? The conclusion I'm coming to is not a fun one. I think Norm has continued with his plan to take Waterbury out on his own. That way, he keeps all the attention of the Syndicate on himself, and we remain uninvolved, which is what he wanted in the first place." Mina hadn't shared with Kaylee the discussion she'd had with Norm this morning. "He was prepared to die the last time but didn't have time to formulate all his plans."

"Die, as in actually dead? Or, 'I'm going to pretend I'm dead so Waterbury thinks I am, and therefore I win, and he doesn't come after me' dead? Okay, so that's not a thing, but I'm hoping it can be."

"He was scheduled to get an echo fib."

Kaylee made a face. "So he was prepared to die, but didn't necessarily want to die die." She waved a hand at Mina. "You know what I mean."

"Pretty much."

Kaylee whistled low. "Jeez. He really wanted to take this guy out. And himself. I watched a screencast documentary about a bunch of different people who tried to take somebody out with one of those. Only one guy survived. He had three heart attacks coming out of it. He was a mess. Those things are so illegal. And there's a very good reason. They don't discriminate who they kill. I mean, most alive people have a heartbeat."

"Yes, they do." Mina chuckled. "That's exactly what I told him. He said he was prepared to take the risk. He was going to rile Waterbury up so that the thing latched on to the faster heartbeat. Or something like that. It was delusional. Thinking you can walk away from something like that is not in the realm of reality. Norm tried to get Wilbert put in a box for a long time. He finally succeeded. But Norm knew once Waterbury was sprung, he wasn't going to let up until Norm was dead. Norm also knew that when they finally met up, under whatever circumstances, Waterbury would search him, so he had to be extra careful. A weapon wouldn't work. So he was willing to go to those lengths to take the Syndicate fixer all the way out."

"Man, what a terrible way to go. Did you tell Webb that we're going to secure Waterbury's arrest? Does he know the plan to take the satellite out?"

"No. Lee and I hadn't gotten that far when we spoke with him earlier. I told Norm the plan would take a while to figure out. I asked him to be patient."

"I'm not sure that old spider knows the meaning of that word."

"It appears that way. If he's not at the residence, he's either staking out Waterbury, getting an implant, or consulting with somebody who can do the job for him. That's my guess anyway."

None of it was good.

Certainly not for Norm and definitely not for his relationship with Mina moving forward. Norm was shredding things faster than Mina could sew them back together.

The proper, articulate voice came back over the drone's aural system. "You are approved to land at the hub. A representative will meet you there. Be timely. The offer expires in three minutes."

She clicked off before Mina could respond.

"I guess we're about to see what this building is really all about," Kaylee said. "I kind of wish we'd weaponed up. That woman sounds a little ominous. Like she loves reading, but she could toss a dagger into an eye socket at a hundred yards if she wanted to."

"That was a visual I didn't need. Thanks. But I am thinking the same thing," Mina said. "We just have to act like we have a few hidden lasers on us."

"Shouldn't be too hard. My swagger is ice."

"It is. You go first."

THEY WALKED INTO the hub, Kaylee's swagger out in front. It was more than ice, it was an arctic blast with a side of hot lava.

No one was waiting for them.

The only individuals occupying the space were a single bot situated inside a box of plexan and an older gentleman reading something off a handheld. He appeared to be waiting for a ride.

Kaylee leaned in. "What are we supposed to do? Keep walking?"

"Let's head to the tubes." Mina gestured to the right. "Maybe Bristol swabbed us in and just had to make a show of saying somebody would meet us."

The hub was modest, decorated very plainly with lots of whites and creams. Very nondescript, perfect for the clientele they thought might be occupying the units here.

The tubes were ten meters away, four to a side.

They were halfway there when a seamless door inset into a wall slicked open, and a man stepped out.

Mina came to a stop, gasping. "Gerald?" Maybe her eyes were deceiving her, and she wasn't really seeing an old manager from the Cullen op.

"Monica? What are you doing here?" Mina's telework manager settled his hands on his hips, his familiar platypus-heeled shoes beginning their double tap on the floor. "But that's not really your name, is it? You deceived us all! I lost my job because of you." He swirled an index finger at her. "The whole place shut down after your little event. Everyone was let go. You ruined people's lives. You should be ashamed of yourself."

The little event he was referring to was when Mina and Lee had brought down Rick the Rat, who had been embezzling funds from customers on Cullen's orders for over a year and a half.

"No shame here. Honestly, Ger, it's a miracle you're not boxed up right now, so maybe you should be thanking me for shutting down a highly illegal operation before you— or anyone else on the floor—became fully invested." There was no doubt Gerald had known, on some level, that illegal activities had been taking place. If someone hung up their coat wrong, he'd talked about it for a week. He'd probably been interested in joining the upper ranks, but they hadn't extended him an invite. Lucky him. Mina had been hoping she'd never have to set eyes on this irritating human again. He'd been a pain in her backside then and would be now.

He sputtered for a moment. It was kind of his thing. "I was unaware and completely innocent of any wrongdoings at Cullen Industries. I ground my fingertips to the bare bones for those people every single day. I was horrified to find that things were amiss! How dare you speculate I was ever involved." His eyes narrowed. If he'd had the ability to produce actual steam, it would be flowing out of his ears at top steam-spewing pressure right now.

"'Amiss' is certainly a creative way to define siphoning trillions of tax dollars out of the hands of the government and into privileged pockets. I skimmed the report the other day. Cullen himself received ten years for that, as did a dozen or so board members. Ricky took the brunt and is now serving fifteen." Rick the Rat was a young, clueless hacker who had been hired to do the dirty work—which he'd participated in happily and been paid handsomely for. "But it looks like you landed on your feet. Good for you." She refrained from making a comment about his large, overly square-toed shoes. "You should be thankful they didn't let you in on it. Instead of a box, you get to work here." She waved an arm around the modest hub. "I'm assuming you were sent by Ms. Bristol to assist us?" She gestured at Kaylee. "This is Agent Poston. We're here to find the resident of unit 107. Time is of the essence, so I'd appreciate it if we could get going."

Gerald cleared his throat, making a show of straightening his purple-and-green-striped overcoat, which was paired with silky navy tuck pants. It wasn't quite a suit, but it had that feel. She couldn't imagine him not dressing up, but she had to admit it suited him.

"I'm supposed to take you up to that residence and let you inside. But nowhere else."

"Got it," Mina said, gesturing toward the tubes. "Lead the way."

He seemed surprised she wasn't arguing for more. He turned and began to walk, high-stepping in front of them, the soles of his shoes literally unyielding. At the tube, he stuck his finger in for a DNA swipe. The door opened immediately.

They all stepped inside.

"Level one hundred," he commanded.

Kaylee had remained quiet but shot Mina a knowing look. Mina had discussed the Cullen case with her bestie over the entire insufferable eighteen months she had spent there, one of her longest cases to date. She'd known the culprit was Rick but hadn't been able to catch him in the act until Lee figured out the code.

In normal circumstances, when an op went on that long, McAllister had the ability to end it or assign someone else. But the siphons bleeding from Cullen had crept into the trillions. That had demanded a conclusion, so she'd endured.

Gerald had been one of the things she'd been forced to endure.

"Do you work directly for Ms. Bristol?" Mina decided to make a little small talk. She was curious to find out how much Gerry knew about his new job.

"I do," he replied. "This is a delightful place to work. I'm an assistant concierge, and my job is to make sure all of our guests enjoy their stay."

The tube doors slicked open, and they stepped out.

"Guests?" Kaylee said casually. "So this is kind of like a pay-a-day-type deal? Not permanent residences?"

Gerald's eyes widened slightly before he got them under control, bringing both of his palms up to smooth the lapels of his coat. Something he did when he was nervous. Mina knew his tells. "Um. No, we have long-term residents. We just have, you know, a lot of turnover." His face brightened like he'd found the right explanation. "Yes, turnover. People come and go a lot."

They walked toward unit 107.

"That's odd," Mina speculated, using a light tone. "Residential lease agreements require a ton of work between the agency and the bank. The average length of stay once a person secures a residence is four to six years. So how often do tenants here come and go?"

Gerald snorted. "You can't finesse me anymore, Monica." Then he growled, "I mean, Agent Kane. Whatever your name is. I don't have to answer your questions. I'm enjoying my new job, and I plan to keep it." He stuck his thumb against the smudger of 107 and leaned in for a retinal. The door clicked, and he turned the lever. Mina knew instantly that Norm was not inside the unit, because that wouldn't have worked if Norm had set the interior security. "Here we are. Take a look around. Then I'll escort you back to the hub."

Mina walked briskly past him, scanning the living area before heading back to the sleep room. None of Norm's things were here. He hadn't brought much, but it was completely empty.

"I got something," Kaylee called from the waste room.

Mina walked in, holding her hand up to Gerald. "You stay here."

Gerry huffed, but remained outside the door.

A set of numbers was written on the mirror in an unknown substance. It wasn't blood. Mina wasn't sure what he'd used. It didn't matter.

"This is obviously for you to find." Kaylee indicated the mirror. "Do those numbers mean anything to you?"

"Not yet." Mina entered them verbally into her cuff. "Looks like a possible street address with an old mail code." She pressed the input button on the side. "Analyze numbers, level five search," she ordered. "Cross-check with numerical addresses paired with old postal codes up to eighty years ago. Display any matches in this city in holo immediately."

"Weren't they called zips or something like that?" Kaylee inquired as they waited. "Why were cities and towns across America parsed into zips? I know they delivered paper mail back then, but you'd think it would be called something like blocks or zones? Zip is weird."

Mina didn't have time to explain it was probably an

acronym. Locations popped up on holo, hovering above her wrist. She scanned the list, then reached out and rubbed the mirror clean with the taper of her shirt. "I know where he is. Come on." She breezed past Gerald. "Thanks for escorting us up and letting us in. We need to get back to the hub quickly."

Kaylee knew better than to ask for more information in front of the civilian. She simply followed Mina out into the hallway as they waited for Gerald to lock up and hail the tube.

"I'm glad you located your friend," Gerald said graciously. "He's quite a character."

It was Mina's turn to narrow her gaze. "You met him?" She saw Gerry retreat inward. She resisted the urge to grab him by the lapels. "Don't lie to me. I'll know it. I need to know what he said to you. Did you order a transpo ride for him?"

Gerald began to sputter. Another go-to for him. "I didn't...I never..."

Kaylee settled a hand on his shoulder, causing him to refocus his attention on her. "Gerald, I know we don't have a past together," she said. "But you seem like a decent enough guy. From what Agent Kane has told me, you were a hard worker who got stiffed by Cullen and his crew. But all that's behind you now. You're on the right track, and I wouldn't want you to mess it up by lying to us. The guy we're looking for is an ex-marshal. A formal federal agent whose life is in danger. You can be a hero and tell us what you know, or we can secure a warrant and bring you in for questioning. Which I'm certain Ms. Bristol would frown upon. What's it going to be?"

The tube arrived, door whooshing open.

"You can't do—"

"We can," Mina said as they stepped into the tube. "This is exactly what I told your boss ten minutes ago. If you don't cooperate, we get a warrant that says you have to, or you spend quality time in a box. You witnessed what happened when my partner and I brought Ricky down. Those same rules apply here. We're on a case, the ex-marshal is part of it, keeping him safe is our top priority. We need to track him down. What you know will help with that. It's all very easy. Anything you tell us will remain confidential, and it will go a long way toward us not bringing back a passel of agents to snoop into what's going on in this high-rise. I'm certain your boss will want you to cooperate."

Gerald appeared like he was going to hold out, then he expelled an exasperated breath. "Fine. He called for a personal concierge. I went up to meet with him. He told me he needed private transpo, and he was willing to pay top currency. It needed to be stealthy and fast." He held up his hand as Mina began to comment. "He didn't tell me where he was going, and I didn't ask. We don't do that here. I met him down at the hub when he was ready. He was all smiles, relaxed, ready to go."

"How long ago?" Mina asked.

Ger checked one of his cuffs. He had two. "Twenty-two minutes ago. I asked him if he'd like me to arrange something for the return trip. He told me he would take care of it himself. He cracked some jokes. Talked about the weather. That was the entirety of our conversation." They stepped off the tube and into the hub. A few paces in, Gerald turned to face them, walking backward. "I cooperated with you, Monica." He swished his hand. "Whatever. You'll always be Monica to me. Now you keep your end of the bargain and leave here without asking me any more questions. And try never to come back."

"We're leaving," Mina said. For now. "But before we go, I'm going to do you a favor." Gerald's eyebrows rose. He stopped moving. "I'm giving you my call address. I want you to use it if you ever find yourself in trouble." Mina surprised herself. She'd never thought she'd feel magnanimous when it came to Gerald the Jerkweed, which was how she'd referred to him in her head for a year and a half. But here she was, feeling magnanimous. "I'm assuming you know some of what's going on in this place, but not all. When you uncover the rest or find yourself in any real danger regarding any of your guests or your bosses, contact me. I'll help if I can."

"I don't need your charity—"

"Take it," Kaylee urged. "Agent Kane doesn't offer stuff like this on a regular basis. You cooperated, now she's matching the favor. Whatever's going on in this place, you're likely to encounter...issues. When you find yourself between an asteroid and a meteor, you'll have somebody to call. I'm pretty sure, at some point, you'll be grateful to have it."

"Fine," he said, lifting up his cuff. "I'll take it, but I'm not giving you mine in return."

Promise? Mina set her cuff next to his, and a soft beep sounded. "Use it wisely, Ger. I wish you luck." She gave him a three-finger salute as they headed outside to catch their drone.

Once the craft doors slicked open, Kaylee muttered, "Everything you told me about that guy was spot-on. Although he became less of an asshelmet once you finessed him. I think there might be a decent guy under all that shellac clomping around in ridiculous square-toed shoes. Who knew?"

"He definitely made work at Cullen interesting every day. Come to think of it, if I'd tried to finesse him back then, maybe my life at Cullen would've been a little easier. But he was too easy to rile. Made every day a little more entertaining than the last watching him overreact to the slightest comment."

"Like snatching a treat from a tot. Where are we going, anyway?"

"Tanks."

"Norm left a clue for us written on the waste-room mirror," Mina reported to her director over the drone's aural system. "A series of numbers that appeared to be a street address along with a five-digit code resembling an old postal designation. I did a search combining those numbers, and one result came back as Tanks. It's the bar where Norm met with Waterbury. We're en route."

"I wonder if he's trying to gather more information. It could be that Waterbury has been to Tanks since he's been released," McAllister postulated out loud. "Whatever the reason, we need to find Webb immediately. I just got word from the committee that they're in the process of approving our plan. I contacted Agent Adams and Ms. Biggins, who informed me that they are able to complete the task without any outside involvement. With this news, I am almost certain approval will come down in the next fifteen. I've reached out to two magistrates I trust. One has an opening to hear this case in thirty. This is going to come together quickly, and we need Norman Webb to make it happen."

"Fully understood," Mina said. "I will report as soon as we have him. We will deliver him to Government One immediately." If everything went according to plan, it was a possibility they could have Waterbury in holding in a few hours. Mina didn't know how long it would take for the stable heart to drop back to Earth, or for Lee and Harmony to work their magic on retrieving the data files, but since it weighed a ton, a two-thousand-kilometer descent should be pretty quick.

"Have you heard from Colonel Kramer?"

"No," she replied. "I'm sure he'll reply as soon as he can." She'd made sure of that, as she'd carefully chosen a few words that would indicate to Vince that it was an emergency. It was imperative he knew that the Syndicate had his identity, or would soon have it, linking him to freeing Norm. Lee had specified a four- to six-hour window. It'd already been two and a half.

"Keep me apprised on that. Good luck tracking Webb down. Hopefully, I'll see you two back here in less than thirty." He popped off.

"Why would Webb go to a bar?" Kaylee asked. "Seems like an odd choice. Maybe McAllister is right, and he's trying to find more information on Waterbury. But that doesn't seem exactly right. Waterbury is being monitored. There's not much to learn at the moment. Other than, you know, his penchant for torturing."

"I'm not sure. They both spent a lot of time there. It's possible Norm got to know the owner or the drink tender. Maybe he was paying them to keep tabs on Waterbury and wanted to check in. Norm has lots of contacts. He pays them well, and as far as I know, once Norm has a spy, they're loyal to him."

Norm was a likable guy. Usually. When he wasn't irritating the crap out of her.

"Landing at public transpo, one block from target location, in thirty seconds," the sim announced.

"I guess we're about to find out," Kaylee murmured.

Mina checked her cuff once more. Nothing from Vince. "Yes, we are."

Kaylee snarked, "Knowing that old spider, there'll be another cryptic note on the waste-room mirror."

"I hope not."

The drone landed, and they departed.

A block in, Kaylee bobbed her head in front of them. "Tell me this is not the place. Don't they know they can print another sign that actually has all the letters? That one looks like it's from a hundred years ago. I bet it used to light up with neon inside. Now it just looks pitiful."

"They probably kept it for nostalgia's sake. Back then, patrons were very loyal to their local bar. It was a big deal."

"The outside glass is tinted. It's not solar-catch either." Kaylee wrinkled her nose as they came to a stop in front of the door. "No wonder a creep like you-know-who wanted to hang out here. No one pays attention. It's a keep-your-head-down-and-walk-on-by kind of place."

"We're paying attention now." Mina swung the door open.

It took a few moments for their eyes to adjust to the dimness. Not more than four ultras were on, all of them at barely there lumen levels. Two customers sat spaced along the bar. No one occupied any of the scattered tables. One drink tender was busy mopping up an area of the original wood bar.

"What can I get you ladies?" he asked genially.

"I'm actually looking for one of your customers. A guy about this tall." Mina raised her hand to just above her shoulder. "Gray hair styled a centimeter off his scalp. He's been a patron here for many years on and off. He would've frequented this place a lot about seven years ago. We have reason to believe he was just here."

The man chuckled. "You're talking about Billy. He said you'd come by. He's nothing if not predictable."

"When did he leave?" Kaylee asked.

"Oh, going on about ten, twelve minutes ago."

"What did he say to you?" Mina asked.

"Came in for a quick hello, like he does sometimes. Said he was expecting guests, didn't know when, likely soonish. At least one would be a female matching your description." He angled his head toward Mina. "Said to tell you not to worry. He's dealing with it."

That only escalated her worry.

"Did he happen to say how we could get in touch with him?" Mina asked. "He's not answering his cuff. It's pretty important we get a hold of him."

"He said you'd be persistent." The man laughed good-naturedly. Now that Mina's eyes had adjusted to the darkened interior, she noticed he was about Norm's age. Taller and skinnier, his hair dyed dark brown. Not too many enhancements, but a few.

"He was right." Mina waited.

"He said that if you looked extra anxious, I was supposed to tell you that he was keeping an appointment he made. And that he wasn't gonna let the same thing happen twice." The man rubbed his chin. "He was pretty vague, but when I pressed him, he wouldn't give me anything else. Except the coin to relay this message to you." The man flashed her a broad smile. He was missing a tooth on the bottom. Kind of went along with the broken sign outside. Not only could you print a sign for cheap, you could also print a tooth. Or, technically, have a dentist do it for you. "What he didn't know is that when he contacted transpo to pick him up, I saw the address he was going to. He typed it out slowly on his cuff. It's dark in here, so he did it on holo." The man shook his head. "Hard to keep secrets at Tanks."

Mina didn't mention all the secrets Waterbury had kept over the years sitting in this very place. Or the fact that Norm was being sloppy on purpose.

"How much do you want?" She wasn't interested in negotiating. Mina needed answers now.

"Billy settled on fifty even. I'm thinking you need this information badly, so I'll give you a deal. How about forty-five?"

"Done."

The man began to protest. "Wait a minute. I was being a little too hasty—"

Mina spoke into her cuff. "I need a coin delivery of one hundred world currency to the main drink tender at Tanks. Approval through Director McAllister. Respond immediately."

"Submitting order. Please wait," a bot at headquarters replied. A few seconds later, it said, "Order approved. Delivery will commence in seven minutes."

The man stared at her cuff in wonder. Then blinked. "Okay, then. The address was an easy one to remember. It's only a couple kilometers away. It's a popular inking emporium called Eclipse Ink."

"Webb's getting body ink done?" Kaylee snorted. "That doesn't sound right."

"He's not getting inked," Mina replied. She debated asking this nice drink tender to give her an alert if Waterbury showed up, but she didn't want to get him on the Syndicate's radar, so she opted against it. "Thanks for your time. Your coin will be here in the next five." She turned and walked out. Kaylee followed.

"Sounds like you know the place," Kaylee said as they began to walk toward the public landing pad.

"I do. I had a case a few years ago involving a crafty

burglar. Traced him back to Eclipse. He was one of their inkers. He was placing microlocators under the skin of his clients. He would grab their skin residue for DNA and their prints off a set special substance he precoated on the armrests. He would chat them up, figure out how secure their residences were, get the name of their sim. With the aid of the locators, he knew when they weren't home. He went for places where the residents used smudgers to get in and out."

"I remember you telling me about that guy. He evaded you for a while."

"He did," Mina said as a government craft set down. "I actually found him in what's called The Underground of Eclipse Ink. It's a space they lease to freelancers. That's why I know Norm is not getting inked. They specialize in performing procedures down there. Body piercings, beauty implants, hair, eyelashes, embedded jewels, stuff like that. At the time, the staff swore up and down those areas were aboveboard and legal. Guess what I bet they also do?"

"Illegal procedures. Like implanting echo fibs."

"Ding, ding, ding. Hand the woman a maple treat."

"Goody, I'm dying for one."

The drone landed, and they boarded.

"If we can reach him quick enough, hopefully we can stop it from happening." Mina was more worried about Norm than upset with him right now. Upset would come later.

"What is your destination please?" the sim asked.

"Eclipse Ink," Mina ordered.

"Eclipse Ink has monitored landing," the sim replied after a few seconds. "You must have an appointment to access its hub."

"Cite a governmental exception," Mina said.

After fifteen seconds, the sim intoned, "Override accepted. Landing in less than one minute."

"I can't believe that devious spider is going to go through with it." Kaylee shook her head. "It's such a stupid thing to do without contacting you first to see if you had a better plan. And you do. A totally better one."

"I can promise you that Norm is not thinking straight." Mina settled back in her seat. "He's likely in some kind of shock from the torture. I should've taken that into account. Assessed his mental health before we started all this. Combined that with all his years he's tried to get Waterbury boxed for good. He wants to stop him at all costs. Norm knows the horrible stuff Waterbury is capable of, and he doesn't want any of us involved. In his mind, the Syndicate will never let up, meaning that all of us will be in their crosshairs forever."

Kaylee gazed out the window. "Do you think that's accurate? Do you think they'll be laser-focused on us for life? In all of my years with the CIU, I've never come up against them before. None of us has, at least that I know of. They've always been exceedingly careful about covering their tracks so they don't get caught. And if they happen to, they always find a way to wiggle right out."

"I'm not sure," Mina replied honestly. "But I can swear to you that I'm going to do everything in my power to make sure none of us ends up at the mercy of the Syndicate. That means keeping everyone involved quiet. If no one knows the identities of the people who brought them down, they can't exact revenge. Exposing this case quickly and making sure it's chaotic will be important. Once Waterbury gets Babble, things will fall apart for them. Hopefully, whoever gave Waterbury his orders, including bosses, will be hauled in."

"When you guys were listening in on the communication between Mr. Frackin' and the guy at Waterbury's, you said he made it sound like they had something big brewing. That would be a benefit. Even better if they blame this entire data grab on Waterbury for deciding to torture a federal ex-marshal. I mean, it was freakishly stupid. Especially since he's still on monitored probation."

Mina nodded. "That would be ideal. This case carries more risk than anything we've dealt with in a long time. We're going to have to be extremely vigilant. There's no way around it. But we took an oath to protect the innocents, whatever the currency expense. This is one of those times."

"Yeah, it's an expensive one. But I'm in it. Knowing we'll be a part of bringing down this massive organization that has killed, maimed, and wreaked havoc for years on end will be extremely satisfying. Maybe the most satisfying to date. I'm kind of shocked we're getting approval to do this. Seems like the higher-ups are okay with us taking down a crime organization that has made a multitrillion-dollar dynasty out of operating in the gray zone of legalized crime. If we're successful, it's going to rock the world."

"I'm surprised, too," Mina said. "I think we might be entering into an era where the world is fed up with coexisting with ongoing criminal activities. It seems the committee agrees. We've presented them with a chance to bash a hole in the Syndicate's titanium shield, and they're allowing us to take the swing."

"I wonder what your faux auditors would say to this," Kaylee snarked. "Certainly whoever sicced them on you wouldn't agree with going after the Syndicate, as they seemed not to want criminals locked in boxes. This kind of proves the audit wasn't from our committee. Is McAllister any closer to figuring out who ordered it?"

"Not that I know of. I'm sure it's been sidelined due to what's happening today. But I'm certain he'll get to the bottom of it. I've never seen him so angry. When I got up to leave the room, and the auditors tried to stop me, McAllister whipped open the door and looked like he was ready to physically fight them." Mina chuckled. "They are going to rue the day they pissed off Duncan McAllister. I can promise you that."

"I'd love to see the ending to that, printed treats in hand. I really would. Our director remains in a constant state of composure each and every day. Thinking of him teetering on the edge is kind of exciting. I hope they come back into the building and demand a meeting." Her glee spilled over.

"It would be at their own peril."

"Landing at Eclipse Ink," the sim intoned.

"Let's go get Norm so this case can begin its free fall," Mina said.

CHAPTER 13

"HELLO, AGENT KANE. How may I help you?" The young woman behind the reception desk greeted them with a tentative smile.

Mina was relieved the woman recognized her from her previous op. Mina couldn't recall this woman specifically, but she wore a very helpful name badge.

"It's nice to see you again, Ramona," Mina replied smoothly. "You can assist me by directing us to the procedure rooms of The Underground. Someone I'm looking for is with a technician down there."

The girl had so much body ink running along both arms that no undecorated skin showed. Her hair was dyed a brilliant cerulean blue to accent her eyes, and her ears were lined with a variety of piercings.

Even under all that ink, Mina could see her pale at the inquiry.

"I'm sorry," Ramona started, "I'm not allowed to

give nonclients access to that area. You have to have an appointment, then that technician comes up and escorts you down."

Mina knew the drill. "Please contact your supervisor. Is it still Roxie? Tell her I'm here and require her assistance." She couldn't recall Roxie's surname, but she was happy that she was able to pull out the woman's first name.

"She's one of them, yes," Ramona replied, tapping a board embedded into the desk. She glanced up, her smile expressing her relief that Mina was letting her off the hook. "She'll be down in a second. Please take a seat over there." She gestured to a small but nicely furnished waiting area.

Mina and Kaylee walked over.

"Are you going to have to call in a warrant?" Kaylee asked. "Or do you think she'll comply?"

"I think Roxie will cooperate," Mina replied. "She's the one who swore up and down the last time that everything that goes on below ground is legal. In fact, she staked her career on it. Because I'd already apprehended the guy I was looking for, I told her she was clear, and I wouldn't investigate any further. But if I had to return, it would be a different story. If someone is performing illegal implants in her building, this will be the second time it's happened."

They didn't have to wait long.

A tall, willowy redhead, dressed in a sheath dress of vibrant, metallic gold that accented all of her decorative ink, strode into the waiting area. Mina saw her apprehension even as she tried to hide it.

She extended a hand. "How nice to see you again, Agent Kane. What brings you by?"

Mina shook the proffered hand. "My partner, Agent Poston, and I are here to pick up a man we believe is receiving, or about to receive, an illegal implant in your basement." She chose not to mince words. She didn't have time to waste.

"That's not possible. We don't condone or approve illegal implants here. I was very clear with you about that last time. Nothing has changed."

Mina knew Roxie was in a difficult position. Mina liked the woman and wanted to work with her. "You were crystal clear. During that conversation, you assured me that all business conducted here is legal, and I took you at your word." Roxie blinked, her expression serene. "But I have intel that suggests otherwise. You can allow me access to continue my investigation, which might lead to inconclusive findings. Or I can procure a warrant to do the same." Mina glanced at her cuff. "I believe it will take no longer than five minutes to procure a warrant, as I'm currently involved in a very sensitive matter. If the warrant is enacted, this place will be shut down so a formal investigation can take place, which is standard procedure. The choice is yours. But I need you to make a decision immediately. The person I'm here for is at risk of dying if something goes wrong."

Roxie cleared her throat, flattening her hand across her chest. The backside was covered in interesting geometric designs. Mina couldn't imagine wanting something like that for herself, but it was beautiful on her. Inking and re-inking was a big business. It'd gotten incredibly easy over the last fifty years to laser off old designs and add new ones.

But that didn't mean it wasn't painful. Needles injected ink under the skin. Nothing else worked as well.

"I will, of course, lead you downstairs. No warrant is necessary." Roxie gathered herself. "But I want to make this very clear before we proceed. If any of our independent contractors are providing illegal services, they are breaking their agreement with us. They will be asked to leave immediately and will be escorted out. If you care to press charges and make an arrest, that's up to you. You have my word that we will cooperate fully. We employ staff on our main and upper floors." She made a sweeping gesture to include the upper stories. "We do full lifechecks, we monitor all procedures, and we follow the law. Nothing happens without our knowledge. Below ground, in The Underground, we procure contracts with independent agents who provide various services that complement our line of work. It helps with the building costs, as upkeep is expensive. Each of our contractors signs a binding agreement with us that everything they do here is completely legal. I can provide those contracts, if necessary. Nothing illegal is condoned nor tolerated by Eclipse Ink. Just as I told you the last time we met, you have my word."

"I appreciate that." Mina inclined her head toward the woman. "I'll give you an address of where to send those contracts, if needed, depending on what we find. I'm certain Eclipse is protected well by the agreements. Independent contractors have a level of freedom that regular employees don't have, which makes them harder to monitor. Right now, we need to get down to those rooms. I doubt the man we're looking for used his real name, but his appointment would have started approximately fifteen minutes ago. He's a little shorter than I am and has steel-gray hair and a stocky build. Somebody will have noticed him."

Roxie nodded. "Come with me."

They followed the manager down a hallway. She stopped in front of a single tube station, DNA-swiping to unlock it.

The ride was short. The door opened, and they had to wait for their eyes to adjust to the lighting—or lack thereof.

"Hey, it's a neon sign." Kaylee gestured to the scrawled letters mounted on a red-brick wall lit by pale pink gas. It read Welcome to The Underground. "We were just talking about those. Somebody should tell the guy at Tanks he can get a fresh, updated sign. So much prettier and full of life."

Roxie didn't comment. She turned down a narrow corridor.

After a few twists and turns, they came upon a small reception area with a desk made out of what looked to be real, reclaimed wood, indicated by all the dents, discoloration, and age that couldn't be recreated by printing. Another neon sign was mounted on the wall behind it, this one pale green.

It simply read The Underground.

A young man with shockingly violet hair standing at least six centimeters straight up and ink decorating every nanometer of his body, including his face, gave Roxie a short wave. "Hey, Rox. What's up?"

Instead of answering, she gestured with a swoop of her arm for Mina to step forward.

"Hi, we're looking for a man about this tall." Mina raised her hand to her shoulder. "An older gentleman with gray hair styled like yours, but quite a bit shorter, no ink, stocky build. Came in about fifteen ago."

The kid, who looked to be no more than nineteen or twenty, shot Roxie a look, his matching violet eyebrows shooting up. "Um, I'm not sure I can—"

"It's fine, Bodie," Roxie told him. "Go ahead and tell Agent Kane where the man is located and lead her back to that room. She's allowed full access."

The kid thought about it for a few seconds, then shrugged, standing. "Okay. He's here. Follow me."

Mina and Kaylee followed him down a short hallway. All the walls were red brick and all the doors reclaimed wood.

Bodie came to a stop and gestured. "He's in there."

"We'll take it from here." Mina nodded at the kid. "You can head back to your post."

He shrugged again. "Man, I always miss out on the fun."

He shuffled away.

Mina rapped a knuckle on the door. "Federal agents, open up."

A familiar voice replied, "Come in."

She opened the door.

Norm sat in a chair next to a patient bed, checking his cuff. "You work quick, you know that?"

"Where's your implanter?" Mina glanced around the small room as she and Kaylee entered, shutting the door behind them. There were no other doors, so the man or woman could not have hidden themselves.

"I let them off the hook," Norm said, resignation in his tone. "No reason to get them in trouble when I'm the one who insisted on having it done. They owed me a favor. I was cashing it in after many years. Not their fault."

"Swear to me you're not already implanted." Mina crossed her arms. "If you are, we're heading straight to the Medi Center."

"I'm not implanted. I swear it," he replied, weariness radiating from him. "I had a change of heart at the last minute. When you called earlier, I was halfway here. I was determined to do this and handle everything myself. Waterbury is my perp, my problem." He thumped his chest, anger sparking his words. "The reason you're all embroiled in this mess is because of me." He rubbed a shaky hand over his face. "But I knew you'd find me before I could get it taken care of. And even if you didn't, my plan had so many holes in it, it wouldn't have held rocks, much less water." The ex-marshal had used up his steam. He slumped back in his seat. The look of defeat was intense.

For the first time, Norm was showing all of his eightysomething years.

Mina wanted to be angry, but she wasn't.

Norm's continued focus on Waterbury over so many years had changed something in him. This wasn't a regular case anymore. The moment Waterbury had been set free, it'd reignited the obsession once again. Norm had a personal attachment to this case because of his niece, and it became even more personal after Waterbury tortured him. He wasn't acting rationally. Therefore, he deserved their sympathy, not their anger.

"How come you didn't contact me to let me know you changed your mind?" Mina asked. "That would've saved us some time."

He shook his head, continuing to look miserable. "I only made my mind up about five minutes ago. I don't know how you tracked me down so quickly. Are you sure you don't have some bloodhound in you? Sheesh."

"You left us a clue on your waste-room mirror, and we got lucky at Tanks," Mina said. "You were sloppy when you typed in the address for Eclipse." She arched a brow. "Or else you did it on purpose because you secretly didn't want to die. I actually prefer that answer to anything else. It's better if we don't know." She gestured for him to get up. "Come on. We need to get a move on. We're taking you to Government One. We have a solid plan, and you play a prominent role. You're due in front of a magistrate in ten so he or she can decide if what we want to do is warranted. Then the plan will be set in motion."

Norm rose off the chair. "That's good to hear. I should've contacted you. I apologize. I just feel all mixed up in my mind about this. There are so many emotions swirling around in there, it's hard to grab hold of any of 'em. They're like a bunch of eels in a bucket. They're right there in front of you, but when you reach in to grab one, they just slide right through your fingers."

"Ew." Kaylee wrinkled her nose. "You gotta work on some better, hipper analogies. Nobody puts an eel in a bucket, much less more than one. You're showing your age, old man."

Norm chuckled.

Kaylee had managed to change the energy in the room with little effort. She was a pro.

"I am old," Norm grunted. "And I like my analogies. They're fitting."

"Only to those who like to grab slimy fish out of buckets."

"Before we head outside of this room," Mina said to Norm, "I need you to swear that the implanter who was going to insert your fib was only doing so at your command, and it's not something they do on a regular basis."

"It was all me. Swear on my honor. What little there is of it left. I called in a favor. They do beauty implants for a living. Nothing more. I brought in the fib. And don't even ask where I got it, because I'm not divulging that. Let's just say the person who procured it for me was also doing me a favor."

"Is it here?" Mina looked around.

"No. I destroyed it." Norm settled a hand over his heart. "I swear it."

"You're a real pain in the backside, you know that?" Kaylee said. "But I'm glad you're okay. Heading to the Medi Center and making them carve it out of you would've lost us valuable time."

Mina gave the ex-marshal who was like family to her a long look. He met her gaze, appearing sincere. She chose to believe him, even if he didn't exactly deserve that from her right now.

Kaylee opened the door, and they exited.

Roxie was waiting for them next to Bodie's desk. The kid wore an expectant look.

"It seems there's been no crime committed here," Mina told them both. "Your independent contractor is off the hook. The implant was not procured by them, ordered by them, nor implanted by them." Mina wouldn't say they were perfectly clean, but it was close. Saying no to a federal marshal when you owe him something would be difficult for anyone.

Norm was likable and very persuasive when he needed to be.

"That's right," Norm echoed. "Don't fire that poor girl. It was all me. She had nothing to do with it."

"I see," Roxie said.

"I told you Verna wouldn't do something like that," Bodie scoffed. "You owe me bronze ink, and I want Felix to do it."

"Thank you both for your cooperation. It's much appreciated," Mina said.

Roxie moved forward, extending her hand once again. Mina shook it. "I was happy to help. You're a good agent who takes her job seriously, and it shows. We were, and still are, thankful that you caught Cameron Tweed. Since his arrest, we have readjusted how we monitor our employees and how they treat their clients. We've added more cams and upped our privacy screening. All of those things have improved our business model, and that was thanks to your diligence. If you ever need anything, feel free to come back. We are open to your future investigations"—she winked as a slow smile spread across her lips—"and any inking needs you might have. We have a temp product that lasts for approximately three months. Can't even tell the difference." She lifted her hand and wiggled her fingers, grinning.

Mina chuckled. "I'll keep that in mind. Hopefully, our paths won't converge in a professional sense in the future, but if they do, I look forward to another positive interaction."

They headed out a small side door across from Bodie's desk and left him happily chatting about his future ink.

"Now why can't every single person we deal with in the civilian world be as professional as Roxie?" Kaylee lamented. "Our jobs would be so much easier."

"Now that's just wishful thinking," Mina said. "I'm calling a craft and reporting to McAllister. This plan is officially a go."

Chapter 14

Mina checked her cuff for what felt like the fourteenth time as she paced back and forth in the middle of a bustling hallway full of litigators, civilians, and government staff.

She and Kaylee stood in the civic area, near pedestrian level in Government One. Norm had been one-on-one with the magistrate for going on thirty minutes.

"You're like a nervous mother about to be presented with a litter of marmots," Kaylee said. "Have a seat." She patted the polymold next to her. "Stuff like this takes time. It's not like we're waiting for a box of chocolate gooeys to be finished being printed. This is a big-time ask. It's going to work out. I feel it in my bones. And my bones don't lie. Well, most of the time. Sometimes they're just creaky. But this isn't one of those times."

"I hope you're right."

"I am right. I feel it deep in the marrow. Not the crunchy outer part. It's no-lie marrow. And it's squiggling around in there, telling me everything is going to be okay."

Mina made a face. "Norm's not the only one who needs some new analogies. Squiggly bone marrow?"

Kaylee huffed, pretending to be offended. "I have magnificent analogies. They're quirky and unique, just like me." She patted her chest as she blinked rapidly.

Before Mina could reply, the door slicked open, and Norm walked out.

He gestured for her to enter the room. "The magistrate wants to ask you a few questions," Norm told her.

"Me?" Mina asked.

"Yep. He has my audio. He asked if you were here, and I told him you were."

Mina nodded. "Okay. Did he give you his verdict?"

"Not yet," Norm answered. "But I have a feeling he's going to approve the warrant. He's being extra cautious, and I don't blame him one bit. You didn't give me all the details of this plan on the way over, but holy wow, if we can pull this off, it will be stratospheric, literally." Norm was showing happiness for the first time in too long. "I've spent my entire life trying to get this guy boxed for life. And, for the first time, it just might happen."

Mina turned to Kaylee. "Contact McAllister and let him know I'm in with the judge. Then contact Harmony and see where they're at. As soon as I'm done, and there's approval, we need to be ready to move."

"Got it," Kaylee replied. "Now go get this done so my marrow can stop squiggling."

Mina entered the room. The reception area was empty. Usually, an air breather or a bot would be stationed behind the welcome desk. No one was here. Two doors were set on either side of the space. One had a blinking red light above it, one had a green.

Mina moved toward the green light.

Behind her, a door slicked open. "In here, Agent Kane," a familiar voice beckoned.

Mina turned, smiling. "Judge Mackey. It's nice to see you again."

Judge Rudolph Mackey was nearly as old as Norman Webb and had held the position of Superior High Court judge for the last forty years. He had an impeccable record and was known to be exceedingly fair. Mina was pleased McAllister had chosen him to oversee this case and that he'd been available. His ruling on this would not come without consequences, which he would be aware of, and he had accepted anyway.

On the rare occasions that Mina had had to testify about one of her cases or provide evidence for a warrant, more than half of them had been with Judge Mackey.

"Sit, sit." He gestured toward one of the big chairs in front of his large, but not overly imposing, granite desk. He wore his official robes in black with silver accents. This testimony was being recorded, the vid feed highly encrypted.

Mina sat. "Thank you for hearing the evidence in this case."

"Comes with the job," he answered genially, even though Mina could sense his tension. "A warrant to take something out of the sky is a new one, even for me, and I've been doing this for a long time. I know it's been legally approved a few times, but this is a tricky space for us to occupy. I've heard the testimony firsthand from ex-marshal Webb against one Wilbert Waterbury and will take that into consideration. But what will put me over the edge in my decision to authorize bringing a satellite down is your testimony on the aftermath of the torture you witnessed and the involvement of, and subsequent threat to, the colonel-in-arms of the French Protectorate, Vincent Kramer." He indicated the wall behind him. "As you know, you are being recorded. Everything you say must be the whole truth to the best of your knowledge. If it's discovered that anything you say in this room was a deliberate lie, it will be held against you in a court of law. Highly sensitive details pertaining to your agency division will be struck from the official report, as deemed by law. Some things are mandated to stay secret. But in order to protect the integrity of this proceeding, and the fact that secret dealings are what could very well mandate this warrant, they must be recorded. To protect us both. I don't need to swear you in, as you are already a sworn agent of the federal government, but if you would like, I can, just as a reminder."

"That won't be necessary," Mina said. "I understand how this works, and I will be truthful and straightforward to the best of my ability."

"Okay, let's begin. You're a federal agent within the Corruption Investigation Unit," Mackey said. "Is this correct?"

"Yes," Mina confirmed.

It wasn't something usually acknowledged out loud, but as Judge Mackey had just explained, this was an exception. Mina wasn't sure if all the magistrates knew about their department, but many of them did.

"The CIU is overseen by a select committee and is legally allowed to operate with exemptions and modifications to current laws pertaining to privacy, acquiring data, secrecy, more so than other departments. Meaning your division is granted a more liberal interpretation of the law, especially when you're involved in a case pertaining to high crime in federally held positions. Are you aware of this fact?"

"I am aware, yes."

Judge Mackey inclined his head. "Because of this, CIU Director Duncan McAllister is entitled to ask for permissions that other directors can't, such as bringing a private satellite down to Earth to be investigated."

Mina hadn't factored that in, but now that the judge had mentioned it, it made sense. It also indicated why McAllister hadn't balked at their request. He knew his parameters better than she did. And it was true—the CIU had been created as a secret agency to fight crime particularly, but not exclusively, inside the government. It came with special legal benefits, such as their get-out-of-a-box-free card, being able to obtain a warrant for a quiet B&E like on the Tedesco case, and infiltrating the workforce with their identities masked—and apparently bringing satellites back to Earth.

"Even though this is within Duncan McAllister's rights to request and comes with full upper committee approval," Judge Mackey continued, "it behooves this court to consider all of the evidence before we make a decision to take what is likely a multimillion-dollar piece of equipment out of the sky. You are here to provide some of that documented evidence, Agent Kane. So let's get to it." He picked up a pen and a piece of paper, rather than reaching for a board. "Ex-marshal Norman Webb cited you as the agent who figured out where he'd been taken after he was kidnapped by one Wilbert Waterbury. Is this correct?"

"Yes."

"How did you figure this out? Be as concise as you can."

"I had just finished a case in which Norman Webb was hired to provide bodyguard duties. I discovered that Webb had confided to someone close to that case that if he went missing, it would likely involve a perpetrator connected to him who had just been released from a box. I narrowed that down to two likely candidates and zeroed in on Waterbury because he and Norm have a shared past."

Judge Mackey nodded. "I heard all about that, and it's been documented. According to Norman Webb, you found him a little less than twelve hours after he'd been taken, and thusly tortured, by Waterbury. When you entered

Waterbury's residence, you did not have a warrant—"

"I did not enter Waterbury's residence. A private citizen did," Mina corrected.

"Ah, yes, this is where the colonel-in-arms of the French Protectorate comes in. Not exactly a private citizen to many—or most—but technically he is while on American soil." At that moment, a green light inset into his desk began to blink. Judge Mackey reached out and pressed a button connected to a small box on his desk. "Perfect timing. Please send in the witness," he intoned to someone on the other end.

The door behind Mina opened a few moments later, and Vince walked in.

Mina had trouble masking her surprise.

Judge Mackey noted it. "I apologize for not telling you sooner that the colonel would be joining us, Agent Kane," the judge said. "But everything we're doing today requires a level of security that rivals any other case I've participated in. Director McAllister has been in contact with the Protectorate over the last few hours and was able to arrange a cloaked transpo for the colonel. It was necessary to have him here to complete this warrant request." The judge turned to Vince, greeting him. "Welcome, Colonel Kramer. It's an honor to meet you. I'm happy that you could come in on such short notice to make a formal deposition."

"Of course," Vince replied easily as he took the chair opposite Mina, flashing her a warm mile. Mina was relieved to see him. He looked tired, but otherwise in good shape. "I came as quickly as I could. I landed on the roof not two minutes ago. I'm here to answer any questions pertaining to the Waterbury case."

"Good, good. It's not every day that an esteemed member of the French Protectorate helps out in a federal investigation." Judge Mackey glanced down at something in his hand. "Escorting ex-marshal Norman Webb out of the residence of Wilbert Waterbury was, in fact, the third time you've been involved in one of Agent Kane's cases recently. Is that correct?" The judge glanced between the two of them, trying to puzzle out their connection. Mina was certain that McAllister had given the magistrate only a brief explanation about their relationship.

"Yes, that's true," Vince replied. "Agent Kane and I are childhood friends. We both ended up in similar jobs, but in different countries. I became involved in the Veritus case, our first time working together, without the knowledge that Agent Kane was leading the investigation here. We ended up on the same ship together and collaborated to bring down Veritus. The CIU's involvement was kept quiet for obvious reasons, which is a shame, because Agent Kane's work on that was brilliant. Since I've been spending more time in America, she has been kind enough to keep me busy, with the blessing of her director, of course."

Mina added, "Colonel Kramer has been a valued asset to us. We are thankful for his talent and his help."

Judge Mackey scrawled something with his pen. He

glanced up. "I'm going to swear you in, Colonel Kramer. You will receive diplomatic immunity if anything about this case ever goes to court, but I'm going to make sure we follow the letter of the law. There is a high likelihood, because of who we're dealing with, that this will be involved in some kind of litigation. Do you acquiesce to that?"

"Of course," Vince answered.

Once Judge Mackey finished swearing Vince in, he began, "Let's get back to where I was with Agent Kane before your arrival to testify about entering Wilbert Waterbury's residence. She clarified that she did not enter the premises, you did. You were alerted by Agent Kane that Norman Webb was missing, and she led you to—"

"I'm sorry to interject, but for the record," Vince said, "Agent Kane did alert me to the fact Norman Webb was missing, but she was not acting as lead. I was in charge of the investigation, as has been fully reported by Director McAllister."

"The correction is noted. From intelligence gathered by Agents Kane, Poston, Adams, and civilian Harmony Biggins, you deduced that Norman Webb was being tortured inside the residence and decided to enter the residence on your own?"

It was a slippery slope, but McAllister had made this account the official one when he'd asked Vince to take lead.

"That is correct," Vince asserted. "Time was of the utmost importance, as I feared Norman Webb was in danger of losing his life. The decision was made quickly. I entered the premises as a concerned citizen worried about a friend."

Judge Mackey nodded. "Protocol for law enforcement would have been to obtain a warrant, which may have been difficult, as there was no clear evidence, no blood trail, no vid or message from the ex-marshal himself, nothing that would indicate that he was inside. But because you are not law enforcement and are merely a citizen, breaking into the residence on a hunch is not considered a crime, especially when your hunch proved to be true. In what shape did you find ex-marshal Webb?"

"He was nearly dead, barely breathing, with multiple wounds and fractures, blood leaking from his side," Vince said. "In my estimation, he was near death."

"All this has been documented by the ex-marshal himself," Judge Mackey said. He turned to Mina. "Can you corroborate the extent of the injuries that ex-marshal Webb sustained inside that residence?"

"Yes. I accompanied him on the drone to the medi-unit at Government Four. The documentation of all his injuries is included in the report, but he had multiple fractures—both legs and an elbow—a puncture wound in his side, and multiple abrasions to his head, neck, legs, and torso."

"While ex-marshal Webb was in the drone, did he tell you how he incurred these injuries?"

"He did. He said he was tortured by Wilbert Waterbury inside that residence."

"Did he explain to you how he came to be there?"

"Yes," Mina replied. "Waterbury approached Norman Webb outside the residence of Harold Hampburg. He then threatened to kill Harold if Norm did not go with him."

Judge Mackey nodded again. "All the details about that encounter have been recorded. According to what has already been told to this court, the cams in Waterbury's home, which are linked to the satellite in question, are believed to hold the only evidence of Waterbury perpetrating this crime, other than the ex-marshal's testimony and you both witnessing his injuries after the deed. Is this true?"

Both Vince and Mina nodded.

Vince answered, "That's correct."

"Yes," Mina said.

"Your knowledge of where the cam data is stored and where Waterbury's internal cams are connected comes from the hacking expertise of Agent Adams and Harmony Biggins, an agent apprentice. They have irrefutably traced the signal from the cams directly inside the residence to the satellite called Currency Reigns." He indicated that either of them could answer.

"That's correct," Mina said. "This signal is verified, and documentation can be produced as evidence."

"I have received that documentation," Judge Mackey confirmed. They waited. He folded his hands in front of him, resting them on his desk. "I feel that procuring the vid evidence is necessary to charge, and subsequently convict,

Wilbert Waterbury for the violent, premeditated crime he committed against ex-marshal Webb. Without it, I believe the Syndicate lawyers may be able to wriggle Waterbury out of this and name someone else as the perpetrator of this crime. Someone who very likely resembles Wilbert Waterbury. Even though we have sworn testimony given to us by Norman Webb himself and eyewitness accounts by Colonel Kramer, CIU Agent Mina Kane, and multiple other federal agents, I believe the vid is the only irrefutable documentation we can obtain. Another reason to approve a warrant to bring a private satellite down is that Colonel Kramer's DNA has been taken from the crime scene and will be identified by a large, very powerful crime family, putting his life at risk. He will be viewed as someone with firsthand knowledge that an individual linked to the Syndicate has committed a very serious crime. Given how the mob has responded to similar events over the years, we have a framework for how they could go about trying to efficiently silence Colonel Kramer. Protecting the colonel-in-arms of the French Protectorate comes under the Allies Act of 2063, which states that if we have knowledge that a visiting official, a guest in our country, could become the victim of a crime, it is our job to intervene. Those two together provide an ironclad defense in your favor for this warrant. Thereby, you may legally proceed in bringing down the satellite Currency Reigns and begin the investigation of the data core located within the stable heart. Subsequently, anything that is found to be incriminating in that core will be held as evidence, and cases will be opened to appropriately deal with those findings."

Pure joy coupled with relief ran through Mina's body.

She scooted forward in her seat. "Thank you. It's my request of the court that once we locate the vid evidence of Norman Webb's torture, Waterbury be brought in with no time to spare and given Babble to uncover evidence of his other violent crimes, including murder. His father has been missing for more than ten years. Waterbury's confessions, under the influence of Babble, of crimes committed on behalf of the Syndicate will be imperative in securing other charges, mainly against those who gave him those orders, and putting an end to some of the major activities perpetrated by this massive crime organization."

"The use of Babble has been formally requested by the CIU director," Judge Mackey said. "I will consider that request but will make a ruling based on the evidence procured from the satellite." He gave Mina a direct gaze. "It will be your job, Agent Kane, to uncover that evidence quickly and efficiently and deliver it to this court without delay. The timing of all of this is very fragile, as you are well aware. I will hold hours here today"—he checked his cuff—"until seven p.m. That gives you just under three hours. After the vid is viewed by the CIU director and is on its way to me, I will issue a warrant to pick up Waterbury, and based on sufficient findings on that vid, I will then rule if he will receive Babble. I shouldn't have to stress how cautionary this case will be. The Syndicate will not react well. We are tasked with defending the law and preventing bad things from happening to innocent people, and sometimes that job comes with a price. Let's hope this one won't be too steep. Good luck to you both. You are excused."

Chapter 16

Mina turned toward the outer door that led to the hallway where Kaylee and Norm waited, but Vince grabbed her hand and led her through the door with the green light instead.

Once inside, he made his way to a tube and placed his thumb on a smudger. "We're cleared to leave through the judge's private tube. I need to keep a low profile, and walking through the crowded hallways is not the way to do that. This tube will take us almost to the roof. We just have to transfer once at a secured floor."

She was familiar with how the private tubes worked. "Just a second. I have to contact Kaylee and Norm, then McAllister." She tapped her cuff. When Kaylee answered, she said, "We have approval. Meet us on the roof."

"Fantastic!" Kaylee hooted. "Wait, what do you mean by 'us'?"

"A surprise witness came to testify. You'll find out soon

enough."

"Gotcha. We'll be there in two."

Before Mina could summon her director, he called.

"I've just received the warrant for the satellite. Good work, Agent Kane," McAllister told her. "I've been in touch with Agent Adams and Harmony Biggins. They are still at the Meridian. Rendezvous with them and keep me informed about the progress and the timing. I'm coordinating other teams to be deployed if necessary."

"Colonel Kramer is with me," Mina informed her boss. "He arrived minutes ago and provided testimony for the warrant."

"I am aware. He has full privilege on this case, but you are running lead, Agent Kane. Let's make this happen. Report back to me once the mission is in motion."

"Will do." Her director popped off.

Vince motioned for her to step inside the tube he held open with his hand.

She boarded, not sure if she should hug him or how she should greet him. Not wanting to be caught on a government cam, she settled on a smile, feeling shy. No surprises there. "I'm glad you're back."

"It's good to be here." He shot her a wry grin. "It took some persuading, but your director might be the smartest man I've ever met. He not only convinced Ambrose that I had to come back immediately to provide testimony, but that the Protectorate would receive an official commendation by the US government for my ongoing work here. Ambrose couldn't pass up the prestige. McAllister also assured him that the cases I'm working on here are legitimate, sanctioned by him, and that you are one of his agents." Vince shook his head. "The entire focus on me changed immediately. It was like a switch was flipped. I wasn't privy to the actual conversation, so I don't know what he said, but that man is beyond intelligent. He's wily."

Mina felt overwhelmed with relief that Vince was safe and standing in front of her. She wove her hands together so she wouldn't reach out. "'Smartest man' is an apt description. Duncan McAllister is a legend. How long are you here for?"

"Hard to say. Things are easier now, but still complicated."

She wasn't expecting him to reveal anything specific in the tube, or anywhere where they could be recorded or someone could overhear. She would have to wait until they were alone for the in-depth story.

"Are you back at The Bella?"

He shook his head. "No. Where I'm staying is up in the strato at the moment. I'm deciding everything as I go. But one thing is for certain, I refused to be watched over any longer. When I left, I informed Ambrose that we were doing this my way. None of my actions have been against the Protectorate or the French, so there is no reason for me to be monitored. He agreed reluctantly. I'm also changing up my routine, given that a crime organization has my DNA. I'm going to have to tread carefully." She was glad McAllister had filled Vince in on the Syndicate having his DNA.

"We'll figure it out," Mina assured him. "Right now, we have a big mission to coordinate and complete, and once that's over, we can discuss the rest." The tube door opened, and they exited. They were on a floor meant for tube shifting. "Follow me."

She wove her way toward the main tube system, DNA-swiped into a tube, and they were on the roof in the next three seconds.

Kaylee and Norm stood by a craft that was open and waiting. Kaylee gestured for them to hurry. "Not exactly surprised to see you here, Kramer. Welcome. While you two were deposing, I've been arguing with this guy." She indicated Norm with a thumb jab. "He's being stubborn, as usual. If we're heading back to the Meridian, the scene of the crime, that's not exactly a great place for Norm to be seen if the goal is to keep him alive."

"They've already been in and out of the Meridian twice," Norm argued. "They're not coming back. That unit will remain empty for months. Waterbury won't be allowed to go back, because they will assume it's being monitored, which it is. It's location non grata for the mob now, basically abandoned. I'd probably be safer there than anywhere else."

"We don't know that for sure," Mina said. "They could send people to check the Meridian feeds or send another crew back for another DNA swab. They could also be keeping eyes on it from afar. Get in the craft, and I'll contact my partner. We may not go to the Meridian if it's not the best place for the hackers to get the job done."

The four of them boarded.

"Destination the Meridian. A roof landing has been approved. Do you wish to make any changes?" the sim asked.

"Yes, hold takeoff until I confirm," Mina said as she tapped her cuff, speaking as soon as she got the signal rather than waiting for a greeting. "Lee, I need an update. We're a go on the mission. Where's the best place for you and Harmony to figure this out? Where you're at or someplace else?"

Mina heard a muffled discussion.

"Harmony's residence would be best," Lee said. "It has the tech we need. It's taking time to talk back and forth between her comps. It's minimal, but it all adds up, especially when we need to be so precise."

"Sounds good. We'll meet you there. Make sure you grab all our stuff," Mina said. "Summon a craft to the roof. We have preapproval for rooftop landings. Make sure the interior cams are looped and that you keep your heads down. We'll see you at Harmony's."

Harmony's voice came over Lee's cuff. "If I hear a single snarky comment about my less-than-adequate unit, I'm moving in with one of you. So make sure you keep your mouths firmly shut."

Kaylee chuckled. "It can't be that bad." She hadn't been

with Mina and the others when they'd gone there the first time.

"It's...interesting," Mina replied, recalling Harmony's teensy residence. "It's in need of a few updates."

"I can still hear you," Harmony called. "It's a stinky rathole. But my tech is A-grade. Signing off. Karmaseeker and I are on our way."

Mina issued new directions to the sim, reinserting her finger into the helix to confirm. Then she sent a quick message to McAllister about the location change. He would get back to her if it was an issue. Mina was happy to switch out of the Meridian. It gave them less to worry about.

Since Harmony wasn't a full agent yet, it was unlikely that the Syndicate hackers could find anything on her. That, and she probably had titanium-coded blocks on her information. Her place was as safe as any, even for Norm.

"I can't believe Operation Drop Zone is a go," Kaylee murmured as the drone took to the air. "It's going to be pretty incredible being part of a mission this big. I conferred with McAllister while you were in with the judge. He's going to assemble a small team of mili to crack that thing open once it hits. They will remain in the dark, depending on your decision. Once we know the location, and McAllister gets the crew together, I'll brief him."

"Military is the right choice," Mina said. "I'll secure the rocket shuttle as soon as we arrive at Harmony's. It'll be ready and waiting. I want us on that thing the moment Harmony and Lee send the satellite tumbling or, if possible, before. I hope the drop zone will be somewhere near us and not halfway around the world. The shuttle can break the sound barrier, but even going that many kilometers an hour, it's going to be tricky to get there as fast as we need. The Syndicate has people stationed absolutely everywhere. I haven't ruled out contacting local authorities to pick it up for us, but we have to have the specifics first and then formulate the best plan."

"How can I help?" Vince asked. "I've been briefed on a few key points by your director, but not much else."

"Norm needs the details, too," Mina said. "I'll run it down quickly for you both. Basically, our extremely talented hackers are going to send the satellite owned by Travis Blade, named Currency Reigns, zooming backward to burn off the fuel, then enact a full system failure. I don't have a drop rate yet, but I believe it will take between ten and twenty minutes to fall the full two thousand kilometers. The moment the satellite begins to thrust backward out of its orbit, and the system subsequently fails, the Syndicate will receive an alert. Since Harmony and Lee are tracking the trajectory ahead of time and can decide the exact moment to disable it, we will know the drop location within a few square meters only minutes before the Syndicate does. Those minutes will determine our ability to get our hands on the stable heart or not. The stable heart is where all the sensitive data is stored and is built to withstand the heat of reentry. The Syndicate will be extremely motivated to retrieve it, as they don't want whatever data is stored inside to be exposed. Once we get our hands on it, we utilize the military to crack it open, analyze the data, then we bring it to Judge Mackey. Waterbury will then be picked up and given Babble, and the Syndicate crumbles."

"One more thing," Kaylee added. "We need cooperation from the media. The breaking story has to be as chaotic as possible right out of the chute. Coverage of the satellite tumbling from the sky, investigating where it came from and whose it is, conflicting reports about who has it in their possession. This all has to come out immediately. Once it's widely reported that the satellite is owned by Travis Blade and that the authorities are investigating, the goss will start to rage because, as you know, all the Syndicate bosses are infamous media stars. Then, not long after, it will be reported that a Syndicate minion has been picked up and given a dose of Babble. All of this will be fed to the media by a reliable source. The story then blows to geyser proportions. If the coverage is done right, it should send all the higher-ups in the Syndicate scrambling. They'll have no time to plan retribution or to even find out who was behind this operation. In order to do that, we have to have a formidable person people trust front and center." She flashed Vince a big smile. "That's where you come in. You're someone who can get people to do things. If you call the media up to inform them of a big, breaking story, they will totally show. If they're getting the scoop from you, they will take it at face value. Because your face has value." She extended her hands out to either side. "All of our problems are solved. Ta-da."

Mina began to object. She wasn't about to let Vince be the face, but he responded before she could say anything. "How about Melissa Socorro? She's a pretty big name. If the story came from her, people would listen."

Kaylee's tongue looked in jeopardy of tumbling out. "Yeah. She would be…ideal. You two, um, know each other?"

"We've met. Once." Vince chuckled at Kaylee's reaction. "It was at Petra's vid premiere. Melissa offered me her call address. Media airmelds work differently than civilian ones. They have broader access. Before I could say yes or no to Melissa, she airmelded her address to my cuff." He tapped his wrist. "Here it is. I have protocols and blocks in place, and my cuff won't accept airmelds from most people if I don't personally approve. But media is classified differently. It's entered into a secure folder." He met Mina's gaze. "We'll have to go over exactly what I'm going to say to her and when. I have no doubt that if we promise her a scoop, she'll jump on it."

"I'm sure she will, especially if it comes directly from you," Mina agreed. "But having it leaked down the jet stream that Melissa received the information from you is not what we're looking for. The possibility of a leak on that end would be huge. You giving them a scoop is also a scoop." Mina could hear the media reports already. International heartthrob and military leader Vincent Kramer secretly informed Melissa Socorro that Travis Blade's satellite crashed to Earth before it exited the strato. How in the world did a colonel from another country know this?

"The Syndicate already has my DNA," Vince pointed out. "I'm in this. It's better me than any of you. If we're going to leave a trail, it should be mine."

Norm snorted. "Not a chance. This is all my fault. The trail is mine. I'm already in their laser scopes. No way to get out of 'em. Even though you rescued me, I'm the key witness. I'm the trouble. I'm the walking, breathing testimony. If it goes to court, I'm the one they need to get rid of. Right now, the Syndicate doesn't know if I'm alive or dead. Once I announce that I survived and the guy who got Babble is the one who tortured me, nothing you say or recall will matter." He wagged his finger at Vince. "My firsthand account is the only ticket in town, and it will keep the focus on me, the way it should be. You fade into the background as some guy who heard my cries for help." Norm continued wagging his finger as Vince started to form a rebuttal. "You'll be surprised to learn that Melissa Socorro also knows who I am. I've given her a couple of juicy tidbits over the years. She'll perk right up when I get a hold of her. She'll know it's something to do with law enforcement and criminal activity, which she loves. It riles her fan base straight through the galaxy. When she sees that thing streaking through the atmosphere, knowing I know all about it, we're all set. I'll even promise her an exclusive about my torture."

Kaylee glanced between Norm and Vince. The colonel-in-arms sat back in his seat, accepting defeat. Then she shrugged. "Honestly, I don't care who gets a hold of her, we just need to make it happen." She directed her comments to Norm. "Contact her immediately when we get back to Harmony's. We need her salivating and ready to pounce."

Norm nodded once. "On it."

The sim intoned, "Public landing in thirty seconds."

Mina glanced at Vince. "This landing pad is only about a block away from Harmony's. I don't think you'll be too noticeable, but just in case, you should probably keep your head down."

He grinned. "That's my go-to these days."

Chapter 16

"OPERATION DROP THIS Sucker is a go in less than forty-five minutes," Harmony hooted from her desk. "Currency Reigns reaches our shores in thirty-three minutes. Drop time is eleven-point-six minutes, so that's actually forty-four-point-six minutes. But that's not even accurate, because it took me twelve seconds to say all that. But we're on the clock here. That's what's important. These guys aren't going to know what hit 'em. One second, everything's printed cake. The next, their satellite is thrusting backward, hemorrhaging fuel, then dirty secrets are crashing through the atmosphere like excrement rain." She rubbed her hands together. Harmony was a hacking ninja who enjoyed the hunt as well as the conquest. She was going to become a brilliant agent.

They'd been assembled in her compact residence for a little less than an hour. Things were moving quickly and efficiently. Mina was pleased. At this rate, they'd be able to give Judge Mackey the evidence with time to spare.

There had been some worry early on that the only option would be an ocean landing, which would have made retrieving the stable heart too complicated. But careful calculations on Harmony's and Lee's parts had the stable heart on track to land on a small island off of the coast of Florida.

Their calculations had to be exact, or there would be issues.

If not the island, they'd have to wait several more hours and retrieve it in the Republic of South America. Or wait a full twenty-four hours for the satellite to circle back around the globe.

They'd all agreed the island was their best shot, even though there was still risk involved. Not only from the chances that the stable heart could still end up in the ocean, but also because the tiny island might not give them enough cover when the Syndicate arrived. They'd have to get in and out very quickly.

Which was why they'd agreed to fly down to be near the island before Harmony and Lee set the full plan into motion.

"Excellent," Mina said. "The rocket shuttle is ready to go. It's just a short ride away, fueled, and ready to launch." Rocket shuttles were leagues faster than the supersonic transport of the past. They used methane, culled from the carbon dioxide in the air, and were very efficient. They traveled at almost ten thousand kilometers per hour, and the g's were pretty intense, but fun. The ride would be so short that as soon as they reached altitude, they would start decelerating for the landing. But it was the fastest way to get where they needed to go.

Kaylee paced the middle of the living area, arms crossed. "McAllister has everything arranged. The mili base outside of Miami is expecting us. Their team will accompany us to the island after go time. They'll provide muscle, tech, and transport back to the base. That's where we'll crack the heart open and get the data inside. It actually works out perfectly, because that particular base operates cloaked at all times. They have what's called a dome perimeter cloak, meaning nobody can see in, and everything's highly encrypted. We have permission to use one of their op rooms to do all the technical stuff."

"We're bringing our comps, which McAllister has already preapproved," Lee confirmed. "Cloaking is a definite asset, but we need to use our own software for this. They don't like foreign comps on the premises, because signals in and out are difficult to manage, but they've approved it. I already checked, and all their hookups are compatible. Not every base has the newest upgrades, but this one does." He smiled, looking relieved and happy. "We are ready to go."

"It's actually stellar how this all worked out," Harmony added. "Trying to coordinate this with the Republic of South America would've been hard, if not impossible. Their government is so conservative, they would've had us signing reveal docs and declaring a bunch of stuff. There would've been no way to keep this under the radar. They also don't have the compatible components we need. This is the best option by far. It's a tiny patch of sand, but I know we can hit it."

Mina nodded. "Let's call Norm back and get moving." She checked her cuff. "We need to be in the air in seven minutes."

Norm had taken a short trip to the basement, where Strum Littlefield, Harmony's father and a renowned hacker, was living. Strum was helping Norm contact Melissa on an untraceable channel. They didn't want Melissa to have any real information until right after the satellite dropped. It had been decided that Strum would be the one communicating with her while they were in Florida. He had volunteered his time and considerable resources, shrugging off any issues involving blowback from the Syndicate, citing that if his daughter was involved, he would accept the risk. That was after he laughed off any possibility that Syndicate hackers could trace where the media summons had originated from.

It seemed they'd landed at the right place.

Mina didn't have to call Norm back. A short knock sounded on the new door the government had provided Harmony—made of honeycombed graphene—after Mina had broken the previous door, before it swung open. They hadn't engaged all the new security features that came standard on it, as Harmony had set up an elaborate alarm system throughout the building. If anyone unauthorized entered, they'd know immediately.

"It's all set," Norm said. "Melissa's interested in the scoop and will be waiting with a crew when Strum contacts her." The ex-marshal chuckled. "She's no pushover. She laid it out for us and told us what she expected. We were vague on details, like we agreed, but we gave her enough so she understood this would be a major break for her. I had to swear on the honor of my deceased mother I wasn't lying. It shouldn't have meant that much, but the way she put it had me thinking about my mother. I'm sure if this doesn't live up to Melissa's expectations, I'll hear about it." He nodded at Vince. "But we did this the right way. If things leak, which Melissa assured me they won't—and, with Strum's help, hopefully that will hold true—this all came from me. Which, I assume, the Syndicate will respect as retribution. They can't expect me to keep quiet and sit on my hands after what I endured at the hands of—"

An alert sounded from Vince's cuff.

It was a short staccato, accompanied by a holo star that flashed once, similar to what the CIU agents used.

Vince met Mina's inquiring gaze. "This only activates if someone unauthorized tries to get inside my personal areas. This alert is coming from my residence in France." He strode toward Harmony's waste room, which was the only place inside her apartment with a door. "Excuse me while I deal with this and see what's going on. I'll only be a minute, then we can leave."

After he left, Kaylee announced, "Everyone in this

room knows that the Syndicate just tried to get to Vince through his residence. It's nighttime in France. They think he's at home. And you know that the colonel-in-arms of the French Protectorate's got an airtight residence. Who would even try that? It's almost for sure that they'd get caught. Which means the Syndicate is running scared and moving too quickly. They're not using their brains. They don't know if Norm's dead, so they're trying to get to Vince. If he's the only witness they know about, and if he disappears, the case is over. Vince was probably seen in France a few hours ago. McAllister got him out quietly. That works in our favor. But now, more than ever, we have to get this stable heart to the ground. We need to get to that base now."

Mina nodded, tapping her cuff.

"Report, Agent Kane," McAllister said.

"The Syndicate just attempted a break into Colonel Kramer's France residence two minutes ago. We're all clear here, media is set, and we're ready to shuttle out. Once we arrive in Florida, which should take no more than ten minutes, Agent Adams is approximating that full timing from hacking in to satellite drop is approximately twenty minutes. Six minutes to hack, three minutes to burn fuel and deorbit the satellite, eleven-point-six to drop. Harmony and Agent Adams need to be in place in twenty, or we miss the trajectory they have planned."

"Good work," McAllister confirmed. "I've arranged for transport to the rocket shuttle. It will land on Ms. Biggins' roof in two. The space up there is extremely small, so I'm sending a stealth drone. It will be a little crowded inside, but it's the only thing that fits. It will get you to the shuttle faster. Report once the hack has started. I plan to come down to see it through. If you have any issues at the base, let me know. Your contact there will be Sergeant Collins. He's leading the small team that will be accompanying you. They are unaware of what they are retrieving. It will be up to you to share details or not. They are highly trained combat soldiers who regularly participate in sensitive missions, which is why they were chosen. Sergeant Collins, who I spoke with personally, has no issues with not being fully informed. He will follow your orders as lead on this case."

"Understood," Mina said as Vince emerged from the waste room, giving her a short nod. "We're heading up to the roof now."

"Good luck," McAllister said. "I have faith that this mission will go off flawlessly, which will kick off a possible takedown of one of the most dangerous crime organizations in the world." He popped off.

Harmony and Lee jumped up from the desk, grabbing their compucases. Other necessary items had already been packed, and everyone grabbed something.

"We're heading to the roof," Mina said for Vince's benefit, since everyone else had heard what McAllister had said. "A stealth is on its way." This type of craft was shaped to be efficiently aerodynamic and go much faster than a regular transport drone. It had propellers, as well as cold thrusters. "They typically only carry four, so two people will have to double up."

"Karmaseeker and I can share a seat," Harmony offered as they walked out of her unit. Lee nodded, blushing heavily. She turned to secure her door, then she led them down a very short hallway and into a stairwell. There were no tubes that Mina could see. This building hadn't been updated in at least fifty years.

Mina was about to offer to share a seat with Kaylee when Kaylee interjected, "You and Kramer can share the other seat, obvi. No reason to make the rest of us uncomfortable when you two clearly want to snuggle."

Mina opened her mouth to deny any snuggling claim.

"Oh, please," Kaylee said. "You can stop right there. Telling us you don't want to sit on that hunk's lap is like telling me you don't want to eat a delicious nonprinted meal or bubble for hours in your soaker. Don't even try." She pointed at Mina. "It's unbecoming of you and untruthful. Which compromises you because you're our truthful leader. We bow down to your truth-telling. So if you lie now, it will besmirch your perfect record."

"I'm not besmirching anything," Mina replied, trying to dig up some indignation, but failing. Sitting with Vince didn't sound too bad. If they'd been with other agents, Mina wouldn't make that choice, as being professional would outweigh any of her wants. But she was basically surrounded by family. "You're assuming that Colonel

Kramer wants to sit with me."

Vince tipped his head back as they climbed the stairs, and a throaty, extremely likable sound came out. "Don't pin this on me. I welcome your company, but it's your decision to make."

"Well," Harmony said as she pushed open the stairwell door that led them toward another door, "you're going to have to make it soon, because we're already here. Four stories up. That's it. I live in the shortest high-rise in the city. Not technically a high-rise. More like a squat-rise."

The stealth drone had already made its landing and was sitting precariously perched on wheels, its tail resting on the edge of the building. It didn't have a standard door. Instead, stairs had been extended from a small opening in the hull.

Harmony and Lee boarded first, Kaylee went next, then Norm. Mina swept her arm to indicate Vince should go next. Before he went up the stairs, he leaned into her, saying, "I'm looking forward to carrying your weight." He winked, chuckling as he ascended into the drone.

Mina shook her head as she boarded. "Everyone is here," she told the sim as she placed her finger in the helix slot.

"Your destination is Avery air base. Do you wish to make any changes?"

"No," Mina confirmed. The drone propellers began to shift, and Mina was forced to pick a seat.

Harmony and Lee were chatting in the first seat on the

right about the mission, their compucases tucked on their laps. They fit side by side in the seat meant for one, no problem. Mina was optimistic she could do the same.

Kaylee caught her gaze from her seat across the aisle from Lee and Harmony, her body sprawled, purposefully taking up the whole space. She threw an arm behind her. "Go find out what happened at Kramer's residence. We're going to be in this thing for less than two minutes. Don't be a baby."

"I'm not a baby," Mina grumbled as she walked past. "I'm an adult woman who doesn't like to be told what to do."

Vince, being the gentleman he was, had scooched all the way to the side and patted the space next to him. "There's no need to sit on my lap. Even though I wouldn't object."

Mina glanced at Norm, who sat in the seat beside him, but the ex-marshal had reclined back, crossing his arms over his chest, his eyes closed.

This must be a conspiracy. Agent matchmakers were not a thing. Or were they?

She took the space next to Vince right as the drone accelerated into the air.

"Travel time to Avery air base is forty-three seconds," the sim said.

"Tell me what happened at your residence," Mina said.

"Not much to tell," he replied, respectfully keeping his hands to himself. "A man was caught on vid trying to pry his way in. He got through the front door by claiming to be from a delivery agency, arriving in the appropriate drone, wearing the right uni. His DNA was a match to the delivery agency as well. I'm assuming it's a Syndicate-owned business in France, of which they have many. Basically, they sent a child in to do their dirty work. The young man is in custody. He had a sear laser in his pocket." Vince snorted to indicate that wouldn't have done much. "I have a few of my trusted captains looking into it right now. I informed them to tell the delivery tech I was inside my residence, and had he gotten inside, he would've found me there. Then to let him go. The tech will take that back to his boss, keeping the story that I'm still in France. I'm not expecting anything else to happen. The next time they strike, it will be when they physically identify my presence somewhere. And since they're looking in France, that won't be an issue for a while."

"Once Melissa Socorro goes public and announces that Norm is alive, the pressure should disappear entirely," Mina said. "That is, if they're thinking rationally. I would say you're going to have to lie low for at least a week until we see how this all plays out."

"I figured as much," Vince said. He reached out and took her hand.

The sim intoned, "Landing in thirty seconds."

Mina gave him a squeeze in response. "Don't worry"—the drone touched down—"we'll work something out."

"I'm counting on it."

"THESE GYRO SEATS are the bomb." Kaylee spun around in hers. Not only did it turn, it swiveled in every direction, like an egg on a spring. "It's been a while since I've flown in a rocket shuttle. I forgot how fun they are. This seat is my own little pod. Now you see me, now you don't." She enacted the face screen that slid over the top of the seat like a shield. Then she opened it. "Now you do."

Mina giggled. "You're such a clown."

"Everybody likes a clown. Wait, no, they don't. Clowns are spooky. Everyone loves a jester. That's a thing, right? I'm a jester. In a fun gyro chair. Doing fun gyro stuff."

"Everyone, please take your seats," the captain, an air breather, announced over the intercom. Even though the rocket shuttle was fully automated, it was mandatory to have a human pilot on board in case anything went wrong. "The seats will align momentarily and lock in the takeoff position. Make sure your feet and arms are clear and that nothing impedes its motion. Our sim will cover the rest. Arrival time will be a little less than ten minutes, as air currents are in our favor today. Thanks for flying with Speedy Shuttle. Have a nice day."

Mina glanced around to make sure everyone was secure. They were sitting two to a row, five rows total. The last two rows were empty. It was costing the government a fortune to pay for the entire flight, but it was necessary.

Mina and Kaylee sat in row one, Harmony and Lee in row two, Vince and Norm in row three. There was no need to sit together, and in fact, it would be impossible. Pulling g's was tough on the body. Everyone needed to be comfortably harnessed in.

A low rumble began. All the seats rotated a hundred and eighty degrees, even the ones with no passengers. When they were locked in position, a loud click sounded, indicating everyone was stabilized. The cushion behind Mina's head began to inflate, bracing the sides of her head. The armrests did the same, as well as the cushion under her.

"Please stay seated," a female sim intoned. "Your safety harness will remain secure throughout the duration of the flight. Please do not try to remove it. If your time on board is longer than thirty minutes, your seat will unlock, but you must remain in your seat at all times. Once descent is enacted, your seats will automatically shift to the correct position and relock. If you experience any displeasure or feel in need of medical assistance, please touch the button on the inside of your seat, or simply speak clearly. Your vitals will be taken, and if necessary, there is a medi-pod on board. Please enjoy your flight."

There was another loud rumble as the ignition engaged.

"This is so cool," Harmony said excitedly. "This is my first ride in a rocket shuttle. And it's not going to disappoint!"

"Mine, too," Lee added, with a lot less enthusiasm. "The statistics on rocket shuttle travel are relatively good. There've only been a handful of minor—"

"No need to cite bad statistics," Mina told him. "Everything's going to be fine. Relax and enjoy the ride."

In a single, powerful thrust, they shot up into the air.

The effect was instantaneous. They were all pushed back in their seats, but thanks to all the cushion, they remained comfortable.

There was no way to hold a conversation, so they just waited.

Five minutes in, the rocket began its descent, the gyro seats spinning a hundred and eighty degrees and locking into place once again.

Five minutes later, they were on the ground.

"Woof," Kaylee said, rubbing her jaw as the rocket settled and powered off, their harnesses popping open. "That was fun, but intense. I feel like elastomer snuck into all my joints, clogging them up." She plugged her nose and blew, puffing out her cheeks. "Ah, there's the pop I was looking for."

"That was incredible," Harmony gushed, her feet

drumming the floor. "I feel great! Can't wait to do it again."

Mina glanced at Lee, who sat diagonally from her.

Her partner looked a little green. "Don't worry," she consoled. "Once you get up and walk, it'll all shake out."

"I'm fine," he said. "Just a little…queasy." He closed his eyes, tipping his head back.

The captain came over the aural system. "Hope you enjoyed your flight. Remember to recommend us on all your boards. If you do, your next flight is half price."

Kaylee rolled her eyes as she stood. "Always an upsell. Can't say I blame them, though. Must be hard scraping up business. No one with common borrows to their name could afford to travel like this. That's what mag-levs are for. Clientele must be sparse."

The cabin door opened, and they disembarked.

A clean-cut man, who looked to be around forty, with zero facial hair and a short, efficient haircut, stood at attention outside the shuttle, hands clasped behind his back. He wore a green regulated uni, a hat with a short brim, and strike boots in gleaming black.

"You must be Sergeant Collins," Mina said, walking up to him. She didn't salute because she wasn't mili. She extended her hand instead, and they shook.

"Welcome to the base," he told her.

"Thank you. I'm Agent Kane, and this is my crew." She gestured to indicate who was who. "Agent Poston, Agent Adams, ex-marshal Webb, civilian Biggins, and—"

Sergeant Collins made a subtle half cough into his fist

as recognition crossed his features. Then the man brought his arm up in a perfect salute. "It's a pleasure to serve you, Colonel Kramer." He stressed the word colonel, even though Vince wasn't in the US military. Clearly, respect for the job crossed oceans. "I wasn't aware that you would be in attendance."

Vince saluted back. "This mission is highly classified. It will require full silence on your part. I was never here."

"Copy that. My men know how to do their jobs. Word won't break."

"Can you show us to the op room?" Mina asked. "We're on a tight schedule."

"Follow me," Sergeant Collins said as he led them to a short concrete building situated only a few meters from where they'd landed. Mina was relieved no one else was around. Even though Sergeant Collins' team would be sensitive to what was happening, and to Colonel Kramer's presence, she wasn't sure about everyone else who resided here. "Everything is secure inside. The whole base is cloaked. It's understood that you need to send a signal out. You do it here and nowhere else. A special line has been set up. No airmelds. Everything is done via cable."

"We've been briefed on all the rules, and we will follow them," Lee said. "We have all our necessary equipment with us. We won't require anything additional."

Harmony entered the room and whistled. "It's all screen in here. Whoa. Is that a Holo Max7000 cam?" She gestured at the ceiling where a gigantic multifaceted camera was mounted.

Sergeant Collins nodded.

"People projected through those are supposed to look lifelike," Harmony said. "Too bad we won't be needing it. I'd love to see that."

Lee had already connected his compucase, along with a couple of other things, to the cable connections provided. He checked his cuff. "Eight minutes till start."

Harmony pulled up a chair as Lee connected her case. Her fingers were typing the instant she sat down. "Plenty of time. There she is. Let's pop it on-screen. Oh, wait." She turned in her seat. "Is he staying or going?"

Sergeant Collins looked on, his face impassive.

It was Mina's call whether to include him or have him wait outside. She looked to Vince. She would let him decide. Vince was good at reading people, and with their shared military background and training, he could choose.

She indicated the decision was his with a subtle bob of her head.

"Sergeant Collins stays," Vince said. "It's my experience that having the officer in command understand the full operation makes that operation run smoother." He directed his comments to Sergeant Collins. "You will receive full intel, but your team is on a need-to-know basis. The less information spread around the better."

"Yes, sir."

"Okay, let's do this," Harmony said. A second later, live satellite feed popped up, surrounding them. This was more than an op room, it was a war room.

A bunker with extraordinary technology.

It was awe-inducing.

Like they were floating around up in space themselves.

"Just give me one second to home in on Currency Reigns," she said. "This live feed is so helpful. Without it, we wouldn't know exactly what was happening. I mean, we could still do it, we would just be doing it blind. I've done plenty of stuff that way, but this is much better for what we need to accomplish."

"Five minutes," Lee said. Harmony and Lee each had their own jobs to complete. Mina didn't know exactly what they entailed. She just knew it would take both of them to make this happen. And her partner was serious about it.

There was nothing left to do but watch.

Mina walked over to one of the numerous tables situated in a U shape around the room and pulled out a chair.

Everyone else did the same.

"Cut the ultras," Lee ordered. "I don't want to miss anything on-screen. If this satellite runs into another satellite or space junk while it's reversing, we will have an issue."

"Ultras off," Collins commanded.

Since there were no windows, the room went black except for the space show happening around them.

"Yowza," Kaylee muttered. "Can you imagine being up there? How many space stations do we have? Fifteen? And a dozen or so science stations? People stay up there for years. They can grow whole ecosystems up there." She breathed out. "It's so pretty. Earth looks like it's a blue beacon floating so peacefully. It's quiet. Kind of spooky."

"It's amazing to actually see how many satellites are up there," Vince said. "Logically, I understand the numbers, but seeing so many in all the different orbits really brings it home. It's incredible they don't crash into each other more often."

"Three minutes," Lee announced. "Trajectory is holding steady. Nothing's changed. We have a clear path backward with a rotation of two degrees. The thrusters have to engage as the right fin comes out. No margin for error."

"I know," Harmony murmured. "There won't be. I'm ready to hack inside the moment you say go."

No one said a word.

Mina glanced over at Sergeant Collins. He was completely absorbed in the scene unfolding in front of him, his face serene. Once he understood the full depth of this op, she didn't think he would have any issues with it. But it was hard to know. It's not every day the government crashed a satellite out of the sky. But for all Mina knew, the military did it often enough, and it wasn't covered by the media or anyone else.

"Ninety seconds," Lee said. "I'll count you down from ten. Once you're in, I'm a nanosecond behind you. You take the thrusters. I'll take the fin."

Harmony nodded. She wasn't going to waste any breath

at this point. Mina knew they'd been over and over this plan.

After what seemed like an eternity, with a slow-moving river of satellites flowing around them, Lee began to count.

"Ten…nine…eight…seven…six…five…four…three…two…go."

"In," Harmony said.

"In," Lee said less than a second later.

"Thrusters engaged," Harmony confirmed.

"Fin out and rotated," Lee said.

"Full throttle initiated," Harmony said. She glanced up for the first time.

Everyone in the room watched as Currency Reigns, situated in a nest of other satellites, began to move backward. Slowly at first, then more quickly.

"They picked up on the problem. They're trying to fix it," Lee said. "Blockers in place."

"Oh, no, you don't," Harmony muttered. "You're not going to get your hands on that." More muttering. Lots of finger tapping. "Karmaseeker, do you see this?"

"I'm on it," Lee confirmed. "They're patching it quicker than I can erase their code."

Mina heard slight panic in Lee's voice. She cheered him on quietly in her brain. She didn't want to interrupt.

"Do a full block erase," Harmony ordered.

"They'll be able to see—"

"No, they won't. I'm coming in after you, copying the code, adding in a teensy error. Do it. Now!"

Everyone held their breath.

The satellite continued to pick up speed, thrusting backward out of the frame.

"We just have to hold for two minutes and twenty-three seconds more," Harmony said. "After that, it's too late. The fuel's gone. They're absolutely producing excrement sandwiches at this point. They know this thing is coming down, and there's nothing they can do about it." Harmony craned her neck around to find Mina. "As soon as we confirm the trajectory, meaning once it starts falling, we need to be in the air, or they're going to beat us to it."

"Sergeant Collins, get your team ready. We're leaving in two. You've already been given the destination," Mina ordered.

The sergeant was up immediately, heading for the door. "The shuttle will be here in one minute. My crew will be ready and waiting."

"I have to hand it to them, they're coming in strong," Harmony said, eyes flicking from her compucase to the screen. "They've probably done drills. We should've factored that in. But their sim training isn't going to help them here, because the satellite didn't have a malfunction. It's being tampered with. As far as I can tell, they have no evidence we're inside."

"Do you see that?" Lee said. "They're trying to reroute the fuel into an extra tank."

"I see it," Harmony confirmed. "I just shut it down. I'm also messing with a bunch of different valves, opening and closing them. This has to look like a rupture."

"The satellite has reached peak speed," Lee said, glancing up.

Everyone in the room watched as new feed came on-screen. The satellite was zooming backward, narrowly missing things in its path. Mina shook her head. "It's amazing you found a clear path through all that."

"Point A to point B makes a straight line," Lee said. "We did it! It's deorbiting. The fuel is almost gone. It will fall immediately. This is going to work." Excitement replaced stress.

"One minute, three," Harmony said. "Come on! You can do it. Hey, stop that." Her fingers flew across the keyboard. "They're trying to enact a power blip. They think that will reset the system. Little do they know the system is about to fail in eighty-seven seconds."

"Fuel a little less than a fifth," Lee said. "It's burning quickly."

"We're right on target," Harmony said. "Fifty-two seconds."

Mina held her breath. She was certain everyone else in the room was doing the same.

"Now!" Lee shouted.

"Done," Harmony confirmed. "Bye-bye, satellite. The system has ruptured."

On-screen, Currency Reigns stopped moving abruptly.

Then it began to drop.

"Destination 476 will be reached in one minute," the sim intoned.

They were all on board a military combat supply shuttle. Along with Sergeant Collins, five other soldiers had joined them. By the looks of them, they were an elite team. None of them made eye contact. No one said a word. They wore specialized equipment, full headgear, face shields, and weapons. The cargo area was loaded with tools and equipment to get the stable heart off the beach so it could be transferred into the craft and back to the base.

"Don't land yet," Harmony said hurriedly from her position hunched over her compucase. "We should wait here until the heart reaches the beach. Just to be safe. I know we said we were going to land, but I changed my mind. Those hackers were on top of us when we were inside the system. I don't think they can change the trajectory, but we can't take that chance."

"Agreed," Lee said. "It just came through the atmosphere." He squinted down at his screen. "Its glides have been enacted. It's slowing. We're right on track. But just in case something throws it off course, we shouldn't be on the ground. Have the craft hover over the water two kilometers north of the island. If anything, it will veer south at its current trajectory."

Sergeant Collins looked to Mina for confirmation. She was the lead, so it was up to her.

"Feel free to take orders from either of them," Mina instructed. "They're the ones in charge until that thing hits the ground, and it's faster that way."

"Destination change, verification 013275," Sergeant Collins ordered as he stuck his finger in the helix. "Head two kilometers north of destination. Hover twenty meters above the ocean until I give new orders."

"Destination change confirmed," the sim replied. "Awaiting orders."

There was a slight tug as the drone repositioned itself, reversing backward at a quick clip. There was a lot of reversing going on today.

"From this angle, we should be able to see it land out the front window," Harmony said. "Or at least streak by."

"It will hit Earth in four minutes, thirty-eight seconds," Lee confirmed. "It's already slowing, coming in at a speed of seventy kilometers per hour, but will slow significantly once its sensors detect the ground within a thousand feet. It will land at about forty-three kilometers per hour. The impact will be fairly intense. It will make a significant hole and sink into the sand." He glanced up. "I hadn't really thought about that. Sand is much softer than soil."

"It won't be a problem," Sergeant Collins replied. "We have equipment that can latch on to it and fly it out if we need to. Even if it's buried, we can get to it. It will just take a little longer."

"We don't have longer," Harmony murmured, her gaze fixated on her screen. "By my estimation, other interested parties will land here six minutes, three seconds after it touches down. That means we have to have it out in three."

"Three is more than enough time. My team has been prepped for this mission. We're aware of the terrain," Sergeant Collins said, completely undaunted. "This is not the first time we've retrieved something like this." That was cryptic. "We have everything we need in the back. Whoever shows up, if we're lingering, will identify us as military and think twice. If anyone opens fire on us, they are fair game. Each one of us is equipped with a mini barrel laser, two heavy artillery hydro-bombs, and a few other classified pieces of tech that are capable of taking out a drone at a hundred meters. Not only that, this shuttle is equipped with integrated firing lasers that can be voice-activated through my cuff." He held up his wrist to display a very complicated military-grade cuff that was three times larger than anything civilians or federal agents wore. It looked complex.

"Okay, then," Harmony said.

Sergeant Collins allowed for a tiny grin. "We have your back. It's what we do. My team is elite force. We're used to doing things quickly. In and out is our specialty."

"Impact in sixty seconds," Lee said.

All eyes were positioned out the front window. The low hum of the shuttle was the only thing making any sound. The drone was a lot quieter than anything civilians used.

A minute later, a large black streak came shooting down in front of them.

"That's a go," Sergeant Collins ordered. "Set down ten meters from unidentified object. Scan from visual three seconds ago, avoid the water. Full speed."

The drone shot forward. Everyone was rocked back in their seats. It wasn't g-force, but it was close.

"Object identified as space debris from scan," the sim said. "Setting down in ten seconds."

Mina glanced out the window. Blue ocean was all she could see from her vantage point. "Myself, Agent Poston, Colonel Kramer, and ex-marshal Webb are going to exit the drone to make sure the debris is the stable heart, then we're back in. Harmony and Agent Adams, make sure you keep the Syndicate's people from erasing what's on that heart."

"We're on it," Harmony said. "They won't get in. It's already repowering and emitting a tiny signal. I'm locked on it. Our proximity helps in this case. The signal is so weak it's not projecting very far. That gives us a huge advantage."

"Don your headgear," Mina instructed her team,

strapping on the helmet Sergeant Collins had provided her with. It had a large reflective surface on the top. Any satellite imagery taken from above would show them as walking, flashing dots.

All of the soldiers wore similar helmets.

The drone set down, and all four doors opened automatically.

Everyone but Harmony and Lee streamed out, four of the soldiers circling back to the cargo space to shoulder bags of equipment.

They all jogged to the stable heart. It was so close it took less than five seconds.

"We did it!" Kaylee exclaimed. "I can't believe it, but we brought a satellite down to Earth. Well, technically not us, because we're not that talented. But as a team, we did it!"

Two of the soldiers immediately got down on their knees. The stable heart had made a small crater, but the top was exposed. One of them reached out with a gloved hand, hovering it a meter over the heart. "Temperature reading five hundred and fifty degrees Fahrenheit. Bring in the coolant."

Another soldier rushed in wearing a pack consisting of two cylinders connected to a hose and a nozzle he held with both hands. He sprayed the entire thing down. A hissing noise issued from it.

"It'll be touchable in seven seconds," Sergeant Collins said. "Probably wasn't hot enough to make glass, but there might be some under there. These things have a protective coating that burns up on reentry, cooling them down. It's helpful." He waved a couple of his men through. They carried what looked to be mini saucers, and another soldier had a remote control in his hands. "Wipe off the foam and connect the wings. We're on the clock. I want that thing inside the shuttle in the next thirty seconds. Then we're out of here in the next ten."

Mina made a motion circling her arm. "Let's get back in the shuttle. We could have company very soon. We need to be ready to fly."

Vince nodded as they all began to walk back. "They've got things well taken care of here."

"Yes, they do," Norm said. "This is a highly trained operation. It's a pleasure to watch."

It really was.

A trained team in action, working in unison, nobody speaking unless they absolutely had to. It was also clear they had gathered up one of these stable hearts before. Maybe they'd been involved in the past government missions Lee had cited, but maybe they had participated in different ones. They would never know. Sergeant Collins certainly wasn't going to tell them about it, and Mina certainly wasn't going to ask.

Once back in the drone, she checked in with Harmony and Lee. "Tell me you blocked access and that thing is going to be full of data when it gets on board."

"We're working on it," Lee said. "So far so good. We expected them to try to access it the moment it came back online and provided a signal. And they have. Harmony had already written some excellent code to block. It's going to appear as another system error."

"Yep," Harmony added. "It's keeping them from latching on to the signal. So far, it's working. But those hackers won't let up. There's a chance they can get around my block. So Karmaseeker's writing new code to trip them up, attributing it to the blips with the landing. Indicating some of the internal structure was damaged. As soon as we get the heart open, and the core data is outside of that three-meter-thick graphene firewall, we can transfer it onto our comps. Then we have copies that can't be destroyed."

Mina glanced anxiously out the door to where the soldiers were working on getting the stable heart out of the sand. They'd attached over a dozen wings to it, but so far it hadn't risen out of the hole. She checked her cuff. They were already a minute in. There was a chance Sergeant Collins would miss his prediction.

Vince settled a hand on Mina's wrist. "They'll get it in here on time. Sergeant Collins is probably right about the glass. There may have been some fusion in the sand below, making it sticky. But like he said, they're used to completing successful missions like this."

A shout sounded from outside. The stable heart was making its way up and out of the sand.

"Those have to be heavy-duty wings. My goodness," Kaylee said. "Those things look so tiny compared to that huge mass."

"We use those in France as well," Vince said. "They're made of a very strong synthetic mixed with the metal, and the adhesive melds right onto whatever metal it's working on and becomes part of the unit. Very efficient and very powerful."

"Here it comes," Norm said. "Right on schedule."

"Uh-oh," Harmony said. "We've got company. I set up a perimeter scan using the stable heart as the guide. Incoming in less than two minutes. Can't tell what it is, but it's moving fast."

Mina went to the door and shouted, "Company in two!"

Sergeant Collins held up his wrist. "I'm aware. It will be loaded in the next twenty seconds. We will be in the air in the next three. Still on schedule."

Several of the soldiers jogged back to the drone, clearing a space for the heart.

It was surreal to see an object that large floating through the air. The soldier who was manning the remote was talented. Everything went smoothly, and the stable heart was positioned onto a metal block that would keep it in place. After it was settled inside, several soldiers hopped into the cargo area to keep watch over it.

Sergeant Collins got back inside, issuing orders quickly. "Destination home base, full power, stealth mode, report any signal interruptions." The doors closed instantly, and the drone took off smoothly a second later.

They went vertically twenty meters, then shot forward faster than Mina had known was capable for any civilian drone.

"Destination confirmed," the sim said. "Signal pings reported. Access denied."

Before Sergeant Collins could report that whoever was on their way to get the stable heart had tried to ping the craft to figure out who they were, Harmony said, "That's a pretty good firewall you've got on this thing, Sergeant Collins. I'm impressed. You must have some good hackers on the payroll."

"Only the best," he replied confidently.

Harmony giggled. "When the best goes up against the best and rebuffs the best, only one will be left standing. And guess what? That's us."

Director McAllister was waiting on the tarmac when they landed. "Have you secured the stable heart?" he asked.

"We have," Mina replied as she moved forward to greet him.

"Excellent work."

"Thank you, sir. All the accolades go to Agent Adams and Ms. Biggins on this. Without them, none of this would've been achievable. Thanks to the efficient work by Sergeant Collins and his team, we got it out in record time and, I believe, stayed under the radar. The Syndicate came in close and was able to detect a military shuttle. They tried to take a closer look but were rebuffed."

McAllister glanced around. "Where is everyone else?"

"They're remaining inside the shuttle. Harmony and Agent Adams can't risk breaking the connection they have established to the stable heart. I believe the elite team is going to try to open it in the back. But I haven't been apprised as of yet."

There was movement happening around the shuttle.

The back end was lofted, and a few of the soldiers were pulling out equipment. Sergeant Collins was issuing orders. When he caught sight of Director McAllister, he stood at attention and saluted. "Welcome to the base, sir," Sergeant Collins addressed Mina's boss. "The mission was a success. We're going to open this up in the next two. If all goes well, the data core should be exposed shortly."

Kaylee disembarked and walked up to them. "The Syndicate hackers are not giving up," she informed Mina and McAllister. "Harmony and Agent Adams are on it, but they're working hard. If the hackers break through, the information will be lost. None of us are going to rest easy until that thing is opened and duplicated."

Mina led the way, and the three of them boarded the shuttle.

Lee glanced up. "Welcome aboard, sir. These Syndicate hackers are aggressive, but we have it under control."

A buzzing sound came from the back as some sort of saw was powered up.

"They're trying to infiltrate our blocks every way under the sun," Harmony said. "The key is to trick them into thinking they should go down one path, but it's really the other one that holds the key. Then you keep changing it up. Everything on their end is reading as a system failure. If they knew we were in here, things would look very different."

Vince stood, reaching out his hand. McAllister shook it. "Thank you for giving me the warning and assisting in my quick departure from France. I owe you some explanations and will give them to you shortly."

"There's no hurry," McAllister replied. "Tomorrow is soon enough. If all goes well with this today, I'll have you and Agent Kane come to my office first thing in the morning for a detailed, confidential debriefing."

"Sounds good," Vince said.

The cargo area was partially visible from inside the shuttle. Mina could see soldiers working, but she didn't have a visual on everything that was happening.

"I'm going to step outside," she said, "so I can see what's happening. If any trouble arises with the hackers, let me know."

"We will accompany you," McAllister said.

Kaylee, McAllister, Norm, and Vince followed Mina outside and around the craft.

The soldiers had already lasered through a few centimeters of the stable heart's outer layer. "We're not going to use a laser all the way through," Sergeant Collins explained. "If we do, we risk damage to the data core. We're going to switch soon to a diamond-tipped saw, the kind they used back in the day. We have several with different widths and thicknesses. We're working efficiently. It will be open soon."

They were making progress, but Mina was still worried. If the Syndicate hackers got through, the entire mission would be lost. Waterbury would get away with his crimes, only to commit more. The Syndicate would be free, and wiser in the future. They would definitely secure their other satellites, possibly putting kill switches inside to wipe out data.

This was a one-time opportunity.

They watched as the team switched out the laser and brought in the saw.

It made a high-pitched grinding noise as it began to rip through the heavy-duty graphene.

Mina almost didn't hear the yelp from inside. She held up her hand. "Cut the saw," she commanded.

Sergeant Collins reiterated, "You heard the agent, cut the saw!"

Everything went silent.

From inside the shuttle, Harmony was saying something.

"What is it?" Mina called.

"I'm picking up on a booby-trap that may be inside. We didn't notice it before. We weren't supposed to. I just stumbled on it now when I was looking at something else."

"I see it, too," Lee said. "I think…it's a bomb."

Sergeant Collins reacted quickly. He lofted both hands. "Everybody set down your tools and back up." His soldiers complied immediately, each of them moving three meters away. "You two must disembark from the shuttle. This is my jurisdiction now, and I'm tasked with keeping everyone on this base safe. This supersedes the lead." He glanced at

Mina.

"We will defer to you on this, of course," Mina agreed. "Our number one priority is to keep everyone safe."

"We need a bomb squad here immediately," Sergeant Collins said. "Leavy, report to Colonel Braxton and bring in the crew we have on base."

Leavy saluted and turned on his heel to complete the task.

Mina rushed to the side of the shuttle and boarded. "I need you two off immediately."

"We want off of this thing, too," Harmony said. "But we can't risk severing our connection. The transition has to be seamless, no blips. If we lose contact, we set off whatever's inside. We're connected to the stable heart, but we don't have the password. If the connection breaks, it ignites." She gazed up at Mina, fear in her eyes. "I'm so sorry I didn't see it immediately. This is something that we should've figured out ahead of time. Not thinking there might be booby-traps was negligent. If they couldn't retrieve the stable heart themselves, this was their fail-safe."

Lee looked equally horror-stricken. "The code was A-grade. The parameters were hidden. It's a good thing we got in first. If they had, they would've ignited it right away. We stopped that from happening. It could've taken down the shuttle or, at the very least, harmed the soldiers when they were getting it out of the sand. We're currently stopping them from activating it. We can't leave until there is a stable connection to transfer to."

"What do you need from me?" Mina asked. "Tell me what has to happen next."

Vince boarded the shuttle. "Why aren't they getting off?"

"They need a secure connection set up to make a clean transfer," Mina said.

Lee nodded. "We need an amplifier. The signal needs to be boosted out here, so we can latch on to it and move our compucases securely. Sergeant Collins is not going to like it. This base is cloaked for a reason. The amplifier will bounce to a satellite connection, instead of using a cable link."

"We'll make it happen," Mina said as she turned to Vince. "Let's go talk to Sergeant Collins."

They walked around to the back of the shuttle. The soldiers had made a large perimeter. Kaylee, Norm, and McAllister stood behind them.

Mina strode up to the man in charge. "We need a signal amp boosted from the op room." She gestured to the bunker they'd occupied. "It has to reach my crew in the shuttle so they can safely transfer signals without a break."

Sergeant Collins shook his head. "I can't—"

"If you don't, the bomb blows," Vince told him. "A signal break for ten to twenty seconds is better than having an unidentified bomb explode. We don't know what the makeup of the explosive is yet. It could affect the whole base. It could be nuclear." He let that sink in. "We can't take that risk."

"As it is right now," Mina added, "according to my specialists inside the shuttle, hackers are actively trying to set off the bomb. They don't want anyone to access the data inside. Which is precisely why we want that data."

Harmony called, "Amp up that signal. Do it now! We're putting blockers in place to keep your base cloaked. If anybody tries to infiltrate, we'll know it. My partner and I are personally guaranteeing that. Anyone who's on a snooping mission is going to get a screenful of white noise until we get inside. Trust us! But we need to get out of here. If our blocks break, that thing is going off."

Sergeant Collins made his decision. He stepped away to speak into his cuff.

Mina and Vince made their way to McAllister and the rest of the group.

"What's up?" Kaylee asked. "We heard some of it, but not all."

"Harmony and Agent Adams need to change signals, from the one in the shuttle to one that's cloaked in the op room. But the cables don't stretch that far, so they're going to need to air-boost it out. It will only take ten to twenty seconds to establish a new connection, but Sergeant Collins has to break protocol to do it. He's ordering it now. Until then, we wait."

"Can those two kids come out of there a little way and still stay connected?" Norm asked. "Keeping them that close seems unnecessary."

"They want to get out of there as bad as we want them

out of there," Mina said. "If that was an option, I'm sure they would've indicated that. They can't risk a break. If that shuttle powers down, it'll be a problem. I'm going to go back on board to stay with them until the new connection is established."

McAllister nodded. "I won't order you to stay out here, Agent Kane. Agent Adams could use your support. I'm going to make a few calls to headquarters and see what we can do from here."

"I'm coming with you," Kaylee said to Mina.

"No, you stay out here with Norm and Kramer," Mina ordered. "You'll be the liaison when Sergeant Collins comes back. Kramer will back you up. I'm not sure what needs to happen, but I want you to make sure they do whatever it is quickly. Nobody else needs to be inside the shuttle."

"But—"

Mina cut Kaylee off. "I'm lead, and that's my order. You're out here, I'm in there. I trust my partner and Harmony. Everything is going to be fine." She turned and walked toward the shuttle without another word. Once on board, she assessed the situation. Both Harmony and Lee seemed stable, not overly nervous. "How's it going?"

She took a seat across the aisle from Lee.

"Man, they're tenacious," Lee said, not taking his eyes off his compucase. "They're making us dance."

"Yeah, but it's an easy dance," Harmony said. "Like those old-timey waltzes and stuff. We're familiar with the steps. We've got this."

Mina stayed quiet. She didn't want to interrupt. She imagined the Syndicate hackers working frantically on their end, knowing they had to report to somebody who could harm them or a family member. She didn't envy them.

"Did you see that?" Lee said. "They're trying to pull a Hannon Maneuver. I blocked with a three Q subratio code."

"Good one, Seeker," Harmony hooted. "Let's throw in some old code. The ones with capital letters with a quotient B. It'll take them a second to figure out what's happening, then just when they think that will continue, let's go into Zenith-level encryptions."

They were speaking a foreign language.

Mina was elated they understood each other so well. They were a symbiotic hacking team. She felt grateful to be working with both of them.

There was movement as Vince boarded the shuttle.

Before Mina could order him off, he held up his hand. "I just came on board to let you know that the amp has been ordered. They've deployed their own computer tech to the op room. It should only be about a minute more." Instead of turning and exiting like he should, Vince took a seat next to Mina. She was about to tell him to leave when he reached out and grabbed her hand. "If you think I'm going to let you stay here without me, think again. Even though you're lead, you're family first."

"Do you want to have dinner with me tonight?" She had no idea where that had come from. It hadn't even been a coherent thought before it had tumbled out of her mouth. "I'm sorry. That came out of nowhere. I mean, I'm supposed to have dinner with my family tonight. That is, if this mission is a success and finishes in time. My brother really wants me to come. He's bringing his new partner." Mina realized she was babbling, but she couldn't stop. "They would love to see you. Quinn said as much. You bringing up family made me think of it. You're family to them, too. And to me." She cleared her throat, extremely aware that Harmony and Lee were listening to this very personal conversation. "I apologize. It was silly to ask you right here, right now. I don't know what came over me."

"I do." Vince smiled. "When people are placed in dire situations, emotions run high. It's happened to me many times. I would love nothing more than to have dinner with you and your family tonight. Thank you for inviting me."

"Just hooked on to the new signal," Harmony called. "Let's get the frack out of this thing!"

THE TEAM REASSEMBLED in the op room. The bomb squad had encapsulated the stable heart. It remained in the back of the shuttle until they could figure out more about what was inside.

"We're almost through the code," Lee said. "Then we'll know what kind of bomb it is. They actually made it look like a flower, if you can believe it. The entire code is written like a cascading flower."

"I see why. Look!" Harmony gestured excitedly at her screen. "It's a stem! That can only mean one thing. It's a stem bomb. The chemis are stored in separate areas called leaves. When activated, they flow down and mix at the bottom of the stem. Then ca-blooey!" She exploded her hands outward. "At least that's my guess anyway."

Lee squinted at the screen. "I think you're right."

That particular kind of bomb wouldn't do as much damage as a hydro, but the size would decide how big the explosion would be.

"Do we have mass or volume?" Norm asked, moving toward Lee. "I've come up on a few stem bombs in my career. The package tends to be pretty small. We need to know how big this blow will be."

"I'm familiar with them, too," McAllister said. "And I concur. Most stems I've encountered have been fairly small, as it's difficult to pack the large quantities of chemis in the leaf areas."

Lee seemed confused at what was showing on his screen. "I'm seeing a 2cc notation. That can't be right. That's too tiny. It's less than half an ounce."

"I think it might be right," Harmony said. "I see it as well. It can certainly be that small. The space inside the stable heart is less than half a meter. I think their plan is to only take out the data inside. That's probably another fail-safe, in case when they recover it and open it, it goes off. Then it wouldn't hurt anyone."

"That size would produce a blast equal to a hydro-cracker for kids," Lee said, scratching his head.

"But honestly, that's great news, isn't it?" Kaylee said. "That means none of us are in jeopardy of dying anytime soon. I'll take a kid-sized hydro-cracker any day."

"It's great news," Mina said. "Now you need to stabilize it. How do we do that?"

"We do that by making it null," Harmony said. "Give me a second. Now that we understand the code, I'm getting to the ignition part. I can erect a blockade around all the stem code." She bit her lip and focused for a few seconds. "That should do it. Now we can safely delete it."

"I'm not sure if we should," Lee murmured. "If we do, they may be able to rewrite that code in a different part of the program. As of right now, they can't duplicate it. It's firm-set on purpose."

"Good point," Harmony said. "My mistake. Thanks for pulling me back, Karmaseeker. You're the bomb. Well, not this bomb, but a total hacker bomb." She glanced at Mina. "Just give us a second so we can make sure it's hack-proof."

Mina nodded. She walked over and addressed Sergeant Collins, who was standing by the door. His distress was apparent.

"We're all clear. You can gather your men again," she told him. "The strength of this bomb is equal to a small hydro-cracker, something a child would play with."

After a moment, he bowed his head. "Order received. I will recall the men and tell the bomb squad to retreat. I have to make a report to my superior. We'll be ready to resume work on cracking it open once you exit the building." He turned and left the room.

Vince walked up, grinning. "You've gained his trust. Nice job."

"I don't know about that," Mina said. "He was listening to Harmony and Lee, so he probably had his mind made up already."

Vince shook his head. "If you'd been unsure of their result, he would be unsure. It's your faith in your team that rings true. He picked up on that."

McAllister joined them. "I have another rocket shuttle standing by. We will physically transport the data core to Judge Mackey after we view it here." He checked his cuff. "If all goes well, we should make it back to the city by five p.m."

"Excellent," Mina said. "I hope what we need is in the core. If not, we miscalculated the need to bring the satellite down."

"You didn't miscalculate," McAllister replied. "Your competent investigative work led us here. As did your intuition and intelligence. We will find what we need on that data core. I'm certain of it."

Since they had a moment or two to spare before Harmony and Lee isolated the hydro-cracker, Mina decided to ask her boss about the faux audit. "Have you discovered any more about the audit? And where those two investigators came from?"

Mina and Lee had participated in an audit aimed at some of their high-level cases, or so they'd thought. It'd been uncovered that the request for the audit hadn't come from the committee that oversaw the CIU, but from somewhere else. So it hadn't been officially sanctioned. All four "official" interviewers had turned out to be civilian lawyers, who had been recruited by an unknown source and brought in to question Mina and Lee on their conduct during past cases. It had become clear that these lawyers had been searching for a way to invalidate Mina and Lee's investigations, which had led Mina to believe that whoever had hired them was worried that the CIU was getting too close, or too good, or too powerful, at combating top-level crime inside the government.

Basically, whoever was behind the audit was likely a criminal themselves.

"I've assigned two agents to the case, as the trail of information has run dry," McAllister said, his voice tense. "But make no mistake, we will find out where this all originated from and who ordered it. Since we last spoke, I've tried to contact all the participating litigators. Their cuffs have been disabled, and their former companies have informed me that they've each taken a last-minute vacation. Nothing about this adds up, but it will."

"I'd love a chance to solve it once this case is over," Mina said. "I'm sure Agent Adams would, too."

Over was a loose term. This case would go on and on, as the Syndicate lawyers would hang up and delay everything they could in court. But the CIU specialized in the legwork. Its agents uncovered the details and evidence needed to make convictions. Once that portion was done, the case would be handed to the appropriate department. In this case, that would be High Crimes.

Mina preferred it that way. It freed her up to do more of what she loved, which was solving the mystery.

"After your debriefing with Colonel Kramer tomorrow, we'll discuss it," McAllister said. "There's a very high probability I will put you and Agent Adams on the case."

"It's done!" Harmony said. "We harnessed the teensy-weensy hydro-cracker. No chance it can go off. Well, unless a laser shoots it or something. Tell those soldiers to be careful. No loose laser play."

"It's completely stable," Lee confirmed. "We aborted the code that would disintegrate the barriers on the leaves. That includes a metal latch attached to a tiny transmitter. As of right now, nothing can ping that transmitter, so the metal latch can't give way to release the chemis. It's safe. But let the soldiers know that the data core will be connected by nanocables, which are connected to powerful transmitters outside the stable heart. Those need to be unhooked carefully. Just make sure they don't yank the data core out before that happens."

"My advice is to do it right now," Harmony encouraged. "Making it bomb-proof doesn't mean these hackers aren't still trying to get in. Go, go! We'll hold down the fort here."

Everyone but the superhackers rushed out of the room. Mina was relieved to find Sergeant Collins back and his team amassed, many of them holding the tools they would need to open the stable heart. The bomb squad had removed the protective container, and a few of them were standing by with what looked to be another smaller box to put the hydro-cracker inside once they opened the heart.

"Don't get any lasers or sparks close to it," Mina warned. "We have to do this as quickly as we can. My team says the data core is connected by nanocables that must be unplugged before extraction."

"None of that will be a problem," Sergeant Collins replied. "We're going to use a shorter saw blade and make a clean line halfway around the sphere. Then we're going to crack it open like an egg very slowly with a specialized separation lever. The bomb squad tells me that a stem bomb will be encapsulated in a silicone sac. It shouldn't rip open, but we're going in slow. Then, when it's open a centimeter, we're threading a robocam in to get a look inside before we crack it all the way."

Mina nodded. "All sounds good."

Sergeant Collins circled his arm high in the air. "Let's go! Get this done. Slow and steady. Henderson and Matthews, you're on the saw. The moment we get a centimeter gap, Marlin feeds the robocam. Patten, I want this on a large screen."

The soldier Mina assumed was Patten gave his superior a short salute and jogged away to find an adequate screen.

Henderson and Matthews started immediately, wearing full face shields enhanced with honeycombed crystalline. Not even a minute and a half later, one of them called, "Centimeter crack, sir!"

Marlin already had the robocam in hand. His face shield looked to be titanium, with a slot for crystalline eye shields. Patten jogged up a second later with a large superboard. They touched the tech together. A low beep sounded. Marlin then threaded the cam into the gap very slowly.

Mina and her team stood back, letting the soldiers do

their work.

"Stem bomb sighted," Patten said. "Encapsulated in what looks to be a clear sac. Data core roughly six centimeters long. No cables visible yet. Nothing else inside."

"Matthews, get the hydraulic pressure pump in that crack. A centimeter is skinny, but it should fit," Sergeant Collins ordered.

Matthews exchanged the saw for what looked to be a metal expander folded up like an accordion. He reached down into the crack and set it inside. It was connected to a long tube, which was connected to a solar-powered air compressor.

"Go slow," Sergeant Collins said. "Three pounds of pressure per square centimeter. We'll go up from there. Instead of cracking it wide, we're going to crane it open to eight centimeters, then reach in and pluck the data core out using the robocam and pliers to unhook the cables."

Everyone waited while Matthews began to exact pressure against the two opposite sides of the stable heart. The noise was like metal tearing. Lots of cracking and groaning.

The entire process took four minutes.

"Eight centimeters, sir," Matthews said.

Sergeant Collins motioned for Marlin to come back in with the robocam. Henderson joined him with long-handled pliers, one in each hand. Patten stood close with the screen, angling it so Henderson could see.

"Henderson has steady hands and excellent hand-eye

coordination," Sergeant Collins said. "Once this is out, I'll have him deliver it to the op room using the forceps. Then I'm going to decompress the stable heart, make sure it's closed, then have the bomb squad take it away. I'm assuming you don't need it for anything more today?"

"It will be entered in as evidence," McAllister answered. "Have one of your official representatives accompany the bomb squad and document the disabling of the stem bomb. Then I want it locked away in your safest bunker. If approval is needed, I can secure that in five minutes. The government will send a few agents down to retrieve it in the next few days."

Sergeant Collins nodded. "Yes, sir. We have several secure sites where it can be kept, including one that's several layers underground. It will remain safe with round-the-clock surveillance until you come to pick it up. No further approval necessary."

"Thank you," McAllister said. "Your cooperation and service are well noted. I will be making a full report to your commanding officer."

"I have it," Henderson called. "All cables disconnected. It's ready to come out."

They watched him tug the data core out of the stable heart sideways, moving slowly and efficiently.

"Man, I thought it would be bigger than that," Kaylee said. "It's amazing what they can pack inside of a small package these days. All that trouble for something the size of a maple pastry."

"That maple pastry is going to bring the Syndicate some much-needed grief," Mina said. "Let's get it inside."

Norm was already at the door of the op room, bracing it open. Mina could hear Harmony's hoots of joy from where they stood.

"I'm already making copies," she cried. "Data is coming in fast and furious. There's a whole bunch of stuff on here."

"The government satellite has been engaged," Lee called. "Official airmeld in process."

"Let's go get these guys," Kaylee said as she swaggered toward the door.

For not the first time, or even the tenth, Mina wished she had a good swagger, one to rival her best pal's. But she was swaggering on the inside.

Mina made her way toward the op room door, with Vincent Kramer by her side. "These guys are going down, I can feel it," she said, her body rippling with anticipation.

"Indeed," Vince said. "I never doubted you for a second."

Data streamed across the screens in the op room. Numbers and files cascaded, while occasional images and vids popped up and disappeared.

"Just a few more seconds until I find what we need," Harmony said. "There are thousands of vids stored in here. These guys liked to record stuff. So dumb. Especially if it proves to be incriminating. I'm sorting by date."

"They obviously thought floating it around in space would keep it safe," Kaylee said. "They're not going to be so confident next time. I wouldn't be surprised if they bring all their satellites down, or at least swipe them clean after this."

The screens stopped flowing all at once, and the same vid appeared on all four.

It was Waterbury's utility room. An empty chair sat waiting.

Three seconds later, there was a loud door slam.

Murmuring voices followed, one arguing, one threatening.

Mina darted a glance at Norm. "You might want to step outside," she cautioned. "I don't want you to have to relive this."

Norm shook his head, even though he looked a little pale. "I gotta watch. I have to know it's on there and that it's accurate. That it hasn't been fiddled with. Don't worry about me. I can handle it."

Vince caught Mina's look and edged closer to Norm. "How about we both sit down? I'm the one who found you, and I know the state you were in. I don't necessarily want to watch it, but I will."

He pulled out two chairs.

"You're trying to nannybot me," Norm groused. "I told you I can handle it."

"Not quite nannybotting. I want to make sure you don't pass out. There's a difference." Vince chuckled. "Stop being hardheaded, old man, and take a seat."

Norm held out for a few seconds, then sat.

On-screen, Waterbury shoved Norm into the chair and proceeded to e-restrain him.

What came next was horrific.

They all watched in stony silence. Harmony wiped away tears. Everyone else was stoic. The brutalization of the ex-marshal, and the glee and calmness with which it was carried out, was atrocious. It was one of the worst things Mina had ever had to witness. Norm pleaded often with Waterbury to stop, bargaining for his life, but he held the agony from the vicious breaks of his bones and the pummeling inside instead of screaming out in pain.

There was no question they had their evidence. Waterbury was going back in a box, hopefully for the rest of his life.

Mina was both relieved that their risky endeavor had paid off and sick to her stomach. The torture went on and on with little break. When Waterbury finally left the utility room, the time he'd spent in there had felt like a thousand years.

It had been only twenty-three minutes.

He came back for another round later that evening. Likely an unauthorized trip out of his monitored residence.

The third time he came back was when he was abruptly called back to the group residence. That's when he stuck Norm in the side with a blade, promising him much worse upon his return.

Harmony fast-forwarded until they heard Vince call his name.

The anguish in Vince's voice, and his tenderness in trying to get the ex-marshal out, even though he had to shock him to free him from the e-restraints, was equally hard to watch. It was a relief to everyone in the room when the ex-marshal lost consciousness.

The vid paused, and Harmony wiped away more tears. Mina exited the building, needing some fresh air. She blinked in the sunshine.

McAllister followed her out, heading off in the distance,

ordering something into his cuff.

Vince walked out, wrapping his arms around her. She buried her face in his chest. She didn't care who witnessed their intimate moment. After a couple of deep breaths, she stepped back.

"Thanks," she said. "I needed that."

"I did, too. Kind of like that time we watched that horror vid after your mom told us we were not allowed. We consoled each other for days."

"Yeah, kind of like that, but this one was real. A real-life horror show."

Norm exited the building next, and Mina moved toward him. "I'm so sorry. It must've been hideously awful to go through that again. I apologize that you had to see it and experience the horror twice."

His shoulders straightened, a firm resolve flashing across his face. "We're going to get that bastard. What I went through was worth it if we can break the Syndicate wide open. I'll wear it like a badge of honor. There's lots more on that data core. I'm going to see this through. I'll be the best witness they've ever had in any courtroom. Nothing will spook me after that."

"You'll be a fantastic witness." Mina reached out, settling a hand on his shoulder, clutching it for a few minutes. They both bowed their heads. "We will work hard to make everything you went through worth it. I promise."

A yell sounded from inside the building.

"We found something!" Lee called. "You have to come

see this."

They all rushed in, including McAllister.

Two men, not readily identified, stood in what looked to be a warehouse, talking.

"Wait, let me rewind it," Harmony said, tapping on her compucase. The vid buzzed back a few seconds and paused.

The men were both nondescript—medium height, brown hair, not many enhancements, clothing shabby. Definitely day laborers.

"I don't think these guys were supposed to be in there, or at least not caught on cam. Somebody must've overlooked this, or it would've been deleted." Harmony gestured to the screen in front of her. "This is surveillance vid from somewhere. It's standard motion capture, full audio. When they walked in, the vid was activated. When they left, it stopped. They're not sneaking around, exactly. Give it a listen."

"If we get caught in here, it's lights out," the guy on the right, who had slightly shorter hair, said. "I can't believe I let you drag me into this."

"Just relax. We're the only ones here," the guy on the left said. "I told you, you have to see it to believe it. They lied to us. They said we were moving standard pharma, but this is not standard." The man walked over to a secured crate and lifted the top off, using a small tool he'd had in his pocket. "Do you see that? Those are airpens full of Plush." He reached in and grabbed one. "Blade doesn't own

Bliss Corp. That's who makes this stuff." He shook the pen. "Nothing in here has a seal on it. It hasn't been approved or nothin'. The outside of the box is stamped as standard biotech. If we get caught hauling this in our freights, we could do serious box time."

The other man shrugged, seemingly unaffected by the find. "That doesn't mean much. Bliss Corp could've hired Blade to do some merchandise delivering. He's a big name in pharma. They could have a contract or something. Maybe it's going for approval right now? And what do you care anyway? We already signed the contract. It's good currency, paid in coin. The chances of getting stopped from here to the border are low. Even if we did, Blade would take care of it. After all, we're not crossing the border. We're just leaving it for someone else. If we get stopped, we tell them we're just the stupid delivery techs." He glanced around the room. Hundreds of crates were stacked up, all bearing the same imprint that indicated they held standard-grade biotech—things that could be sold to the public without a prescription, not top-grade, unapproved, highly regulated pharma. "What did you think when you signed the contract? That everything would be on the up-and-up?" He slapped the guy on the shoulder playfully. "This is what you get." He gestured in front of him. "Nothing is what it seems, and they like to keep it that way. So let's get out of here and get the job done."

Harmony paused the vid, glancing over her shoulder at Mina. "This seems pretty big, right?"

"Yes," Mina said. "The fact that Bliss Corp is using Travis Blade as an illegal courier for secret, unauthorized doses of Plush adds to the picture that's already forming about Bliss Corp testing out a new serum on unsuspecting people. But without getting our hands on one of those airpens, we won't know for sure what's inside. They could be legal. Just like that guy said. Or they could be heading for inspection right now. The Syndicate could argue that they were shuttling them off to be approved. Or anything else, for that matter."

Since the two men hadn't given any clues to which border they'd been referring, there was no way to know where they were going.

"Speculation won't hold up in court," Mina went on. "Travis Blade has plenty of litigators on his payroll. They could claim dozens of scenarios to say what they were doing was completely legal. One thing is for sure, Blade and Bliss Corp definitely have a contract together. To be able to do anything, we would need hard evidence, as in the pens themselves, and witnesses, like those two. But they'd have to be willing to testify against the Syndicate. I can't see that happening. They wouldn't want to forfeit their lives for something like this."

"I'm running facial rec on the two men right now," Lee said. "So far, no hits."

"We need to get moving," McAllister said. "Agents and analyzers have downloaded the airmeld and are now combing through the data. Each vid, all files, images, and anything else will be authenticated and categorized. Anything that flags as criminal activity will be forwarded to me immediately. Let's get the core on the rocket shuttle and to Judge Mackey immediately. Waterbury has already been detained. I had agents stationed outside of his residence to make sure there was no interference by the Syndicate if the evidence came through. He is boxed securely underground in Government One, awaiting Judge Mackey's ruling. High Crimes will meet us at Mackey's office. I've arranged for the judge to have a twenty-four-hour protection from now until I deem the threat of Syndicate retribution has subsided. They are already with him."

Mina glanced at Norm. "We need the media. The shakeup needs to happen now."

Norm nodded. "It's all set. Littlefield's already been in her ear. The moment I step off of that shuttle, I'm meeting with Melissa Socorro at a secure location. I'm giving her an exclusive live on cam. She was given prior notice to film on the south tip of Florida and aim for the air. I'm certain they caught the streak of the stable heart falling on vid. She'll use her considerable resources to identify what it was, if she hasn't already. That woman is beyond resourceful."

Mina knew many people had likely caught the streak on various devices. Right now, speculation would be ramped up all over the boards. The quicker the story broke in their favor publicly, the better.

They gathered up their supplies, carefully placing the data core inside a titanium box that Sergeant Collins had provided.

He stood at attention, saluting them as they boarded the shuttle.

"Thank you for your time and coordinated effort," Mina told him. "As a precaution, I would increase perimeter and air surveillance for at least a week or so. The people who lost this data want it back. They may wrongly assume it's still here on this base until the story breaks wider."

Sergeant Collins nodded. "Don't worry about us. We will remain on lockdown, fully cloaked, as always. Nothing gets in or out without us knowing."

Everything witnessed by these soldiers would stay here. The Syndicate had no doubt identified the retrieval shuttle leaving the island with the stable heart as military, but it would be an unlikely move for them to retaliate directly against the base. It was government protocol to deploy soldiers to investigate a satellite crash to Earth. It couldn't be proved that they knew anything ahead of time. Just that they were a well-run group who could react to a threat instantaneously.

The entire mission had worked out in the CIU's favor, keeping them below the Syndicate's notice, and Mina hoped it would stay that way. She was thankful that Judge Mackey would receive protection. The agents would be taking him and his family to a safe house. Once Waterbury confessed all on Babble, the Syndicate members would scurry for cover.

The rocket shuttle touched down in the city eleven

minutes later.

They'd landed at another secure military base. Mina wasn't surprised that McAllister had taken that precaution. They disembarked, walking under an awning that had been erected to protect them from any notice from above.

Several unmarked drones were ready to go.

"Agent Kane, Agent Adams, Colonel Kramer, and I will head out on one shuttle," McAllister said. "Agent Poston and Ms. Biggins on another. Norman Webb on the third." McAllister addressed Kaylee. "You and Ms. Biggins will be in the last shuttle. Your directions are to tail Norman Webb to his location with Ms. Socorro and provide discreet backup. If any issues arise, call for support immediately." He turned to Mina. "In order for us to continue staying well under the notice of any inquiring minds, our shuttle will set down at a safe house location. From there, we will board a mag-lev train that will take us to Government One. Until this data core is safely secured as evidence, we are not taking any chances."

Mina nodded. "Sound thinking." She was completely on board with staying well under the radar.

Once everyone had boarded the unmarkeds, they took off. No one spoke.

At the safe house location, they landed on the roof and made their way underground and boarded the waiting mag-lev. They were its only occupants.

"You have arrived at Government One," a sim intoned as the mag-lev slowed.

Once on the platform, McAllister said, "We will each approach Judge Mackey's office from a different direction." He handed the data core to Lee, who tried not to gape, but managed to anyway. "Agent Adams, I'm entrusting you to get this to the destination safely." He ignored Lee's expression like a pro. "Your face is the least recognizable as an agent in this department. I will approach the offices in full public view, monitoring for any tails. Agent Kane will as well, from a different direction. Colonel Kramer will act as your backup. You should both go completely undetected, as I'm having you take a tube up to level three-ten. Once there, you will transfer to Judge Mackey's private tube and take it directly down to his office, as Colonel Kramer has already done today. If anything goes wrong, tap the alarm on your cuff. I will order the building into lockdown. Do you have any questions?"

"Ah, no," Lee confirmed. "I will deliver this to Judge Mackey immediately."

McAllister nodded. "See you all there."

Chapter 22

"THE SATELLITE CURRENCY Reigns, owned by Travis Blade, crashed out of the sky this afternoon with no warning whatsoever," Melissa Socorro reported to her audience, her voice severe. "Before it was identified, the widely viewed UFO streaked through the air over the southern tip of Florida, causing alarm and unrest. It was immediately retrieved by the US military, which was deployed moments after its landing. It was safely recovered, the data analyzed, and what was found inside could very well shock the world." She stared into the cam, unblinking. Her body language, her restrained hair, her dark, modest clothing, and mild enhancements told viewers all they needed to know—whatever she was saying was extremely serious. "Stay tuned for my exclusive one-on-one interview with ex-marshal Norman Webb, who was the subject of vicious torture that was documented and stored on that very satellite. The perpetrator has been taken into custody, and there are murmurs he might be given Babble, the truth-telling serum that has only recently been reinstated for violent criminals, not just murderers." She let that sink in during a prolonged pause. "Given the satellite's owner and his rumored ties with the crime organization known as the Syndicate, we are expecting the fallout to be earth-shattering, similar to the impact of the satellite's return home." She was having a hard time containing her glee. This was indeed a huge scoop. "Tune in at ten and hear the harrowing story right from the ex-marshal's mouth. Viewer discretion is advised."

The newscast cut to a flashy ad about enamel-growing toothwash.

"Mute newscast," Mina instructed the comp.

"This has blown up all over the boards, too," Lee said. "Everyone's talking about it. There's massive speculation about what's going to happen to the longest-running crime organization the world has ever seen."

Mina, Lee, and Vince sat in a conference room at headquarters, two hundred stories up from the office where approval had just been granted for Waterbury to receive Babble. Wilbert was going to be dosed immediately by a team of doctors and analysts, with a heavy guard stationed outside a secured medi-room.

The Syndicate's lawyers were already swarming, placing legal objections and demanding stays, all of which had been overruled by Judge Mackey.

"Once Waterbury gets his dose, and the confessions

are recorded," Mina said, "there will be a mad scramble. High Crimes has at least twelve teams at the ready to pick up associated criminals. If Melissa Socorro thinks her interview with Norm will be explosive, wait until they find out who's going to be boxed next. I don't think Travis Blade himself will avoid this fallout, but he may." She turned to Lee. "Has Harmony uncovered any more on that Plush airpen trail?"

Kaylee and Harmony had gone somewhere secure so Harmony could keep analyzing the data on her own. Norm had given his interview to Melissa and had refused a government safe house option afterward. Instead, he had assured them he had a safe place to lie low. He had promised Mina he would check in hourly, and that was as good as they were going to get, at least for today.

Lee shook his head in response to Mina's question about Harmony. "Not that I know of." He checked his cuff. "No facial recs have come back on either of those men from the vid, which is strange. If those techies run deliveries for a living, they would be picked up by surveillance at nearly every stop. Something should've already popped."

"That doesn't bode well for them." Mina shifted in her seat. "If someone watched that vid and reported it to their bosses, the odds are that something happened to them. Then the Syndicate hackers wiped their lives clean."

"That's what I'm thinking, too." Lee gazed over Mina's shoulder. He was momentarily lost in thought. "When I get home, I can enter their images into an age modifier and do a sweeping face rec search on them as younger men. The images won't be a hundred percent, but it usually works well. At least enough to get a few hits."

Mina knew Lee was excited to get back to his new residence. He'd had only a short time to enjoy it.

"We're just waiting on McAllister to excuse us," she said. "Then you'll be able to get back to your new awesome residence. Clearance to leave should come shortly. I don't think we'll receive orders to retreat to a safe house, as we're not known to the Syndicate." It would be McAllister's call. But because they had stayed below the radar, that should make them relatively risk-free. At least for the moment. Waterbury had seen both her and Lee, but he likely still thought they were counselors. His residence wasn't equipped with any tech, and he was in custody now. That meant he had no way of gathering their images or reporting them.

At least not a way they knew of, anyway.

Mina's cuff buzzed. It was the sound for her mother.

She stood. "I'm going to take this. It's my mom. She doesn't usually tag my cuff. I need to check in and make sure there's no emergency." She tapped her cuff for voice only. "Hi, Mom." Mina walked out into the hallway, shutting the door behind her.

"Hi, honey." Her mom sounded cheerful. "I'm sorry to bother you at work, but you haven't replied to any of my messages today, and we're about to eat a meal here in thirty minutes. Quinn told me you were involved in something and might not have the time, but that you also might invite Vince to join us? Your brother wasn't exactly clear, and he's not answering right now. If you're still planning on that, I need to know if I should set an extra place. Or is Vince taking your place? We would love to see you both, of course. It would be great to catch up. We miss you."

"I miss you, too." It'd been at least a month since she'd seen her parents. "I should be finishing up here for the day fairly soon, so there's a chance I can make it. I won't know until I get a formal dismissal from my boss. Don't get your hopes up. There's a possibility he has more work for us to do tonight." How much should she tell her mother about the colonel-in-arms? "As for Vince, I'm actually with him right now. He's…um…helping out the government while he's in town. It was kind of a coincidence how things came together." Not exactly a lie. More of a sidestep. "We worked a case today."

"Well, that's nice. How fun to reconnect. Bring him along if you can. We would love to see him," her mother said. "Even if you're working a case, you both have to eat. If you leave again quickly, that's fine. We understand your job parameters. We just haven't seen you in so long. Your father and I are planning to take another trip next week. It would be nice to see you before we leave." She chuckled good-naturedly. "I think I might've forgotten what your face looks like. Last time I checked, it was a pretty good face. Looks a lot like your nana Leeds."

Mina's parents enjoyed traveling. Her father, Damon,

made extra borrows writing about the places they visited. He had a very active social board about it that brought in substantial revenue. They weren't fully retired, but they were close. They were gone a lot, which worked for Mina since she didn't have a lot of time to spend with them at the moment.

Vince stuck his head out of the door. Mina could see worry creasing his brow. She hadn't come back yet, so he'd assumed there had been an emergency.

She mouthed, "Everything's fine," before telling her mother, "I'll ping you back in a few minutes if we can attend. If you don't hear from me, it's unfortunately a no. But I'll make it up to you soon. I promise. Work has been hectic. And if you need one, I can send you a still image of my face."

Vince stepped out into the hallway with her, shutting the door behind him.

Her mother said, "I'd rather see that face in person. We hope to see you both tonight. If not, let's arrange a vid chat sometime this week."

"Will do," Mina said. "Love you."

"Love you, too."

"That was about dinner tonight," Mina told Vince. "She's hoping we can still come by. They're eating in about thirty."

"Lee just got a message that McAllister's on his way up."

The tube door dinged, and McAllister stepped out. He made his way toward them. "Agent Kane, Colonel Kramer." He bobbed his head at each of them. "Excellent work today.

Babble is being administered as we speak. The doctors believe the confessions will take a while, as Waterbury has been working for the Syndicate for many years. We won't have information on arrests made until early morning or possibly tomorrow. High Crimes is ready and waiting. They'll be handling this case for the foreseeable future. It seems our journey here has ended for the moment, but that's not to say we won't continue investigating things found on that data core. With committee approval, of course."

"What are our orders?" Mina asked.

Behind them, the door opened, and Lee stepped out.

"You are all excused for the evening," McAllister said. "Remain on high alert. If anything suspicious happens, or you detect a tail, alert me immediately and request backup. As of this moment, I believe that the Syndicate does not know who is connected to their case. Until I receive news saying otherwise, you will remain cautious, but can resume normal activities." He turned his attention to Vince. "You are not directly under my command and are capable of making your own decisions. I would, however, recommend that the Protectorate confirm that you are in France for the immediate future. That will give you more freedom while you are here."

Vince inclined his head. "It's already been reported." He lifted his cuff. "As of seventeen minutes ago, the French Protectorate gave confirmation to the public that my residence was broken into and that I was on base dealing with the perpetrator. Our rules on Babble are still far stricter than yours, so that's not an option, but the investigation is being handled by very capable officers who are loyal to me. I will be going over the vid of the attempted break-in shortly. Anything that correlates to what's going on here, you will be given a full report."

"I appreciate that," McAllister said. "I will pass it on to High Crimes. Anything validating this case will be of great interest to them." He addressed Lee. "You have my full authority to go over every centimeter of the data core. Contact Ms. Biggins and coordinate your efforts. If anything of interest comes up, contact me directly. I will be available throughout the night." He turned to Mina and Vince. "I'll see you both in my office tomorrow morning for a full debrief. You're all excused."

He walked back to the tubes, already on a new call.

"I'm going to ping my mom and let her know we're on the way," Mina said. "Lee, you're welcome to join us at my parents' for dinner."

"Ah, no, that's okay," Lee said. "I appreciate the invitation, though. I'm kind of excited to get back to my residence. I also want to see what Harmony has uncovered so far. We'll probably do a holo thing so we can discuss the data core. My residence has holo capacity right in the living area." His face was one big grin. Mina was glad to see happy Lee was back. "I've never been able to do that with any accuracy before. But maybe we'll just do screens. If she's not at her residence. She hates her screen." He shrugged, still grinning. "But I'm excited to get home."

"Summon a craft to the roof," Mina said. "But make at least three stops at various public landings to make sure you don't have a tail. You heard what McAllister said—we stay on high alert. The Syndicate is wily. We take that seriously."

Lee nodded. "Will do. I'll be careful."

"I know you will. Once you're home, enact all your new security protocols." Lee's face lit up as he remembered he had new government upgrades. "Vince and I are going to take an underground mag-lev. We can't land at my parents' public hub." She indicated Vince. "He can't be recognized there, and we have to make sure we don't pick up a tail ourselves."

The last thing Mina would ever do was put her family in jeopardy. Absolutely making sure she didn't have a tail was her number one priority. Making sure Vince's cover wasn't blown was her second.

"We'll touch base after our meeting with McAllister tomorrow morning," Mina told Lee. "Let me know if you find anything of significance on the data core."

"I will." Lee smiled. " Enjoy your date."

Mina arched a brow as her partner chuckled, enjoying her discomfort.

"It's not actually a date," Mina began to protest. "It's—"

"Actually a date," Vince confirmed. "And we plan to thoroughly enjoy it."

THE MAG-LEV DROPPED them at a private, secure stop. They wove through a long hallway and up a narrow stairwell, exiting through a nondescript office building and finally out a side door.

They had emerged a few blocks from Mina's parents' high-rise.

Now came the tricky part.

Mina glanced around as they began to walk. There was no one around. The public thoroughfare for this area was a couple blocks away. Office buildings and vacant space took up this area. There wasn't much commerce here. That's why it worked as a private government stop for agents entering the field secretly.

"It's too bad we don't have Phineas Raphael's blazer, hat, and sunshades," she told Vince. "We should've picked up a disguise for you from Tech. But then Tech would know you were in the building. I trust them, but they're Tech. I could've said it was for me—"

Vince tugged her gently around a corner and into a narrow passageway in between buildings.

A public grinder and recycler had been placed here, and a few bins awaited public pickup. These spaces weren't used for much of anything anymore, but years ago, cars would've driven through here. The building next to it had grabbed the extra space over the years, so the passageway was only two meters wide.

Before she could protest, he gathered her into his arms, murmuring, "I've been waiting for this since I saw you in Judge Mackey's office today."

His lips were electric.

So much better than pretend lips.

Mina had forgotten all about the phantom sensations until right this very second. Leave it to a hard case to get in the way of romance.

Before she completely gave in to the urge to wrap her arms around him and kiss him back, she whispered, "Are you sure we should do this right here? It kind of goes against my training to make out in a pass-through zone."

He chuckled softly, kissing her again. "No one's around. It's just a few kisses. It's not like we're planning to disrobe." Another kiss. "Unless, of course, you think that's a good idea—"

Mina playfully slapped his chest. "I know you're kidding." She quirked her brows together. "You better be kidding." All she got from him in return was a wicked grin.

She scanned the alleyway. "I don't see any cams, but shop owners and retailers can get tricky with placement."

Vince nuzzled her neck. "We aren't around any retailers. I checked. I didn't spot any cams either. If we keep our heads together, no one is likely to recognize us, even if there are any." He bent down for another delicious kiss. His tongue did some exploring. It was hard not to get lost in the sensation. She and the colonel-in-arms of the French Protectorate were stealing kisses in a back alleyway. He broke away from her, a slow smile playing on his lips. "I can see you're still worried. You have a little crease right here." He lightly caressed a fingertip between her eyebrows. "It's your worry crease." He bent down and kissed it. Then he settled his nose on hers. "The sun is almost below the horizon. There's no direct light here. If anything picks us up, it will be dark and grainy. Retailers are notoriously cheap on paying for tech. Their average software is twenty years old. And as a bonus, this is the perfect place to wait and see if anyone is following us."

"Okay, so you're right." She kissed him long and hard, feeling breathless. And joyous. "You've thought of everything, haven't you?"

"It's my job to stay five steps ahead. It's what I do."

"I feel like a naughty teenager. That's the last time I snuck into a pass-through zone for a kiss."

"I do believe his name was Ryder Tims. Or was it Dev Reddy?"

Mina looked up at him in wonder for the second time

today. "You remember their names?"

"Of course I do. At the time, I don't think I was jealous of the romance aspect, but I was jealous of the time you gave to them. And you were not shy with your details either." He chuckled. "I have vivid recall of your delight in kissing both of them."

She wound her hands up into his hair. "That was childish delight. This is something far greater than that." She proved it to him, moaning softly. The man was an expert kisser. His lips were firm, yet soft. They moved with hers like they were coordinating a routine, his tongue slow and methodical. She was pretty sure she could do this for the rest of her life and be perfectly happy. She broke away, needing to catch her breath. "It's not like you were innocent and kiss-free. I seem to remember an Annika something or other and a Willa. There was definitely a Willa."

"That would be Nakita and Lilly." His laugh was a deep rumble. "I can see you were equally affected by my teenage trysts."

"It's not my fault I don't hold on to things like that," she protested. "I'm not an incredibly sentimental person, but that doesn't mean I don't care. Kaylee was just giving me crap today about not dotting my residence with precious mementos. But I do have a box of keepsakes somewhere in my utility room. I know it's there. I just can't remember what's in it. I wonder what my eighteen-year-old self thought was important to hold on to."

He brushed an errant strand of hair away from her face.

"I would love to discover what's in there with you." He bent down for another soft kiss. "As much as I don't want to leave, we promised your parents we would arrive shortly. I do believe we're at least ten minutes late already."

He was right. "Okay. Let's go. Once we get close, I'm tagging Quinn. He's coming down to let us in the side delivery door. It's the best we've got."

They moved through several alleyways until they were across the street from her parents' high-rise.

She tapped her cuff. Her brother answered immediately. "Hi, sis. Are you here?"

"Yep," she said. "Come and let us in. Bring one of Dad's caps, his sunshades, and that old ratty raincoat he likes." Vince raised his eyebrows. "And a scarf. The purple and yellow one."

Quinn didn't question her. "Got it. I'll be right down."

"A purple and yellow scarf?" Vince asked. "And a ratty raincoat?"

"The perfect disguise. The purple and yellow scarf will cloak those perfect, heart-shaped lips. If people can't see those lips, they won't know it's you."

He made a play to reach for her, and she danced out of the way. "I'm pretty sure that's not the only thing that gives me away."

"You'd be surprised," Mina said. "People tend to home in on the face, particularly eyes and lips."

Quinn pushed open the service door a few minutes later, handing out the garments. Vince took them and put them on, shrugging his large shoulders into her dad's raincoat. It was a snug fit, but it worked.

"Daphne's holding a tube for us. Come this way." He ushered them inside.

They made their way down a short hallway and into a tube Quinn's friend Daphne held open. She was a petite brunette with a pretty smile.

Once the door was safely closed, everyone inside relaxed.

"Hey, man, it's good to see you." Quinn reached out and shook Vince's hand. "It's been a minute. Glad you could join us tonight." He placed his arm around Daphne, pulling her close. "This is my friend Daphne Rogers."

"It's very nice to meet you," Daphne said with a slight catch in her voice. She placed a hand on her chest to steady herself. "I'm sorry. I've never met anyone famous before."

"Yes, you have," Quinn said. "At Primal. Last week, that vid star came in. What's his name again?" He snapped his fingers a couple times.

"Knuckle Knot?" Daphne said. "That's not exactly the same. He's a vid star celebrity, but Mr. Kramer is in a whole different strato." Mina was going to let the mister stand, even though Vince's title was colonel. She knew Vince wouldn't want to make a big deal about it.

"I'm not so sure about that," Vince answered easily. "It's nice to meet you, Daphne. It's good to see you, too, Quinn. I'm happy to have secured an invite for tonight."

Daphne turned her attention to Mina, reaching out to

give her a quick hug. "It's great to see you again. I'm really glad you're here."

"It's nice to see you, too. I'm happy we could make it," Mina said.

"Mom's been bouncing all over the place," Quinn said. "She's beyond excited you're coming and bringing Vince. She keeps saying it's like old times again. I even caught her with some liquid in the corner of her eye."

Their mother, Rose, wasn't one to hide her emotions. She was definitely a crier.

The tube door opened, and Mina gestured for Quinn to get out first.

"It's clear," he said, taking Daphne by the hand.

There were ten residences on this level, five on each side.

"Why are we being so careful, again?" Quinn asked as they moved toward their family home. "Everybody knows Vince is in town. He should be able to meet with old friends if he wants to."

Mina had told her brother very little, only that they had to get Vince in unnoticed. He also wasn't aware that Mina worked for a secret agency, and therefore, being seen with Vince would ruin her undercover status.

"At the moment," she explained, "Vince is working on something top secret for the Protectorate, and everyone thinks he's in France. We want to keep it that way." She glanced at Vince for approval. He gave a short nod. "So it's really important that you guys don't say anything to anyone. Particularly not at Primal, but no one can know he's in town or that he was here."

"Cool. We get it," Quinn said. "I explained how it all works to Daphne. We already do all that for you, so we can do it for Vince. We're good at keeping secrets after all this time."

Before they got to the door, Mina's mother whipped it open. She spread her arms wide. She had the same coloring as her daughter and son, was a bit shorter than Mina, and her long, undyed brown hair was showing its gray.

Mina went in for a hug. Everyone else followed. Quinn shut the door.

She held on to Mina's face for a couple beats, then kissed her on each cheek. "It's so good to see you. I've missed my firstborn. You look healthy and glowing. I love it." She dropped her arms and turned toward Vince. "Come here and give an old woman a hug."

Vince had already unwound the scarf and shrugged off the coat, cap, and glasses, which were now dangling over one arm. Quinn took the garments, and Vince obliged, giving Rose Leeds a very nice embrace.

"It's wonderful to see you, Rose. It's been much too long."

She patted his back while wiping away a tear that had leaked out. "You've gotten so big since I saw you last. Not a little boy anymore, but a grown man. How did that happen? It feels like only a blink of time has gone by." They separated. She grabbed on to both of his hands. "I only recently found out about your parents. I'm so very sorry. I was getting ready to send you some sort of note of condolence, but it felt hollow after all this time. I can't believe we didn't know. It was shocking to find out. They were so terribly proud of you. When they went to France, we lost touch. But I've never seen two parents more proud of a child. They adored you. They would be exceedingly proud of the man you've become."

"Thank you for that," Vince replied with some emotion. "I deeply apologize. It was my fault you didn't know. I shut down with my grief, rather than reaching out. If I had it to do all over again, I would've made their death ceremony a celebration of their lives. But I was young. Too young to know any better. Too lost in my own sadness. The very small gathering was held in France, only immediate family. My parents were very fond of you and Damon. They talked about you often. I wish it could've been different."

Footsteps sounded from the short hallway, and Damon Leeds walked into the room. "Vincent Kramer!" he called genially. "How wonderful to see you. What a career you've made for yourself. It's been impressive to watch your progress. Congratulations." He grinned at his daughter. "Mina Patina. We've missed you. It's been too long between your already sparse visits."

Where Rose was slight, Damon was robust. He was tall, with broad shoulders and a thick waist. Like his wife, he eschewed enhancements and was aging gracefully, his black dark hair streaked with gray.

"It's good to see you, too, Dad," Mina said. She hadn't realized how much she'd missed seeing them. This was just what she needed.

He wrapped Mina in a hug, rocking her back and forth. "We have to make this a more-often occurrence."

"We do," she agreed.

He turned toward Vince and gave him a thorough handshake.

"It's wonderful to see you, Damon," Vince said. "Thank you for letting me crash your dinner tonight."

"You are always welcome in our home. After all, you're family. You were a constant here for many years, and we hope for many more to come." Damon Leeds was never one to leave anyone out. He turned toward Daphne, reaching out his hand. She took it, smiling shyly, and he guided her into the meal-prep area, saying, "Come on, everyone. We've made a feast, and Quinn has brought the guest of honor. Daphne Rogers, we formally welcome you to our home and hope you enjoy our food and company. In honor of your visit, Rose and I decided that a real meal was in order, so this morning, we flew to the fresh market upstate, and we've prepared some delicious dishes. A nice baguette topped with fresh tomatoes and basil." He gestured toward a plate of dazzling red tomatoes. "And an apricot tart."

Mina's parents actually had an old-fashioned oven. And by the smell of the tart, they had just taken it out.

"We had something like this on our last trip to Istanbul,"

Damon said, "and it was amazing. I hope we were able to create its equal here. And there's much more to come. Sit, sit." He gestured to all the stools around the comfortably sized island. "Who wants wine? It's printed. Real is beyond our budget. You can't win them all."

Mina and Vince took seats next to each other in the same polymolded seats where they'd sat together so often over the years. He leaned over to whisper, "I forgot how much fun your parents are. They always made me feel so welcome here. You're lucky to have them."

She whispered back, "Hey, you heard my dad. They're extremely excited to have you back. Even if we don't work, they'll be happy to keep you in the fold."

He winked. "Oh, we're going to work."

Chapter 24

"WE SPENT SO much time in here." Mina paced around her old room, which was now her father's office. Her old sleep pod had been removed long ago, as well as all of her toys and wall decorations. "It feels like another lifetime, yet like no time has passed at all. Remember my orange tent? The small triangle one that zipped up the front?" She walked to the corner of her room, indicating with her hands. "It sat here for years. I spent so much time in that thing imagining I lived in different worlds and far-off places. It was a magical hideaway. I'm sure that's where I came up with Princess Priscilla of the Poconos and Sir Servant of Seville."

Vince sat on her father's office chair, grinning. "I do remember that tent and playing make-believe. I was delighted to be knighted Sir Servant of Seville. It felt important. I also remember you had actual paper books. That was an anomaly, even back then. We would bring stacks of them inside and read together, even when we were far older than the content. It was such a pleasure to turn the pages. I think we even slept in there a time or two when we were younger, curled up side by side."

"The books were fantastic. My mom collected them. She would drone hundreds of kilometers to pick up one." Mina remembered it fondly. "Feeling the heaviness in your hand with all the bright, detailed pictures was the best. I bet she kept some of them."

"I'm sure she did," Vince agreed. "She would want her grandchildren to experience the same thing we did."

She glanced at Vince. "I never thought of that. You're right. I'm sure she still has them."

Vince rose off the chair, moving toward her, grabbing her hand, and leading her to the middle of the room. He gestured toward the ceiling. "This is where we let the holo butterflies loose. I wish I still had that old holo box. I wonder what happened to it?"

"I have no idea," Mina murmured, resting her head against his shoulder. Being together in her childhood home felt so natural. Just like it had back then. But this was different. They were adults in the process of forming a new, different connection, built upon all the mutual love and respect that they'd shared for years. "It was yours, so I'm sure you took it home."

"I likely did," he murmured into her hair. "I just know that when I saw the wonder on your face, I wanted you to enjoy it forever and ever."

He tilted her chin up and gave her a slow, lingering kiss.

There was a short knock at the door, and Mina spun away from Vince like she'd been pronged.

The colonel-in-arms chuckled, letting her go easily.

Damon Leeds stuck his head in. "I just arranged a drone pickup on the roof for you two." He smiled. "It should be here in a few minutes."

"Thanks, Dad," Mina said.

"It's no problem. We understand the need for secrecy. I've gotten to know the maintenance manager here. A good fellow by the name of Carmine Kennison. He called it in, claiming we had some furniture to haul in. He didn't ask too many questions and promised it wouldn't be a problem in the future if we needed to do it again." He inclined his head. "I'm hoping we get to do it again. It was such a pleasure catching up with you, Vince. The stories of your life will stay with us for a long time."

"The pleasure was all mine," Vince answered as he and Mina made their way out to the living area to say their goodbyes.

Quinn and Daphne stood by the door.

Daphne stepped away to give Mina a quick embrace.

"Thank you for being so kind to me," she whispered in Mina's ear. "Your family is absolutely lovely and so generous. I had a wonderful time. I appreciate you not bringing up, you know, my past…episode."

Mina smiled warmly at this sweet girl whom her brother was so obviously over the moon for. He'd doted on her the entire night. "Daphne, your private life will always remain private. I promise. I don't discuss cases with civilians, including the ones who birthed me. You decide what you want to share with them, not me." Mina lowered her voice even further so no one could overhear. "And for the record, trying a dose of regulated Plush doesn't sound like such a bad idea at the moment." She winked.

Mina wasn't about to take a dose of Plush. And because of what Bliss Corp was doing, she probably never would. But she wanted to let Daphne know that when you were with the right person, trying things like a pleasure enhancer was perfectly normal.

Daphne grinned, bowing her head. "Thanks for that." She glanced up shyly. "I've never experienced a stable family life, or ever had anyone who would keep my secrets. That means a lot. I promise to also keep yours." Her eyes flicked to Vince, who was in an animated conversation with Mina's parents, her mother clutching his sleeve.

"We both appreciate that more than you know. And just so you understand," Mina murmured, "we are still investigating what happened to you. I'll keep you informed with what we uncover and will try to keep you out of it as best I can. There are bound to be more cases like yours, and those will be documented, which will take the focus off of you."

"I hope you discover what's going on. Having those doses out there is scary."

"I agree."

Quinn eased Daphne away, giving his sister a quick hug. "Thanks for showing up and bringing the entertainment." Quinn chuckled. He turned to Vince and shook his hand. "It was amazing catching up with you. It felt like we were back in the old days. We'll have to do it again soon. Daphne and I are heading to our first night at Harri's unit. We'll have you all over for dinner next."

"That sounds like a plan." Mina gave each of her parents a quick hug.

Her mother held on for an extra moment. "We'll be back from our next trip sometime next month. I'll be in touch."

"We look forward to hearing about your adventures," Mina said. "And tasting some new recipes."

Rose Leeds embraced Vince and gave him a kiss on each cheek. "Take care of yourself. Don't let those media buzzards peck at you too much. I hate how they go after you with such glee. "

"I won't," Vince said. "Thank you for a wonderful evening, Rose. The food was delicious, and the memories were priceless."

Quinn, Daphne, Mina, and Vince exited the unit together, along with Mina's dad, who went to the line of tubes and swiped for one.

When it opened, he stuck his hand in to keep it open. "This one will take you up to the roof."

Mina and Vince stepped on, saying their goodbyes to Quinn and Daphne, their heads down because of the cam set high in the corner. "Thanks, Dad. Hope your next trip is amazing."

"I'm sure it will be. We're going to Bali. This is the fourth time, but it's such an enchanting place. I'll send you some images when I can."

"Can't wait to see," she said.

The tube doors closed.

Vince draped his arm around Mina's shoulders, both of them facing forward.

They exited onto the roof three seconds later. The drone was just setting down. It was from a fancy private shuttle service company called Lux Rides.

"My dad spent some nice currency on this," Mina commented. "Nothing but the best for the colonel-in-arms."

"More like he wants to spoil his daughter." Vince grinned.

"I don't think so. If you weren't here, I'd be taking public transpo home, like Quinn and Daphne. Do you think we should make a few stops or just go through to The Spire?"

"Since your father ordered this, we should be fine," he said. "It's up to you."

"Let's head there and wait. We need to be cautious. We can check with the transpo hub and see if there were any unauthorized drones that have requested to land."

"Sounds good."

The door rose, and they boarded.

Vince ordered the drone to land on the executive level at The Spire, where he'd already been approved by Suzanne,

Mina's mega rep.

Mina snuggled into Vince's side, basking in the happy glow of the evening. It had gone exceedingly well. The conversation had flowed, the food had been excellent, and the family time had nourished her. She hadn't known how much she'd needed it.

She glanced up, noticing Vince was lost in thought. "What's up?"

He pulled her closer. "I'm imagining faraway places. Nothing I can speak of at the moment."

"Understood." It was illegal for transport companies to record conversations inside operational vehicles, but since everything was voice-activated, a record could be stored for a while. "It can wait until we get home."

"Home? I like the sound of that."

"Don't get ahead of yourself, French boy. You're staying with me tonight, because it's the best option, but you're going to have to find your own unit soon enough."

"I've been thinking about that." Vince lazily rubbed Mina's arm, head reclined. They were both satiated and relaxed. "I'm planning to give Suzanne a call. If I secure a residence in The Spire, we'll be able to see each other much more easily."

Mina lifted her head. "I'm not sure I'm ready—"

He kissed the top of it. "I don't plan for us to move in together or to invade your space. I'll likely be back and forth from France quite a bit. There will be long periods where we don't see each other. But when I am in town, you and I both know that keeping a low profile is our number one priority. To do that, proximity will be our best ally. Residing in the same building will give us that. We don't have to make any decisions tonight. It's just a thought."

"It does make the most sense," Mina said, snuggling back in. "But we also promised each other we would take this slow. You moving into my building doesn't feel slow." It was more like a mag-lev humming at top speed.

"No, it doesn't. But it doesn't feel like the wrong choice either."

"You're right." Oddly, it didn't. "Let's let it sit for a few days and see how we feel."

"Deal."

Mina wasn't sure how this comfort and calmness with him had happened so fast, but she knew the night with her family had aided it by a great degree. She wasn't complaining. It was nice.

"Landing at The Spire, executive level, in thirty seconds," the sim intoned.

They exited and separated, as there were a few people around. Vince hung back until it was clear, while Mina made inquiries at the transpo hub. No unusual landing requests had come in. They waited for a full fifteen just in case.

It was quiet.

Once they were down on her level, Mina opened the door to her unit with relief.

"Welcome home, Mina," Veronica said. "Is there

anything I can do for you?"

"Not at the moment," Mina replied as she turned and secured her residence with a few extra measures, enacting a whistle alarm that she usually didn't activate. If someone tried to break in, they wouldn't be the only ones to hear it.

"Very well," Veronica said. "Just holler. I'll be around."

Vince chuckled. "Your sim already has you figured out."

"She does," Mina agreed. "I lucked out with this program."

All the ultras had popped on low. It was her nighttime setting. It made her residence feel warm and comfortable. Instead of heading to the living area, Mina took a turn and went straight to her utility room. Vince followed.

Once inside, she began opening doors, searching. "I'm sure it's here someplace. I just don't know where they put it."

Vince stood in the door, his shoulder rested against the jamb, his arms crossed. "What are you looking for?"

"My box of mementos. We've had a full night of reminiscing. Why stop now? This place isn't that big." Mina spun in a circle. "Where could it be?"

"It's likely behind your laundry unit." He gestured toward the largest cabinet.

"Why would it be behind there?" Mina hadn't even known such a place existed.

"They have to be tricky about storage in places like this. When Suzanne showed me the unit next door, she demonstrated that the whole thing pulled out, and there was more storage behind. Laundry units are fairly shallow."

"Huh." Mina walked over and opened the door, then grabbed on to the protruding side and yanked.

Lo and behold, the entire thing swung open, revealing a bunch of aluminum storage boxes stacked inside.

"See?" Vince chuckled. "They're even stamped with the word 'storage.' The bot movers knew where to place them."

"If you weren't here, I never would've found them," Mina mused. "This one has an old tag on it." She gestured at a box in the middle. "It looks like the one I packed when I left home. This other stuff is from the training academy, and the top one is from my last residence."

She went to grab the middle box. Vince had to help her by holding the other two up so she could grab it out. It was heavy and awkward. She brought it back out to the living area, setting it on the thick pile floor covering. She knelt next to it, Vince coming to sit next to her in the chair.

"I was smart enough not to add a lock to this thing," she said. "I would've forgotten it by now. I didn't have enough money to buy a fingerprint or DNA release at the time."

The lid popped open with little effort, and she peered inside.

It was filled with her childhood.

A few favorite toys, some old pieces of tech that would take some charging to reboot, a bunch of digijournals, images of her and friends throughout the years, encased in crystalline for presentation and preservation.

She reached in and pulled out a plush toy. "I got this

at—"

"The annual school programming carnival. I think the year was '94 or '95."

Mina gazed at him in amazement. "How do you remember this stuff? I barely can. Though"—she turned the pink bear around in her hands—"I think we were together when I won this. Something to do with driving a simulated drone through an obstacle course?"

"Yes. You aced it the first time through. I was surprised they gave you such a small prize for such precision flying." He grinned.

She set it down and began to move things around. There were a few keepsake boxes decorated in colorful patterns, then at the bottom, she spotted a small black box. "Oh." She lifted it out. Her eyes darted to Vince's. "I guess you let me keep it after all. Do you think it still works?" She held the little holo box in her hand like it was a bar of gold.

"It's been years," Vince said. "The battery will need a charge." He reached out and took it from her, sliding the bottom piece out easily. A small standard coin battery fell into his palm.

"I have a replacement. Let me go get it." Mina made quick time back to her utility closet, grabbing a battery from her stash. She came back and handed it to Vince.

Her chest suddenly felt tight. Her keeping the holo box meant something special to them both.

Vince set the replacement in and glanced up at Mina. His expression matched the feeling in her chest. He placed the box on the floor in the middle of the room and stood.

"I'm so sorry I didn't remember I had it. It's been so long," she said. "I'm not good at—"

He reached out, pulling her close, his lips on hers, seeking and demanding.

Vince didn't hold back. They were in private, just the two of them. She matched his intensity, their tongues intertwining, their mouths hungry for each other. Her hands gripped his chest, needing something to hold on to. Her legs felt weak.

After a long moment, he arched away, winding his hand up her neck and into her hair. He rested his forehead against hers. "Never apologize." His voice was barely above a whisper. "I don't care if you hold on to the past. All that matters is right now."

Her throat was full. She nodded. "Ultras off," she managed.

Vince reluctantly let her go, reaching down to flip the switch on the holo box. As the three microcams triangulated upward, fluttering butterflies filled her living area.

"They're much smaller than I remember. But the details are perfect. They look real." She laughed. "They're every bit as magical as when we saw them for the first time."

"You're the one who's magical," he whispered.

She looked at him, seeing the love and longing in his eyes. She knew they matched her own.

"How you look at those butterflies is how you look at

me now. And I've never been happier about anything in my entire life." His voice was full of emotion. "All I've ever wanted, now that I look back, is to make you feel like you did when you first saw these butterflies."

She wrapped her arms around him. "The butterflies are a wonderful memory, and I'm so glad I kept the holo box. But I can promise you that how I look at you is a million times more special than I'll ever feel about these butterflies."

The kiss was spectacular. Starbursts went off in her head.

"Shall I have Eggie print up some champagne?" Veronica asked. "Or a sweet cake to celebrate?"

Mina and Vince separated, laughing at the interruption. Veronica really did get her.

Normally, Mina would take the champagne. But instead, she grabbed Vince's hand, leading him down her hallway. "No, thank you, Veronica. We plan to be busy for the rest of the evening."

"Then perhaps tomorrow morning we can celebrate with some nice mimosas?" the sim added.

"Perhaps."

Sneak Peek

BOOK 7

A MINA KANE NOVEL
BOOK SEVEN

AMANDA CARLSON

Chapter 1

"Keep your voice down," Mina shushed her best friend, gesturing toward her hallway, her voice low. "He's in the sprayer, but he could still hear you." She idly slid a wet lock of her hair behind an ear, hoping her pal wouldn't notice how damp it was.

Kaylee snorted. "Who cares if he hears? I'm not saying anything you two don't already know." Instead of quieting, Mina's one-time partner, fellow agent, and best friend opted to pace back and forth on screen, her vibrant blue sleep wrap flowing out behind her. "It's not like it's a secret to him he's there. I mean, the guy is in your sprayer. He spent the night in your platform. It's not my fault you have a more intriguing personal life than I do right now. I'm just helpfully pointing out that you have a man in your unit. And I would like to know where else he visited. It's an easy question to answer. And while we're at it, did the man use his unit or did you two opt to stay unit-free—"

"Stahp!" Mina sputtered, giving in to laughter, which was the norm around Kaylee. It was a good thing she didn't have a mouthful of coffee. "That's way too many units. I can't keep up." Kaylee in the morning was almost better than caffeine. Almost. "I didn't tag you this early to go over any, um, units. I tagged you because you sent a cryptic message in the wee hours of the morning about something Harmony found on Blade's data core." Harmony Biggins, Kaylee's superhacker mentee, was reviewing information that'd been recovered yesterday from Currency Reigns, Travis Blade's satellite, after it jettisoned out of orbit and crash-landed on a deserted island off of the coast of Florida. The stable heart, which contained the data core, had been retrieved by Mina and her team with the help of the military. "I just listened to it and need to know more before we see McAllister. We have a meeting with him in thirty."

"My message wasn't cryptic," Kaylee corrected, her finger wagging. "It was precise and lacking in specifics because I didn't want to horn in on your night. Literally. It was not my place to horn. That space is raised reserved for someone else who's hair is as wet as yours. Because, let's face it, it's been much too long since you've been horn—"

"Okay you win!" Mina cried, tossing up her arms, giving in like she usually did when Kaylee wanted details. Her pal was the queen of persistence. "Yes, we were intimate. A single blissful completely satisfying unit was involved. It was amazing. Best night of my life. Having him here is like a dream. I'm happy we're giving it a shot. But that doesn't mean I'm not scared. This whole thing could crumble down around us as quickly as Blade's satellite dropped out of the sky. But after last night, I can say for sure it's worth the risk of us possibly not making it." So worth it.

The night had been spectacular in every way. Vince had been a kind and generous lover. So generous. Her body had exploded like a hydro-cracker a hundred times. Okay, not triple digits, but definitely double. Shivers ran up her arms. She shook them out as nervous energy rushed through her. Maybe she should go for a run? People still did that, didn't they?

"Wow." Kaylee leaned into the screen, examining Mina up close. "The hair on your arms is literally standing on end." Her face softened as she paced back to her comfortable, overstuffed chair. Her lovable dog Dag was curled up on the floor, not bothered in the least by either of their antics. It was too early. Dag was lazy in the mornings. Kaylee tucked her feet underneath her, rearranged her sleep wrap, her straight, dark shoulder length hair looking perfect even though she'd just woken up. "Of course it's worth it. If you hadn't given this a shot, you would've regretted it for the rest of your life. And don't worry about what the future holds." She swished a hand dismissively. "If you decide to part ways because his persona is too grandiose—because, let's face it, the man is splashy—it'll be in a mutual, loving way. I'm absolutely pos. And, damn, the sex is so good you're humming with it. That's a pretty sweet problem to have."

"I'm not humming—"

Her finger arched up looking huge on Mina's full wallscreen as she shook it twice. "Yes, you are. Not only that, you're wound up tighter than a piece of carbon loaded into a high-velocity slingshot ready to zing itself to Mars. Steam is practically shooting from your ears."

"I don't have any steam—"

Finger shake. "So. Much. Steam. It might be from your superhot sprayer sex, though. But whatever." Another hand swish. "My advice? Revel in it. Embrace it. Roll around in it. Enjoy your time with him without overthinking things."

"That's easy for you to say—"

"No. It's easy for you to do. This is the honeymoon dating phase. Honeymoon it up. Don't think about anything other than when your next trip to Unit Town will be. That's all this stage requires."

Mina blushed absentmindedly running her fingers through her still wet hair. "Maybe you're right."

"Of course, I am. I'm always right."

Honestly, she usually was.

Sound came from the hallway as Vincent Kramer, the colonel-in-arms of the French Protectorate, walked into Mina's meal prep area with a plushy dry wrap casually knotted around his waist, his dark hair fingered back away from his face, beads of water still slowly dripping down his back.

"Yowza, Kramer," Kaylee hooted. "You could give a girl

some warning. Please tell me you have a brother or sister packed away that I don't know about."

"Sadly, no," Vince replied with a chuckle.

"Damn," Kaylee lamented.

Mina grabbed the two coffees she'd ordered from Eggie, her Magnito meal printer, out of the warming area. No mimosas, as Veronica, her home sim had cheekily suggested last night. No alcohol when they had a meeting at headquarters. Vince was set to debrief Mina and her boss, Duncan McAllister, about the Fiefer case.

Fiefer was not an actual case. Fief was their code word for double agent.

Vincent Kramer, the hunk of a man wrapped in a violet plush wrap, had a suspicion that Ambrose Bernard, the leader of the French Protectorate might be a double agent.

It was a huge, startling accusation that needed to be addressed immediately. Even before they dealt with what had been found on the data core of the satellite owned by Travis Blade.

But Mina still needed to know what Harmony had discovered. She handed Vince a cup of coffee, made the way he liked it with a shot of dairy-sub, no sweet, just like she did. "Let's get back to the reason I called," she addressed Kaylee as she took a sip from her own mug, trying not to mew. Eggie was the best. Then she took another. "What did Harmony find on the data core?"

"It wasn't a huge discovery, which is why I didn't alert you in a worrying kind of way," Kaylee answered. "While she was running through vids last night, she caught sight of one of the guys from the first one we watched while we were at the mili base. The one where the two guys found those Plush airpens in the wrong crates and were supposed to deliver them to the border. She spotted one, not sure which of the two, at another undisclosed location. Looked like they were in the process of interrogating him before the vid cut out. He looked roughed up, clothes were torn, blood on his face. She's trying to pin down the location now. With her wizard brain, I'm sure she'll figure it out soon."

Bliss Corp, the big pharma company who was likely testing illegal pleasure drugs on unsuspecting people, looked to have a contract with Travis Blade to move unapproved airpens full of Plush discreetly under the nose of the government. Two delivery techs had stumbled on the loot and were caught discussing it on vid.

It seemed having that discussion hadn't boded too well for them.

"Lee was running face recs on them last night," Mina told her pal. "He came up empty, but he was going to age alter them younger and try again when he got home. Make sure Harmony and Lee are sharing info. I have no doubt they'll uncover their identities. I'm going to get a hold of Lee on our way to Government One." She took another sip of coffee and held in a sigh. "Have you heard how many Syndicate members they've arrested yet?" The data core contained a lot of incriminating evidence. High Crimes was ready and waiting to round up all the guilty players.

"Nope," Kaylee said. "All's been quiet. I wouldn't be surprised if McAllister orders us to lay low for a day or two to see what splashes back from all this." She yawned. "It might actually be fun to have some time off. I haven't had a proper day to myself in what feels like years."

"You hate days off. You find them aimless and unexciting. Those are your words, not mine."

"Hate's a strong word." Kaylee grinned, unfolding her legs from beneath her, her toes faintly blinking with an aged blue hyperglo that matched her sleep wrap. "I adore being busy, but it would be fun to take Daggie on a nice long walk through Atlas Park today and breathe in some nice, fresh air. I haven't been down there since they slapped all that greenery on top of that giant eyesore." Atlas Park was located on the southern tip of the city atop a large seawall that had been erected over sixty years ago, and had been added onto over the years, making it an enormous ocean barrier to keep the rising seas as bay. Last year they decided to cover the top of it in lush plantings, grass, and trees, effectively installing large public park. It'd been a massive endeavor. It was actually pretty now. Much less of an eyesore.

"Don't get your hopes up," Mina cautioned. "We rest when there's a break between cases."

"You're right," Kaylee said. "But until we know if the mob is going to try to extract justice, a break—or at least modified casework—is what I would do. McAllister's smart like that. He won't put any of us at risk if he doesn't have to. Mark my words." She lofted a finger in the air. "We're going to get a day off. I feel it in my bones. And as you know, they don't lie—"

Mina chuckled. "Yes, I got a very clear understanding of how your bones don't lie yesterday when you explained it in excruciating detail. Vince and I are heading in soon to discuss the Fiefer case. Then we'll know what McAllister is thinking."

Kaylee leaned forward, a frown forming on her lips. "I know I'm not going to be privy to all the stuff you three discuss today, but please be careful. That goes for you too, Kramer." Vince glanced up from his cuff, giving Kaylee a quick nod. "This kind of intel gets people killed. It's big trouble if the wrong people find out what you suspect."

"We'll be careful," Mina assured her. "Nothing will go further than McAllister's office." She shot Vince a worried look. She couldn't hide it. Kaylee was right. These kinds of things got people killed. If Ambrose Bernard felt like he was backed into a corner and was worried about exposure, and Vince was to blame, there would be retribution. It would be swift and calculated.

"I plan to fully cover myself," Vince said. "I trust my soldiers. If what I suspect is true, stopping Ambrose Bernard will become my number one priority. But I won't get caught." He moved closer to Mina, his expression soft, running a hand up her forearm, grasping it lightly. "That's a promise."

"You can't promise something like that," Mina argued. "Like Kaylee said, this is big trouble. Even if you trust your subordinates, things can and do leak."

"Nothing gets out if I do it my way," Vince said.

"What way is that? The magic way?" Mina placed her hands on her hips.

Kaylee cleared her throat. "This is probably a great time for me to bow out, so I don't intrude on your first lover's quarrel. Because, you know, you're lovers now. Just pointing out facts. You guys have a good meeting with the boss. If you need to find me, I'll be at Atlas Park. Ta-ta! Kevin, end vid."

"Sure, darlin'." She popped off waving.

"Did that sim have a southern accent?" Vince leaned in to give Mina a kiss.

Mina accepted the kiss, but made it brief, even though her inclination was to yank off Vince's plush wrap and situate herself on top of the meal counter. "Yes, Kaylee's sim Kevin has a southern accent. But you're not getting out of this by changing the subject. Nothing about investigating a double agent is foolproof. No matter how careful you are. And once we go into McAllister's office, and you tell us what you know, it can't be undone. It's like Norm said yesterday, if we do this, you have to be prepared to stand on old train tracks and get hit by a passing freight."

Vince grinned. "Not sure I'm familiar with that saying."

"Never mind. It's not a saying, exactly." She shook her head. "He was trying to warn us away from gathering his testimony against the Syndicate. This is kind of like that, but you're going against the powerful leader of the French military, instead of an age-old crime organization. Same rules apply. Once the information is out, there are no second chances, so you have brace for the train. I want you to be absolutely certain you want to do this before we go in. If you don't want to tell McAllister what you know, he won't press you. You're basically giving him international intelligence of your own free will. You're entitled to change your mind."

"I can, but I won't. I understand your caution. But having your director hear a firsthand account is going to help keep me safe. It's part of my plan. I can use it as a bargaining chip if I ever find myself in need. It would be useless for Ambrose to kill me if he knew the US had information that would expose him."

"You just finished telling me you wouldn't get caught. You actually made a promise." Mina slid her hands up is very ample chest which had just enough dark hair covering it to make it completely sexy and not overly furry. Vince could laser it off very easily, but she was glad he didn't. When she reached his shoulders, her hands continued, splaying around his neck, drawing him down as if to press he lips against his. Instead, once he got close, she whispered, "If you go back on your word, you won't get another taste of this." She kissed him deeply.

He drew back from the embrace slowly, grinning, running his arms around her waist, pulling her tightly against his still damp chest. "My word will hold." His lips were mere millimeters away from hers. "Now that I've had it, I'm not sure I could live without the taste of you."

About the Author

Amanda Carlson is a graduate of the University of Minnesota, with a BA in both Speech and Hearing Science & Child Development. She went on to get an A.A.S in Sign Language Interpreting and worked as an interpreter until her first child was born. She's the author of the high-octane **Jessica McClain** urban fantasy series published by Orbit, the **Sin City Collectors** PNR series, the contemporary fantasy **Phoebe Meadows** series, the dystopian **Holly Danger** series, and the futuristic thriller **Mina Kane** series. Look for these books in stores everywhere. She lives in Minneapolis.

FIND HER ALL OVER SOCIAL MEDIA

Website: amandacarlson.com

Facebook: facebook.com/authoramandacarlson

Twitter: @amandaccarlson

Instagram: @author_amanda

Nothing is completed without a great team.

My many thanks to:

Awesome Cover design: Damonza
Digital and print formatting: Author E.M.S
Copyedits/proofs: Joyce Lamb
Final proof: Marlene Roberts

*Head to my website to sign-up for my Book Alert
newsletter to receive new release info in your inbox so
you don't miss a thing!*

www.amandacarlson.com